JAN TURK PETRIE

FALLING APART

ALSO BY JAN TURK PETRIE

Until the Ice Cracks – Vol 1 of The Eldísvík Trilogy

No God for a Warrior – Vol 2 of The Eldísvík Trilogy

Within Each Other's Shadow – Vol 3 of The Eldísvík Trilogy

Too Many Heroes

Towards the Vanishing Point

The Truth in a Lie

Still Life with a Vengeance

Running Behind Time – Cotswold time-slip series Book 1

Play For Time – Cotswold time-slip series Book 2

Turn Back Time – Cotswold time-slip series Book 3

Time to Choose – Cotswold time-slip series Book 4

Contents

FALLING APART

"Chaos was the law of nature; order was the dream of man."
– Henry Brooks Adams

"Civilization begins with order, grows with liberty and dies with chaos." – Will Durant

Chapter One

Outer Hebrides archipelago, Scotland, UK.

Ash

Shivering, he crawls out of bed still in his sweatshirt and jogging pants. During the night, while the storm gripped the island, the timbers around him had creaked and shuddered like the whole thing might take off. Now all he can hear is seabirds calling and the familiar rhythm of breaking waves.

His fire will need resuscitating before he can boil the kettle on the stove top. Over last night's embers he lays dried moss and blows until a few sparks ignite and a weak column of smoke begins to rise. He builds a Jenga frame of kindling and, once that catches, sits back on his haunches to watch the flames take hold.

After throwing on more logs, he shuts the door. Though the blaze is now roaring in the chimney pipe, it will take time for his one-roomed hut to warm up.

He straightens up, arching his back to unknot his lower vertebrae. Through the salt-encrusted glass this morning's view is all horizontals. Under a weak sun, the sea is level and grey, the high ridge to the left hidden in mist. A new layer of flotsam has been deposited along the high tide line – there might be things he can use amongst it. Nothing much out on the water except for a handful of bobbing birds.

Wait a second!

He rubs his sleep-deprived eyes before checking again. It's true – there's a moving vertical over by the rocks. Some distance away, a lone figure is walking along "his" beach. And they're not alone. A smaller object – could be a dog – is trailing some distance behind.

The shock hits his stomach then spreads through his body. Heart thumping, his trembling hands locate his binoculars. He focuses in. First thing he picks out is not an animal but a small, fair-haired child in a brown coat, running to keep up with what must be its parent. Way ahead and paying the child no heed, the adult is striding on, their long dark hair streaming out behind. A flapping, navy jacket, rolled up jeans, barefoot in spite of those sharp-as-hell rocks. He can't see the face. From their slight build he guesses it's a woman. As yet no sign of the boat they must have arrived on.

He scans for more invaders. None immediately visible. The ruins of the old tythe barn shield much of his view. Thankfully, that works both ways.

Through the lenses he watches the woman head towards the sea. What in God's name? Ignoring the trailing child, she's already over the tangle of last night's jetsam and advancing on the breaking waves. It's late March and, despite the trend towards warmer seas, at this latitude the water temperature will, at best, be around eight degrees, yet, without hesitation or reaction, she wades straight in.

The child's had the sense to stop near the water's edge. What the hell's the woman up to? Could be trying to rescue someone, or something, from the water.

He pulls on his boots before again checking the wider landscape for any sign of more interlopers. Satisfied, he hangs up his binos and opens the door. The bitter air hits him. After a steadying breath he breaks cover, racing down the track towards the beach.

Where the shingle turns to sand, their mismatched foot-steps form a trail he automatically follows. He reaches the child first. A shivering little girl. Skinny as hell. At a guess, around four or five. Breathing hard, he grasps her shoulders. 'Stay here. Don't move from this spot, okay?' She looks up at him wide-eyed with no indication she's either understood his instructions or is going to comply.

He needs to prioritise and right now her mother is the one waist deep in icy water. His teeth already chattering, he knows too well how cold water shock can kill a healthy person within minutes. Overhead a swooping, black-backed gull barks its disapproval.

'Stop!' he shouts from the shoreline. 'You're going to freeze to death out there.'

No response. Did she even hear him over the sound of the waves? The weight of her wet clothing is slowing her progress though she seems determined to wade in deeper.

'Fuck sake,' he mutters. Then louder, 'I can help you.' Taking a risk, 'I've got a boat.'

Her head slowly turns in his direction. 'No one can… help me,' she yells back. 'Leave me alone.' Her face is ashen, wet hair hanging about her shoulders like kelp.

Damn it. He kicks off his boots, launches them towards the safety of the dunes, then wades into the water. The icy shock robs him of breath. It's an effort to raise his voice. 'Stay there!' he shouts. 'I'm coming.'

She's shaking her head. 'Too late,' she yells backing off. 'This… only way…' Her voice blends in with the shrieking of gulls, the last part of what she said lost.

And now she's turned her back, seems determined to drown herself. His legs are growing numb as he wades deeper. Up to his waist, he's aware that his blood will now be racing away from his limbs to protect his vital organs. 'Don't!' he pleads, for both their sakes. The wind's whipping hair into his eyes, the sand shifting under his feet. He's too far away to grab her.

When he checks behind, the child's still on dry land. 'Think!' he shouts. 'Your little girl…'

Water up to her chest, she's really struggling to breathe. 'Maia…'

He's so cold he doubts he can get to her before his legs stop working. 'Think of your daughter,' he yells. 'Maia needs you.'

It takes him a moment to realise that her snort was an aborted chuckle. She screams at the sky, 'Mea culpa!'

Christ, she's lost it. The incoming tide is now buffeting her shoulders. 'She's an abomination,' she yells, both arms raised above her head. 'We both are.' Her words are not for him but the elements, maybe the deity they represent.

She's shutting her eyes, getting ready to surrender to the ocean.

His strength's ebbing fast. 'Don't! Please!' It takes a supreme effort to wade towards her, the weight of water insurmountable. 'Stop! Your daughter…'

'… not mine.' The woman's staring into the swell. Raising her eyes to the sky, she cries out, 'God… Mercy on me,' before her gaping mouth and then the rest of her head disappears beneath the surface.

Gone. The sea's swallowed her whole. He scans the shifting, swaying water for any sign of her.

This is happening too fast. He's dreaming, that's it – she's a figment of his isolated imagination. He's almost convinced himself when he looks back to where the child is still at the water's edge, watching him.

He tries to peer beneath the restless surface but can't be sure in those surging waves of the exact spot where she disappeared. Shouldn't the incoming tide be carrying her towards him? Gazing into sand-clouded water, he can see only strands of uprooted weed.

Does he have the strength, or the will, to plunge into its icy depths? He's already some way from the beach. Fighting the tide, if he uses up what's left of his energy searching for the woman, odds are he'll drown in the process. Is he prepared to take such a risk for a suicidal stranger?

And then there's the child. If he doesn't survive, she'll most likely die of exposure. Or hunger.

Their two lives outweigh the one as good as lost. And yet he continues to check in a wide arc, hoping her head will bob up. Did she weigh herself down – fill her pockets with stones like that famous writer? He's forgotten her name.

Successive waves are nudging him towards the shore. He can't tell how much time has elapsed, but it must be too late to save her.

Mustering the last of his strength, he hauls himself towards the tiny figure standing alone on the empty beach.

Chapter Two

He staggers towards the child. Getting closer, he can see she's not staring at him but past him out to sea. The wind is tugging her flaxen hair, her unbuttoned coat billowing around her. That wan face is expressionless. Shock, he imagines.

Reaching her and dry land at last, his spent legs give way. Felled by exhaustion, he collapses onto the sand at her feet. She doesn't flinch but continues to stare beyond him.

He groans, rolls onto his back, shuts his eyes, and succumbs to exhaustion.

Coming to, he's appalled to find himself beached like a stranded porpoise. And cold right through to his bones. He swallows the taste of salt, his throat parched dry. The nightmare that just happened comes back to him in a rush.

The girl is still there. Black ankle boots, goosebumps on her bare legs. Blinking into the low weak sun, he looks up at that thin coat, the cotton dress, her lost, pale face. The two of them need to get off this damned beach – and fast.

He scans the length of the beach and then the rising land beyond. All clear. Reassured, he struggles to his knees to match her height. Ice tremors run through him like blades. To her blank face, he says, 'You're freezing,' in as soft a voice as he can muster through his knocking teeth. 'I am too.' He raises a numb finger to point. 'My hut's over there. It's warm inside.'

She doesn't look at him or show any understanding. Traumatised, no doubt. When he offers his hand, she doesn't respond; has probably been taught to be wary of strange men. With his sand encrusted hair and his wet clothes sticking to him, he easily qualifies. To her he must look like some sea monster. In her place he wouldn't go into his hut either.

'Let me help you,' he says – an unfortunate echo of what he'd said to her mother. When he reaches out to close her flapping coat, she shrinks back. Those aquamarine eyes swivel to meet his, an unspoken accusation at their pin-prick centres.

Could he have done more to rescue the woman? Not really. She's one fatality he's not responsible for. Suicide might be common these days, but how could a parent, or any adult, abandon a defenceless child in this remote and hostile environment?

If others landed along with them, there's no sign of them now in any direction. He rakes his hair away from his eyes, runs a hand down his face to brush some of the sand off. His skin feels like it will crack when he smiles. 'I'll make hot chocolate. You like chocolate, right?'

She must have understood something because she takes several steps backwards while shaking her head. Her knowing gaze offers no absolution.

What now? If he leaves her here, she could head out into the sea in search of her mother – if that's who she was. Tide's coming in fast; the water will be on them in minutes. He doesn't want to use force – doubts he can summon much of that in any event.

The woman's footprints – her last traces – are still visible where the shingle gives way to sand. Hers and the child's intertwined. His own prints coming in at an angle, overlay both of theirs before disappearing at the water's edge. Evidence of what's occurred here will be lost with the advancing tide.

How's he going to persuade the child to go with him? He recalls the wild-born kitten his family adopted – how they'd lured it out of hiding with scraps of food and kindness. But time and tide won't wait on such subtleties.

'I'm going to my hut,' he says. 'It's warm inside.' The old barn's hiding it from view. 'I know you can't see it from here,' he tells her, 'but if you look hard you might spot the smoke from my fire.'

Her eyes seem to flicker like it's an effort not to follow where he's pointing. That small mouth is set against the idea; against him.

Less than an hour ago his life was uncomplicated – a long succession of days and nights witnessed only by calling seabirds and basking seals.

After hauling himself to his feet, he stumbles towards the dunes hoping she'll follow. His boots are lying amongst the jetsam and weed of the high tide mark. With no strength to pull them on, he picks them up and carries them. Reaching the track, its sharp stones begin to dig into the soles of his feet. He drops the boots and squeezes his damp, sand-crusted feet into them.

When he looks back the child is rooted to the same spot, and now the lace edges of the incoming tide are lapping at her boots. Any second one of those incoming waves will sweep her sparrow legs out from under her.

Damn it. Fuelled by panic he breaks into a run. Reaching the beach, he scoops her up just as the water hits and drenches him all over again.

She's lighter than he'd expected and yet in his weakened state it's a struggle to lug her inert body up the beach and over the dunes. She doesn't kick or scream, but neither does she hold on to him to make it easier.

Reaching the track, he sets her down to walk the rest by herself. One boot has fallen off revealing her achingly vulnerable, bare foot. Once he's warmed up, he'll come back to look for it.

The girl turns around and heads straight back towards the beach and her vigil. 'Oh no you don't.' He grabs her around the waist more roughly than he'd intended. Her 'Ummf,' is a forced exhalation not a protest. Is it only shock that's prevented her from speaking so far? She could be deaf. Or dumb. Maybe both. She goes limp in his arms as he carries her the rest of the way to his hut.

Inside it, a blast of hot air hits his frozen cheeks. He sets her down. She seems not to register her new surroundings but instead stares at the door he's now closed behind them. He kicks off his boots. Before the girl can bolt, he flips the catch at the top to lock it. 'Just keeping you safe,' he says, with no hint of the remorse he feels. That catch is beyond her reach.

Steam is beginning to rise from his soaked clothing. He

would strip off on the spot except that would confirm the girl's worst fears. She's still staring at the door catch as if, by sheer willpower, she might be able to move it.

Finally, she turns around, her look an unspoken indictment. 'Okay, okay.' He raises both hands. 'Guilty as charged. Though you have to admit this beats freezing our arses off out there.'

Maybe not the right tone to use with a child. He wishes those pale eyes would stop looking at him like that. She might be outraged, but at least she's now stopped shivering.

He rubs his hands together. Like the jovial uncle he never had, he says, 'Right, then. I seem to remember I promised you hot chocolate, young lady.'

She's following his every move as he crosses the room to fill the kettle from the jerry can and place it on the top of the stove. 'Let's find you a cup.' It takes a while to locate the spare tin mug. 'I've got a sachet or two somewhere,' he says, checking one of the tins. 'We're a long way from a shop here.' He finds them. 'A long way from Kansas,' he mumbles though the reference will be lost on her.

While waiting for the kettle, he spreads his hands to the warmth radiating from the stove. His mind rushes ahead to the many possible repercussions now his total isolation here has been breached. With feeling returning to his fingers, he rips the top off a sachet and pours half the chocolate powder into each mug.

Standing like a sentinel, the girl's turned her attention back to the door catch. Her shoulders flinch when the kettle whistles. Not deaf, then.

He pours hot water into each mug and stirs, his mind straying to the many ramifications of this new situation.

The smell of the hot chocolate begins to colonise the air. He inhales the steam from his mug before taking a sip. Too hot. He pours a little cold water in and takes another sip. A fierce warmth spreads down his throat and into his chest.

His fingers struggle to prise open the lid on the hardtack biscuits. He snaps one in half and puts her portion on a plate. Approaching her slowly, he places the drink and her half of the biscuit on the floor a short distance from where she's standing.

Taking another sip of his own drink, he says, 'Mmm – delicious. Still a bit hot though, so be careful. You might need to blow on it.' He blows on his own to illustrate.

She hasn't moved, is staring at him like he's a wicked warlock attempting to lure her deeper into his hut. A woodcut illustration from Hansel and Gretel pops into his head – a childhood memory he'd all but forgotten. Do they read scary stories to children anymore, or does the grimness of real life preclude the need? If he was a kid in these troubled times, he'd want to retreat to some cosier, safer world. He looks over at his precious books wondering if any of them might be suitable for a child.

Chewing on his half of the biscuit, he swallows it down with a gulp of hot chocolate. Feeling a lot better, he strolls across to the alcove where he sleeps. After putting down his mug he pulls out the drawer that contains his spare clothing.

He's reluctant to undress with her there but needs must. He turns his back before peeling off his sweatshirt. Once he's dried his hair, he rubs the towel over his smarting torso. The residue of sand begins to scour his skin and gets his circulation going. When his top half is dry, he pulls on a t-shirt and then a sweatshirt. He wraps the towel around his waist before divesting himself of his soaked joggers. Before he's fully dry, he pulls on clean underpants and then his jeans.

He rubs the remainder of the sand from his face. Perhaps he'd look less of a threat if he cut some of his dark beard off? In the wall mirror he can see the girl is now a few steps closer to the bait.

He keeps his back turned while her reflection snatches the mug and sniffs its contents. At the first tentative sip, her face shows surprise. Could this be the first time she's tasted chocolate? Emboldened or desperate, she gulps down the rest of it, draining the whole thing then running her tongue around the rim.

The biscuit is subjected to the same sniff test. Though nutritious, they don't smell of much and are so compressed they're difficult to swallow. Having struggled to bite into it, she decides to gnaw at the edges like a mouse might.

He runs a comb through his hair to dislodge some of the sand still clinging to it. The girl is watching him while nibbling the edges of her biscuit, then turning it over as if looking for a softer side. It's not long before she's eaten the whole thing.

She's startled when he turns around, as if she'd momentarily forgotten he was there. Wariness haunts her eyes. She's vigilant, suspicious just as she should be. The innocence of childhood is one of the many causalities of this last decade.

'I expect you feel better after that,' he says, taking a couple of steps towards her. 'In a while I'll make us some soup.' He remembers to smile. 'The great thing about soup is you can put anything in it, and it still tastes good.'

Her undone coat, lack of socks and the too-thin material of her dress all suggest she'd put them on unaided – or in a hurry. The woman she was with had killed herself not caring what would happen to this child, unconcerned with whether she'd survive or not. What the hell had possessed her? It might be better not to imagine what this little girl has endured in her short life.

He's assaulted by a vivid flashback to the moment the woman's head plunged under the water and the absence of the usual last minute instinctual struggle to breathe – an animal reflex that can thwart the most determined suicide attempt. She'd called herself and the child *abominations*. In her dying moments, she'd bequeathed this little girl, possibly her own daughter, that ugly accusation.

Abomination is an extraordinary word to have used. It suggests something unnatural, or illicit. He rubs at his beard. In religious-speak it means people who possess some innate evil or wickedness – a person, or thing, cursed from birth. The damned.

Taking another step forward, he puts a hand to his chest. 'My name's Ash,' he tells her – the single name he goes by these days. A choice that seemed appropriate for the times. He's trained himself not only to respond to it, but to take ownership of this new, simplified version of himself. 'I'm Ash,' he repeats, then pointing at her, 'What's your name?'

Her lips remain closed. Did she understand the question? Surely someone must have given her a name and taught her to say it.

'I'm Ash,' he repeats. 'Pleased to meet you.' He extends

his hand for a shake. She looks right through him, her tiny swaying frame defiant. That closed-off expression could be a way of hiding how vulnerable she feels, how terrifying it must be to be dependent on a total stranger in this isolated place.

Chapter Three

A shaft of light penetrates the window, highlighting his outstretched hand while hers are held stubbornly by her side. How mismatched the two of them would seem to an onlooker – if such a person exists; not a possibility he can dismiss since the woman and this girl arrived here in spite of his vigilance.

The girl's long, fair hair is burnished by the sunlight. As she gazes out of the window, her pale eyes are alight with energy. Questions crowd his mind. Does she expect someone to be searching for her? Are they already here on the island? Time and habit have made him complacent. Comfortable even. He needs to adjust his thinking, and fast.

The expression on her face is unfathomable as she scans the beach and the sea beyond it. Is she expecting the woman to rise from her watery grave, or does she know someone else is out there?

The smoke from his fire would be a dead giveaway. Should he douse it? Not yet – it's too soon to panic. Through the binoculars he focuses in on the shoreline half expecting to see a search party heading their way, but the stretch of sand he can see is clear.

He lowers the lenses and lets the regular sound of the surf soothe him. He's safe here. The two of them are – for the time being at least.

The girl was bone dry when he reached her, which suggests she and the woman had landed in some kind of craft. Steep cliffs surround most of the island making it a natural fortress. It's unlikely they came ashore on this beach given he'd seen no sign of a boat or any wreckage. There's one other inlet, a narrow creek. Navigating any boat into the mouth of it is tricky in daylight, almost impossible in darkness and in a storm like the one they've just had. Did they wait it out before heading ashore? He needs to check.

The woman and the girl could have been fleeing for their lives. Not an unlikely scenario. Then again, why would the woman commit suicide *after* she'd managed to escape?

If the child would only speak, he might be able to get a clearer idea of what happened, what led them here amongst all the other islands in this archipelago. Had they set out on a deliberate course for his tiny island? Unlikely. So maybe they were blown off course and landed here by chance.

This island – *his* island – is officially designated as unin-habited and has been for many years. The original crofters abandoned it for the mainland more than a century and a half ago. Their cottages now lie in ruins. His hut is the only hab-itable dwelling here. It's shielded by the walls of the derelict tythe barn because the conservationists who built it wanted it to be less visible from out at sea. From the things they'd left behind, he's learnt that the hut was once used by volunteers posted here for a month or two to survey the breeding colonies

– back when folks had the time and resources to care about such things. Left to themselves, the birds and animals here are doing just fine.

He scans the same section of beach again and finds nothing untoward. To be certain there's no one else on the island, he needs a much better vantage point. There's no time to take the long way around, but he can't climb a sheer rockface with a small child in tow.

He'll have to leave her here – there's no other option. He'd promised her some soup a moment ago but that will have to wait. The door opens outward, its lock rusted away so it can't be secured from outside. She'll be safest in here if he barricades the door so she can't escape. He's not used to being in charge of a small child, but he's pretty certain barricading one inside an empty building by themselves is inexcusable. But needs must. And it won't be for long.

Everywhere he looks there are hazards – the most immediate being the red-hot stove. More barricading required. Various sharp objects are lying around; he needs to make sure all of them are out of her reach before he leaves.

The child didn't follow the woman into the sea, so he has to assume she doesn't share the same suicidal impulse. 'I'm really sorry, but I need to go out now for a little while,' he tells her. She stares up at him showing no emotion. 'It'll be better, a lot safer, if you stay here,' he says, hoping it's true. 'I won't be gone long, I promise.' If he's quick, he can be back inside an hour.

It's a familiar climb, the series of handholds and ledges he's using are embedded in his muscle-memory. He needs to concentrate, but his conscience – it seems he has one after all – keeps nagging away at him. It's hard to shake off what happened when he left the girl – her desperate blows on the other side of the door. The scream that might have come from her instead of one of the gulls whirling overhead.

Reaching the summit, he pulls himself up onto level ground and pauses for breath before taking in the view. The earlier mist has lifted to give clear visibility in all directions. Water's calm except for a few white horses further out. He extracts the binoculars from his backpack. Through them he can see there are no boats approaching. And none passing on the horizon. If he's facing a threat, the chances are it's already here.

He focuses in on the beach in front of his hut. As far as he can tell there are no fresh tracks and no signs of anything out of the ordinary. Another time he might try to spot the dolphin pod that regularly frolics just off shore.

Moving the lenses through 180 degrees, he surveys the mouth of the inlet and part of its meandering creek. He can see no boats or craft of any kind. He scans the surrounding marshland. Still nothing. Above the shingle, he picks out a line of crushed vegetation. Yes, there's a discernible trail of minor destruction through the rushes and up into the heather. Someone's recently dragged something up there.

His own boat is hidden inside a dilapidated boathouse at the very end of the creek. The surrounding trees help to shield it from view.

Studying the heather, he spots where some small branches have been snapped off and laid down to disguise a dark shape that's more than just shadow. From its size and basic outline he must be looking at an inflatable craft.

Would the woman have had the strength to singlehandedly drag it that far? Doubtful. And why would she go to all that trouble only to subsequently commit suicide? It doesn't add up. If it wasn't the woman, then another person, or persons, must have tried to hide any sign of their arrival.

Ash lowers his binoculars. He'd intended to abseil back the way he came, had promised the girl that he wouldn't be long, but that was before this discovery.

Looking out to sea again, he gets that familiar, prickling sensation – a warning that he's being watched. Easy to dismiss, but such instincts have helped him survive against all odds.

One thing's for sure – silhouetted up on this ridge he's an easy target. He drops into a low crouch. Scanning his immediate surroundings, he comes up blank. To properly defend himself he needs to get back to his hut and pronto, though maybe not by the most exposed route.

He stows his binoculars and shoulders his pack. In front of him there's a narrow pathway – one of a network on the island created by feral sheep. With the bracken still only half grown, the precipitous slope on that side will be much easier to navigate. He can then approach the clearing where his hut is through the woodland.

It's only a three metre drop from the ledge he's on. The soft ground helps to absorb the impact. He makes good progress downhill despite having to skirt around various rocky outcrops and thicker clumps of juniper and gorse. The sheep – descendants of the ones left behind by the crofters – have grazed down the land at the bottom of the slope. Once he reaches it he breaks into a run heading straight for the trees.

He's almost there when his eye catches something blue lying in bracken to his left. He slows to a jog, steadies his breathing as he approaches. The blue takes on the shape of two legs ending in a pair of stout boots. The legs disappear into an olive green, oiled jacket. Above this, there's a man's face twisted to one side.

Coming to a halt, Ash takes in the dark hair ruffled by the wind, the open brown eyes staring up at the sky. His body is slightly arched, the fingers of his visible hand open as if he's trying to catch something. Or some prized object has been wrenched from his grip.

He's dead – the blue tinge to his face and lips make that unmistakable. Even so, Ash checks his neck for a pulse. He feels nothing but icy cold flesh. It's not obvious what killed him until he rolls the man over and sees a hefty handle protruding from his back, a dark red stain discolouring his jacket. No other visible wounds. The blade must have severed a vital organ or blood vessel. A single lucky or unlucky strike, depending on whose point of view you take. The perpetrator must have used considerable force to penetrate his heavy clothing plus his ribs.

He rolls the man back into the face-up position. Studying his features, he tries to imagine how he might have looked when animated. He's pretty sure he doesn't recognise him. Aside from encounters with sheep carcasses, it's been a while since he looked death full in the face. Up until today this island has been his refuge from all that.

He straightens up. This is no time to ponder the fragility of life or the finality of death. Could the woman have done this?

Did she kill herself out of remorse? It's tempting to believe such a scenario, to conclude the loop has been closed.

As he breaks into a run, he pictures the family of three heading here in the inflatable. Having successfully navigated the inlet, they stash their craft out of sight and set off to explore the island. The woman's been biding her time, waiting for this degree of isolation and its opportunity. Once the man's back is turned, his guard down, she plunges the blade she happens to have about her into his back. It would have taken remarkable strength, or extreme passion, to bury the blade that deeply.

He ducks down to avoid a low branch. Maybe the weapon was his and she grabbed it from him. Afterwards she turns him face up – possibly to make certain there's no pulse. The woman and child then head into the wood and, once through it, walk through the clearing almost passing his hut before taking the path to the beach where, overcome by guilt, or the madness that drove her to stab the man, the woman decides to drown herself. Murder/suicide they used to call it, skipping all the in-between, unnecessary words to explain a common enough sequence of events.

If his working theory is correct, with the ground soft after the storm, there might be tracks to prove the woman came this way with the child hurrying behind her.

He's grateful for the cover of the trees. Planted as part of a "rewilding" scheme, the woodland is dense having never been thinned. In places it's difficult to find a way through. He searches the ground for tell-tale signs but finds only confirmation that some sheep had sheltered here during the storm. A closer inspection might reveal more, but he can't afford to slacken his pace, or risk looking down instead of up.

Halfway through the wood, he stops to listen. Above the ever present sound of breaking waves, he hears rustling nearby. It turns out to be just a squirrel frolicking in one of the birches.

He presses on. The leaf litter has been churned up so much by the animals it's impossible to pick out any human prints. He scans for intruders before he steps out into the clearing. Here the grass has been close-cropped by the sheep. Where the ground is really sodden he spots a few boot prints, though from their size and shape they could be his. As he passes the row of ruined cottages, he can almost picture a gun barrel protruding from one of those glassless windows.

He glances over his shoulder several more times before he dares to approach the crumbling barn that shelters his hut. Once he's reached the old barn, he tucks himself behind its high stone wall and peers around it to be certain no one is following him.

There's no smoke rising from his stove's vent pipe, though that's not too surprising since it will have burnt down by now. The hut seems unaltered, the big water container he'd used to bar the door is exactly where he left it.

Shifting it to one side, he opens the door. The air inside is warm, redolent of woodsmoke and wet clothing. At first he thinks the girl's somehow escaped, but then he sees she's curled up in his moth-eaten armchair, fast asleep with her mouth slightly open. She must have taken off her coat before pulling it over her like a blanket. Her remaining boot lies on the floor – useless without the other one.

Satisfied there are no intruders, he shuts the door then turns the stave that acts as a lock.

He studies the sleeping child. Her unguarded vulnerability really gets to him. Where her bare forearm is exposed, he spots discolouration – a series of unmissable bruises above a livid mark encircling her wrist. His heart beats faster thinking about how someone had recently tied this poor child up.

His eyes dart to the cupboard above his bed. In a few strides he's across the room. Wrenching open the cupboard, he gives a sigh of relief that it's still there along with the precious ammunition stowed on the shelf below.

During his training, the weapons instructor liked to remind them that the highly sophisticated metal and polymer instrument in their hands was useless if it wasn't ready and loaded. He's never stopped practicing, can still assemble and load this rifle blindfolded in less than 45 seconds.

Chapter Four

Provence, France

Guy

He's chosen his position with care – a vantage point from which to observe anything and everything that moves within the target area. Though his boots have trampled wild thyme and marjoram, the scent trail will soon dissipate.

Through the morning mist, the mountain peaks are a blue graph-line on the horizon. Within an hour those rock faces will be exposed and rippling like gold. The emerging sun is behind him so there'll be no tell-tale glint from his telescopic sights.

Guy rests his back against the powdery wall of the ruin. The sharp end of a stone block digs into him. He welcomes the slight pain this produces – it will help him stay alert.

Life in these remote mountain villages goes on almost un-touched by events elsewhere. A metallic peal reaches him from across the valley. From here he has a clear view of the ancient church tower. Seven o'clock and on this fine spring morning the population is beginning to stir. A grey vehicle looking the size of a toy is raising a dust trail as it winds its way up the hill behind the huddled houses. In a changed world, this place is set in amber.

He's wearing his hunting jacket and, though it's getting warmer, he won't give up its familiar ripeness just yet. A stray cicada lands on one of the stones in front of him and begins its rhythmic song. The other day old Menard told him, in all seriousness, that God put these creatures on earth to stop men from sleeping – to save them from the temptations of idleness. For such small insects, they've got a lot to answer for.

Menard is one of a group that includes big Girard, Andre the waiter, Bertrand, who likes to call himself a painter, and Laurent the shepherd – the men who nod him a "soir" when he enters the bar. In their fitful conversations they *tu* one another and, through familiarity, this now includes him. Whether they like it or not, he's an integral part of their community – a necessary safeguard in these troubled times. He's grown used to being "Guy" and their pronunciation – rhyming it with oui not why. It makes him smile that he's chosen a name that means everyman.

An hour passes in which he hasn't moved except to flex his toes to stave off cramp. The sun is strengthening, warming the back of his neck through his frayed collar. Crouching, he takes off his jacket and stows it in a crevice before resuming his position.

Just because he can, he pivots the barrel to the left, focusing on the church tower before swooping down into the square. The café's chairs have been set upright and are beginning to fill with customers eager for their morning fix of what now passes for coffee. Andre appears with a tray at his shoulder. The man likes to flit and flirt between the tables, presenting each order with an old-school professional flourish. That waistcoat helps to hide the weight he's put on.

Guy moves the barrel a fraction until the crosshairs are dead centre of Andre's head, trained on that bald patch he tries to disguise. The slight breeze that's ruffling his own hair won't be strong enough to deflect his aim. No correction needed.

'Boom!' He chuckles to himself, his index finger stroking temptation on the curve of the trigger. 'And right now you'd be dead.'

Movement catches his attention. A woman comes into hard focus. Madam Le Gall – Giselle – is crossing the square in a hurry to get to the store though it won't open for another hour. What excuse did she offer her husband this morning? Sporting her smart skirt and polished shoes, who would guess her dirty little secret? He aims the sights at her chest, though now she's sideways on, the shot would be trickier.

As Giselle strides off on her cheating way, she's overtaken by a couple of children running ahead of their mother. He recognises Fontaine's wife and the bouncing curls of Bastien – their son. The boy's little sister is trying to snatch something in her brother's raised hand. Bastien is holding what appears to be a doll out of reach above her. Positioning the crosshairs on the crown of the boy, he allows himself to imagine the boy's arrogant father brought to his knees by grief.

The town is within his power; on this glorious morning he can decide between life and death – thumbs-up or thumbs-down. He's aware of his quickening heartbeat. Given free rein it would pump more blood into his muscles, raise his glucose levels and expand his pupils to darken his eyes.

He wills himself calm. He's a professional on a mission, even if this one is unsanctioned. Once it's done, he'll make the call – a rendezvous already arranged in a drinking hole due east of here. Leaving nothing to chance, he's checked the place out. Entering its dim interior, he'll order a gut-rot drink and take it to a table in the far corner to wait.

His client will arrive, his hat pulled down lower than usual. He'll take the chair opposite without a word. A creased envelope will emerge, placed between them on the table's sticky surface ready to be exchanged for verification – a trophy from the kill.

"Merci bien, Monsieur" he'll say, tucking the payment into his inside pocket. Better not check its contents there and then with so many eyes about. He'll grin and say, "Je vous fais confiance" – though nobody trusts anyone these days. The other man will give a nod to the lie.

Taking his leave, he'll pause to lean in close. Trusting his French, he'll add, "C'etais un plaisir".

He's brought out of this reverie by the mournful call of a buzzard circling overhead. Around him the chorus of cicadas is swelling. He's read somewhere that these insects spend years underground before they emerge for one brief season in the sun.

Hold on.

The head of the nearest ewe is up from the lush spring grass she's been grazing. Others in the flock follow suit – alert to something on the far side of the pasture. He moves his sights and re-focuses. Two rounded off ears are just visible above the rippling grass, followed by the outline of a brindled back.

Controlling his breathing, he waits. The wolf hesitates as if sensing the trap. Its full head emerges and turns in his direction, eyes trained on the half-ruin borie he's hiding in. Hunter to hunter. Turned to stone, he waits. Against its instincts, the wolf will eventually succumb to the temptation of such easy prey.

Meantime, the dumb-ass flock has gone back to grazing. As he knew it would, the allure is proving too strong, and the wolf's attention turns to the sheep and their heedless lambs. Keeping low, it eases forward, ruffling scarlet poppies as it passes. In a matter of seconds it's reached the stock fence that will be no barrier to its formidable agility. Muzzle now raised above the grass, it's scenting its prey on the wind. Then it holds position, marshalling the force needed to propel it's body at speed.

He too is trained in patience. As it creeps forward, more and more of that fine pelt is exposed. He trains the crosshairs not on the head, but on the pale bib at its throat. About to take the shot, he notices the line of pink teats hanging loose from the animal's belly.

What difference does it make that this she-wolf has pups? He's not paid to have a conscience, is happy to leave questions of morality to others.

With young to feed, what choice does the wolf have? His hesitation has allowed her to creep closer and now she's poised, ready to make her final move and so distracted this will be an easy kill.

He doesn't expect the she-wolf to turn her magnificent head in his direction. As if every solid stone that shields him melts away, those amber eyes know him for what he is.

The merest increase in pressure is all it takes. A blunt crack resounds off the hills. A second makes certain.

Birds have taken flight in every direction. He lowers his weapon. A whole family for the price of one – by rights he should demand a bonus.

Chapter Five

Ash

He's ready. Rifle's loaded with a twenty-round clip. His body thrums with fear and excitement – a response as ingrained as the grooves in the butt against his shoulder. He keeps well back from the window, trains the sights on the immediate foreground and sweeps the old settlement in a wide arc.

Asleep in the armchair, the kid adjusts her position then settles down again. While he's geared up for a fight, she couldn't be calmer.

All evidence suggests nothing untoward is happening out there. At least not yet. No sign of any camouflaged unit heading his way or a blacked-up bunch of assassins getting ready to storm the place.

He slows his breathing, takes a moment to size up the situation. That hidden RIB suggests they'd feared others could come looking for them after they landed here. There's no connection between himself and the new arrivals, no reason to believe their pursuers will be looking for him.

The girl is another matter. From out at sea his hut is

shielded from sight by the substantial walls of the old barn. If they land, they'll eventually spot it. With only one exit and wooden walls, storming this place would be like shooting a fish in a barrel. Correction, make that two fish.

It might be safer not to venture outside for a while, but his food stocks are low, and the fresh water won't last long. He's grown fond of this hut, but now it feels like he's caught in a trap. If it was just about him, he'd leave this minute, take his chances out in the open. But he needs to factor in the kid.

Since he got back he's made a fair amount of noise, and she hasn't woken. Must be exhausted. No reason to drag her into his unconfirmed fears.

With no immediate threat out there, he lowers the gun, turns it over, reacquainting himself with how it feels. That sweet spot weight – light but substantial enough to have some heft. Back in the day he came to think of it as his Significant Other. The two of them against the world. He snorts remembering how he used to quote that line from Catch 22 to his team: "Just because you're paranoid doesn't mean they're not all out to get you." A joke that's no joke anymore. As recent global events have demonstrated, it's better not to underestimate the power of paranoia – the way it can take people's sanity.

Currently, a tiny sleeping child is the only new arrival he needs to be concerned about. It feels wrong to be looking down at her with a weapon in his hands. What's she going to think if she opens her eyes and sees him poised above her with a gun?

Her regular breathing is in sync with the rhythmic sound of the breaking waves. With her fair hair and scrawny little body, she's the least threatening intruder his imagination could have conjured up.

Until today his time here has been uneventful. With two deaths in the space of a few hours, he wouldn't be human if it hadn't unnerved him. Doesn't mean he should give in to panic and do something rash he might later regret.

The girl could be the only survivor of a troubled trio who set off on a sea journey. They then got blown off course and randomly washed up on his island. The murder-suicide hypotheses is not an unreasonable one, though he's kicking himself for not checking through the dead man's pockets while he had the chance. A missed opportunity that might have yielded clues to the corpse's identity and/or what he was up to. Face it, he'd made a major error.

He runs a hand down his face. The fact remains that some-one – not necessarily one of the two dead adults – tried to hide the boat they'd arrived on.

And there's still the girl – her existence a problem he needs to deal with. If he accepts there's no immediate threat, his dwindling supplies won't stretch for much longer. From time to time he's been forced to head off to one of the larger islands to stock up on essentials. Predictability is a habit that can get you killed. Always better to mix things up. When he leaves the island he never heads off to the same place twice.

The wind is picking up, whistling in the woodstove's vent pipe like it's getting ready to break into a tune. Except for wading birds, there's not a single soul out on the beach. The only object circling above is a white tailed eagle high over the cliffs with its barn-door wide wings outstretched.

Why isn't he reassured? Countless hours in this shack and he's never felt this anxious and claustrophobic before. Some switch in his brain has been flicked to the on position. He wants to pace, but there's no room to do much of that.

The temperature's dropped now that the fire's gone out. He can't risk sending up a smoke signal so instead he pulls a blanket off his bed and lays it over the girl, relieved to have covered that small arm with its bruises and telltale marks.

Would he look less sinister in her eyes if he cut his beard? He's never wanted kids. In these troubled times he's been thankful not to be responsible for anyone else's welfare. Having her here is a major complication – a burden he could do without. Whatever the three of them were running away from, he's guessing their pursuers could rock up here sooner or later.

Damn it. While the kid is catching up on her sleep, he might as well check the hut's immediate surroundings. Re-assured by the tranquil view through the window, he flips the catch on the door. Deep breath. Gun raised, he pushes the door wide, checks left then right.

Clear.

Crouching, he scurries over to the barn wall. By balancing on an old stone trough, he gains enough height to train the rifle through one of its arrow-slit windows.

All clear on that side as well.

He jumps down. Hugging the walls, he then tucks himself behind the remains of the barn's once massive doors. It's clear from that angle too. And no sounds out there except for the usual surf and seabirds. In the old days he would have sent up a drone to make certain. If only.

He lowers his gun a fraction. Through his hut's open door he sees the girl is now sitting bolt upright and staring out at him. No – more like she's studying him.

'Had a good sleep sweetheart?' he asks, mustering a reassuring smile. He jerks a thumb backwards. 'Just checking everything's okay out here. Can't afford to be too careful – under the circumstances.'

No response. No sign she'd understood what he said. She can't be more than five years old so phrases like "under the circumstances" will be beyond her vocabulary. He doubts she can comprehend what happened to the woman she was with. In any case, death is always unimaginable for the living.

It's possible she witnessed the man's murder, though that's not something he intends to interrogate her about. Out on the beach, he hadn't noticed any blood-spatter on her clothes. Given the state they were both in, he would hardly have spotted a thing like that. If she was nearby when that knife was plunged with force into the man's back, a few stray droplets might have landed on her clothes. Something he should check for later.

Ashamed of his train of thought, he says, 'I promised you soup, didn't I?' She's staring wide-eyed at his gun with what appears to be recognition in her eyes. God alone knows what associations she's making. Under that unblinking gaze he's being judged and no doubt found guilty. A verdict that would be hard to defend.

He goes back inside the hut and shuts the door. When he turns around the girl is standing up. Without her coat, in that flimsy, summer frock he can see just how bony she is.

Turning away from her scrutiny, he stows the rifle out of her reach. If his fears are unfounded and, assuming their immediate situation doesn't alter, why not go off in his boat to get supplies and use the opportunity to drop the kid off somewhere safe? Kills two birds with one trip.

The logs in the stove are still glowing at the edges. There might be enough residual heat in the top plate to warm the soup. He tests it with a touch. 'Shit!' Sucking his finger, he dances on the spot. It takes him a moment to realise the sound he can hear is coming from the girl. She's giggling – though when he looks at her she stops. It's been a while since he heard the sound of someone laughing.

Hmm. Somewhere safe – now there's a challenge he'll need to think about. He rubs at his beard wondering whether to shave it off for this trip. Then again, it might be better not to draw attention to what an ex once called his duelling scars.

Chapter Six

The kid is watching his every move. To get her to his boat without a struggle, he needs to gain her trust. Remembering his promise, he knocks up some "soup" – a concoction made from an unlabelled tin of hard to identify vegetables with a handful of flaked oats thrown in to bulk it out.

When it's warm enough, he gives it a final stir then divides it between two mugs which he places on the counter some distance apart. 'This one's yours,' he tells her, tapping the side of one mug. 'It's not too hot so you can eat it right away.'

She takes a step towards the food but is reluctant to come closer. He sips from his own mug. 'Though I say it myself, it tastes pretty good.'

The girl's shivering, either from cold or fear – possibly both. Two more steps and she's close enough to reach out and snatch the mug. He checks out her dress for any blood spots. None that he can see.

Once the soup's passed her sniff test, she takes a sip which she rolls around her mouth like some picky connoisseur. She must have liked it because she then gulps the rest down. When she's finished, she tips the mug upside-down to swallow the last dregs.

While sipping his, he checks the clearing and the beach and, once again, everything looks much the same as always. No unusual activity out there or on the water beyond.

The girl's pale blue eyes stare up at him before travelling down to regard her empty mug. 'I'm guessing that means you're still hungry,' he says. Between them they've finished the soup. All he can offer her now is another half of one of his precious dried biscuits. He breaks one in two then puts her half down on the counter in front of her.

She makes a grab for it. 'No rush,' he tells her. They're a challenge for even the strongest teeth though she nibbles away at it. 'A bit dry, aren't they?' he says. 'I reckon some water would help to wash it down.'

She shrinks back when he stretches to pick up her empty mug. He fills it from the jerry can. Instead of drinking, she stares suspiciously at it. He pours himself a mug full then raises it towards her like he's offering a toast. Her eyes study him closely as he's swallowing as if she wants to be certain it's safe to drink. What can have happened to make a child of her age so wary? Has she been drugged or poisoned in the past? The marks around her wrists suggest she was recently held captive and, judging by her hunger, kept half-starved.

He shakes his head. Christ – what is the world coming to? Since he's been living in isolation, he can't begin to answer that question. If he's going to help this girl he needs to learn more about the current state of play in the big wide world out there.

With both hands raised to show her he's no threat, he makes his way over to the alcove where his bed is. Kneeling down, he pulls out one of the drawers tucked underneath it and moves aside his summer shorts and t-shirts to check on the field unit. It's still safely inside its metamaterial container. Like Pandora's box, opening it could have dire consequences. He hasn't dared to use it in a long while. All the same, he should probably take it with him when they leave. It could be useful.

For the journey she'll need an extra layer of clothing. He holds up one of two identical navy t-shirts. 'You could wear this over your dress,' he says.

She's not looking at him or the t-shirt but staring past him to the closed door. He'd turned the piece of wood at the top to lock it. She must be thinking of making a run for it – weighing up her odds of success.

He'd locked her in here earlier – not the best way to build trust. In her position he'd be feeling the same impulse to escape. Right now, with her being nearer to the door and him on his knees, she might just make it over there before him. What then? She won't be able to reach that stave. What if she waits until he's asleep and drags a chair over and opens it? The last thing he needs is a game of hide and seek around the island.

He holds the garment out – a peace offering. 'I don't mean to frighten you, sweetheart,' he says, 'but it's likely there are some bad people out there.' She's staring at him, weighing him up. 'Believe me you're a lot safer in here with me.'

Her eyes flick to the door and back. He arranges his face in what he hopes is his least threatening expression and takes a punt. 'It's hard for me to figure out how I can help you if you won't talk to me.'

She's listening. Assessing. 'We got off on the wrong foot earlier,' he says looking down at her bare feet. 'Sorry about shutting you in here like that.' He smiles. 'Shall we start again?' He lays a hand on his chest. 'Let's begin with the easy stuff. Like I told you, my name's Ash.' He repeats it, taps his breast-bone then points a finger at her. 'What's your name?'

A frown creases her forehead as if she's struggling with the whole concept. It's possible she doesn't know. Seems unlikely she's never been given a name. He'd initially thought the woman referred to her as Maia. Then she used the phrase "mea culpa". I'm guilty. Up to his waist in freezing water, he'd guessed she meant the child's existence was her fault, her mistake. Was it simply a case of mishearing her, or had she intended some kind of sick pun on the girl's name?

Either way, it might be better to let "Maia" die along with her mother and likely tormentor.

Careful to make no sudden movements, he puts the t-shirt down on the bed and reaches for the pad and pencil resting on his bedside table. He turns the page on his sketch of a basking seal and draws a stick man, then gives him a beard. Alongside the man, he draws a stick girl with long hair. Angling the drawing towards her, he points at the man. 'That's me. Not the best of likenesses.' Too wordy – he needs to keep this simple.

He taps the stick-girl with her triangular skirt. 'That's meant to be you.'

The girl stares at it for a moment and then nods like she's understood. 'So what should I call you?'

Her mouth opens as if she might be about to reply, but no sound comes out. 'Okay, maybe that question wasn't as easy as

I thought.' He runs a hand over his face. 'For now, why don't I just call you Lass. That's what they call all the girls in this part of the world. If you want me to call you something else, you'll need to tell me what.' His thumb and index finger form a ring shape. 'Okay?'

Though her arm is down at her side, he sees the same two digits come together on her right hand.

It's a start.

He picks up his sketchbook and turns to the next blank page where he draws a box for the hut and lines for the barn walls. He taps the hut square. 'This is where we are now, okay?' He draws an irregular circle to represent the island adding a few trees and some sheep. With his pencil tip resting on one of the sheep, he tries a couple of baas.

Her eyes light up. Then her lips form a thin smile. To make his map clearer, he adds waves to represent the sea surrounding them. Thinking of those old sailors' maps, he's tempted to draw a few dragons at the edges of the page.

Anticipating what could be about to happen, he adds a group of stick men hiding amongst the trees, then gives them turned down mouths and big guns.

He draws the winding inlet. 'My boat is over here,' he tells her as he sketches a childish boat with a sail it doesn't have. He adds a dotted line leading from there into the waves. To make things clearer, he makes his two fingers walk from the hut square across the island to his cartoon boat. With one finger following along the dotted line, he adds, 'Once we get to my boat, we'll sail all the way down here to the sea. And the good news is we'll be well away from all those bad men over there hiding in the woods.'

Did she understand any of that? 'Is that okay?' When he makes the OK sign again, her little fingers show no response. Has she failed to comprehend, or does she have reservations about his plan?

He looks down at her tiny, bare feet, that one boot still lying on the floor. 'Before we go anywhere,' he says, 'I'll need to find that other boot of yours – the one that dropped off when I carried you up here from the beach.' It would be quicker if he goes by himself, but counterproductive to shut her in again.

He picks up the t-shirt. 'It's cold out there.' In a decisive tone, he tells her, 'Put this on over your dress and you'll be warmer. Before we go to look for your boot, you'll need to put your coat back on. And we'll make sure it's properly buttoned up this time.'

She takes the t-shirt he's holding out. After sniffing it, she hesitates for a moment before pulling it over her head.

Chapter Seven

Guy

The music they're playing is sentimental to the point of maudlin – old songs to reassure their dwindling clientele nothing much has changed. All accordions should be strangled at birth. It's a mild evening so the pall from their foul tobacco smoke is drifting in from outside. Conversation tonight is sparce and mundane, punctuated with more than the usual volleys of coughs and grunts. No wonder few women choose to waste their evenings in here.

At times like this Guy misses real bars – joints where you're forced to shout over raucous conversations and pulsing beats. Places where they share the same fucking language, where a man can casually pick up someone for a wild and sweaty night without risking the outrage of their relatives in the cold light of day.

In this village he'll never be fully accepted, which is more than fine by him. Integration – now there's a concept folks like to wrestle with. He snorts into his drink. Though he's been forced to endure the odd spit aimed at his boots, most of the people hereabouts have chosen to tolerate him. He's the "necessary evil" around here. Perched on his usual stool at the bar, the other customers tend to pass the time of day with him when they come up to order. But tonight it's different. Tonight you'd think he was invisible. At the same time he's been on the receiving end of way too much side-eye – not what a man needs when trying to unwind after a taxing day.

By this time of an evening, faces and voices tend to merge together. In their mostly dung-coloured clothes, collectively they reek of the land – the famous "terroir" of the region that finds its way into the taste of the wine and liquor they serve here.

He's intrigued – which one of them will have the cojones to confront him with whatever's praying on their collective mind? These country folk! He shakes his head. They share a hive mentality – groupthink that gives the weak minded the backup they need to hold on to their precious beliefs or opinions.

The usual suspects are standing in a close huddle some distance away from where they habitually congregate. A while back he'd attempted to train up that lot, along with some of the younger villagers. Tried to make them into an effective fighting force. Fat chance. With no immediate threat to their comfortable lives, most weren't prepared to put in the hours or commitment. A couple of individuals had showed some promise. Next thing, they had their weapons confiscated by the other locals because of their so-called "psychopathic tendencies". In his experience, that's a definition that depends entirely on who's judging who.

What's got them riled up tonight? He attempts to meet the eyes of this potential posse. Heads in a huddle, they're most definitely avoiding his gaze, though from time to time they can't resist a glance in his direction. Seems like he might have been schooling his potential enemies. Good job he did a bad job.

What's their beef on this fine evening here in the back of the back of beyond? He's taken care to keep his unsanctioned activities below the radar – or so he'd thought. It's possible word's got around about some of his sidelines. Chances are they're pissed at his unauthorised use of the ammo the commune likes to keep close tabs on. In the past he's fobbed them off with some bullshit about needing those missing rounds for target practice – honing his skills in readiness for dot, dot, dot. He'd let them fill in the blanks. Like the latest circulating virus, bad news spreads to even the most remote places – and there's been plenty of bad news lately. Every man, woman and child must have heard tales rising up from the lowlands like the foulest of farts. As their protector, his harshest critics would find it difficult to argue against him being prepared for the worst their primed imaginations can conjure up. Pity the same can't be said for the rest of that rabble.

Right now they're definitely psyching themselves up to stage some sort of intervention. Big Gerard's shoulders are raised and flexing. They must have chosen him as tonight's message bearer.

Wait up. Holding him back with a firm, though farcically much smaller hand, Fontaine has more to say on the matter. It's impossible to make out what it is from this distance. With faces obscured or turned away, he's having trouble reading much on their lips. Their body language is way easier to interpret. Fontaine's holding court. Not an obvious alpha specimen, he's nonetheless honing his rabble-rousing skills to the max.

Guy turns his back on them, acts like he's unaware of the mood music playing in here. If only. 'Bring it on,' he mutters in English to the mirror behind the bar. The wild-haired individual staring back at him could be a stranger. Not that he's overly concerned about losing the smooth looks of his youth.

As yet, no one's broken out of their tight little cluster. They're biding their time, waiting for the place to clear out a bit. Maybe sensing something's about to go down, other customers are draining their glasses and staggering off to their beds.

He makes the odds eight, possibly nine, against one. He's faced worse. Since they know all about his specific skill set, they're bound to suspect he's armed.

Any mass-brawl needs to be carefully choreographed. With one of those whiny songs still assaulting his ears, it gives him a degree of pleasure to decide which individual he'll pick off first. Fontaine's not going to be a problem since he's more likely to begin with a tongue-lashing. If their chosen delegate is that brute Gerard, it should be easy enough to sidestep his lumbering moves and avoid contact with those meaty fists.

They might decide to come at him all at once on the basis that there's safety in numbers. The adrenaline now flowing through his veins is delivering more of a buzz than the shots he's tossed back. Maybe they just want to parley. He apes the famous French-shrug. 'Peut-être ils veulent parler,' he mutters out loud. Too bad – he's in no mood to justify his actions. If he refuses to answer their accusations, will they have the necessary balls to risk using force?

Fisticuffs – now there's a word and a concept that's gone out of use. Against this tanked-up, half-trained mob, physical force should be sufficient. If necessary, he'll flash the knife strapped to his ankle – an ugly blade that should prove an effective deterrent. If they pile in all at once, he might need to brandish the handgun tucked into the back of his waistband. Perhaps he'll need to fire it, make a few new holes in this low, smoke-stained ceiling.

He nods to the server. 'Encore.' Then giving it a bit more finesse, 'Une autre, s'il te plait,' addressing the lovely Théa in his never-going-to-be-good-enough French. A full glass of liquor in the eyes works wonders as an aperitif if it seems like things are going to kick off.

Truth is, after all this sitting around he welcomes the prospect. He lifts a glass to his own grizzled reflection, 'Santé!' What the hell are those cowardly bastards waiting for?

Chapter Eight

Ash

They slip silently away from the land. No lights when he looks back at the island, no tell-tale glow from an intruder's fire. The inlet, the towering headland and then the last of the rocky outcrops are gradually swallowed up in darkness.

Once they're a safe distance from shore, he stows the oar and starts the engine. It settles into its usual chugging rhythm.

A calm, clear night, the moon's light dappling the waves. Countless stars pattern the heavens reminding him of his insignificance, of the entire planet's irrelevance. He doesn't believe in any sort of cosmic purpose.

Now they're in open water the boat is being tugged by the tide. He's soothed by the gentle slap of the waves against the bow. While he's standing in the open wheelhouse, the kid's chosen to huddle down in the narrow gap between the storage lockers on deck. Well wrapped up, with both of those little boots back on her feet, she appears to have fallen asleep – no doubt worn out from their hurried trek across the island. In the end she'd offered far less resistance to this trip than he'd anticipated. She'd even allowed him to pick her up and set her down in the boat. It seems the girl's beginning to trust him. That possibility and the fact that he's about to offload her onto strangers shames him to his core.

They can't drift for ever. He gives a long sigh. No point in prevaricating – it's time to steer a course for the island he's decided on. As soon as he does, he gets a sense of foreboding. Right now, with nothing but open water surrounding them, there's plenty of time to change his mind. All available evidence suggests there are no other intruders on "his" island, nothing to stop him simply stocking up with provisions and heading straight back. At the last minute he'd grabbed a pile of his precious books to exchange for supplies. He has to hope people still have an appetite for fiction.

But then there's the problem of this girl. He can offer her no sort of life on his tiny, remote island with no one but him for company. After what she's been through – some of which he can only guess at – she deserves a lot better.

The kid's made herself so small she's almost invisible in the shadows like some tiny stowaway. This trip is mainly about her, for her. At least that's what he's been telling himself since they set off. Just when he's gaining her trust, he's about to betray it by taking a massive gamble with her future.

The girl stretches a little then settles back into sleep again. He's grown used to living alone. With all the dramas of the past behind him, since landing on his island he's known only peace – an uncomplicated existence that's pacified him beyond any substance man can concoct. He's not a fan of hippy shit, scoffs at all that stuff about Gaia or Mother Earth, yet he can't deny he's learnt to live in harmony with the elements instead of always pitting himself against them. Nature can be harsh, downright brutal at times, but there's a logic of sorts to it – a balancing act. Left to itself, life finds a way to flourish even under the harshest conditions. They say deeds speak louder than words and, judged by their collective actions, it's impossible not to see homo sapiens as a blight on an otherwise perfect planet. Man as a species deserves the extinction they appear to be hurtling towards.

He's not proud of his own part in that process. He shakes his head as he stares into the unfathomable depths of the black ocean. No point in picking apart all the rights and wrongs – the dark deeds and darker responses of the last few decades. Though they weren't aware of it at the time, it turned out his unit had played a part in destabilising things. Along with others, he could make a fairly valid claim to being one of the many who have helped to bring this new world into existence. But hey, don't shoot the midwife.

After what happened on his last mission there's no going back. So he'd checked out – traded in the few chips he had left and sailed away in this stolen boat having left it all behind for good. Or so he'd imagined.

An alert flashes and he makes a course correction to avoid a trio of half-submerged rocks. They're making reasonable progress though he can't decide if that's a positive. Truth is, he has only the vaguest notions about the place he's set course for.

Judged solely on his superficial impressions during a fleeting visit to Dumna Novus, the people there appear to be bucking the trend and leading a relatively harmonious existence. As a response to all the unrest, they've fallen back into the age-old pattern of eking a living from the surrounding land and sea. For everything else, they barter with what they can spare. According to the fisherman he'd shared a drink with, the Dumnami seldom visit any of the larger islands. They leave home only to trade their hand-woven fabrics and leather products in return for fuel for their boats and what the fisherman called "other necessities". He hadn't explained how they reached agreement on what constitutes a necessity.

On that same trip he'd acquired the handmade, leather gloves he's wearing. Making a fist, he stares down at his hand – the stout stitching that's lasted longer than on any other pair he's had. The fact that someone on Dumna can produce a highly serviceable pair of gloves is no recommendation of anything else. And the drunken musings of a fisherman would hardly stand up as evidence in court. He has no reason to believe the islanders will welcome an anonymous, non-verbal child into their midst. Even if she gets lucky and some good-hearted souls agree to take her in, can they be trusted? How's he going to know whether they'll treat her well?

If he's learnt anything from history it's that outsiders are seldom regarded as equals. There'll be nothing to stop them exploiting her in ways it might be better not to contemplate. However unlikely, he's acting in loco parentis though he has no rightful claim to such a role. No guarantee that leaving her to the mercy of other strangers will turn out to be in the girl's best interest.

Events during the last year and a half have literally passed him by. Life may have stood still on his island, but it's a safe assumption many things will have changed. He doubts it's for the better. He's watched larger vessels making their way along regular shipping routes and often speculated about what was being traded and with whom. It can't bode well that, in all his time on the island, his sole visitors have been a man who gets murdered, a deranged, suicidal woman and this mute child.

When they reach Dumna, they'll need to look acceptable. Though she's dressed in a rag bag of clothes, with her blonde hair and blue eyes, the girl is undeniably cute. Appealing. Feeling the sea wind on his face, he rubs his hand across his newly shaven chin. As well as revealing a few scars, the blade has left its mark here and there. His skin is deeply tanned, his self-administered haircut ragged. He's noticed grey creeping into his dark hair. Safe to say his 42 years haven't been kind to him but he's not alone in that.

It's possible Dumna is no longer the peaceful and stable community it was. There's no way he's going to sail blindly into an unknown situation.

He takes off his gloves before extracting the field unit from its box. Weighed in his hands, it seems insubstantial but carries so much weight. Once he switches it on, he'll be able to discover what's been happening in his absence. At the same time, his present location will register as a ping and then a pulsating dot in this vast archipelago.

Will anyone flag it up? There's no way of knowing if the organisation he last worked for still exists. Are any of them left alive?

Such a small device and yet it will set off a homing beacon leading them straight to him. If he's lucky, his whereabouts will be of no further interest to anyone. If he's unlucky – watch this space.

He studies the unit, turns it end to end as if this might offer the answer to his dilemma. The current's getting stronger. With the next big wave, the boat lurches before righting itself. If he were to drop the device overboard now it would be irretrievably lost and that would put an end to his deliberations.

Quite a thought.

Legs braced, he takes a steadying breath. He's kept the damned thing against all the odds and in spite of its potential value to the highest bidder. No point keeping it if he's not prepared to use it.

'Okay,' he says out loud. 'I guess there's only one way to find out.' From this point on the risks for both of them are about to increase.

Chapter Nine

Guy

The movie-cop siren bores its way into his brain – his own stupid choice of ringtones. It doesn't let up. 'Fuck off!' Guy shouts at it.

The noise carries on. Groaning, he opens one eye then snaps it shut against the day's awful brightness. His mouth tastes of raw metal. When he moves, a jagged pain splits his forehead. Ears ringing, he stuffs the pillow over his head, but that fails to block out the racket.

Waa! Waa! Waa!… Whoever it is, doesn't give up easily. Squinting, he remembers his satphone is on a table that's just out of reach. He lunges at it, muttering a string of oaths. Half out of bed and after a great deal of fumbling he switches it off, stops just short of hurling it across the room.

Though peace is restored the ringing in his ears persists like tinnitus. He closes his eyes and tries to get back to sleep.

No good – he's too awake. And now some fucker is banging on his door. Wishing them to hell, he pulls himself upright though every movement causes a different part of his body to protest.

A quick recce confirms he's in his own bedroom. He touches various parts of his face, wincing at each new swelling he discovers. One thing's for certain – he won't be a pretty sight. His knuckles are raw and caked in dried blood – some of which is probably his. Looking down he discovers an array of livid bruises peppering his torso; they continue all the way to his genitals and beyond. Today he's sporting more spots than a leopard.

His visitor appears to have given up and gone away. Pinching the bridge of his nose, he can't recall how he made it back in one piece. Did he have help? Seems unlikely given the level of hostility towards him last night. He's naked, his clothes abandoned in a trail across the floor. Did he undress himself? There's no hollow in the other pillow, no tell-tale whiff to his sheets and no sounds coming from his only other room. If he had company last night, they decided not to sleep over.

He can hear someone pottering around in the old cart shed down below and concludes it must be Arnaud working on that ancient truck of his. Like he's told him many times, that thing has had its day.

Now his eyes have adjusted to the light, he peers through the window at the framed view of mountains shimmering against a clear blue sky. A view picturesque enough for one of those wish-you-were-here postcards no one sends anymore.

He's tempted to go back to bed and hunker down, pull the covers over his head and write the day off – except something's nagging away at him.

He needs to recalibrate. Snatches from the previous evening come back like scenes from a movie he'd dozed off to before the end. As far as he recalls, he'd taken on and bested the men who came at him in the bar – inflicted more injuries than he received. Ironic that they were the same men he'd done his best to train in combat. Good job he's a lousy teacher. In spite of his sore jaw, he chuckles remembering how he'd easily floored most of those bastards. Who's the fucking daddy?

Down below Arnaud is whistling some godawful tune as he works. It's not long before he hears him close the outside door and lock it – a pointless exercise since you'd have to pay someone to take that old wreck away.

Hearing heavy boots on the stairs, his smile drops. Arnaud's always been a tenacious old bastard. 'Guy! I know you're in there Guy,' he shouts through the door in his heavily accented but otherwise impressive English. 'It is time for you and me to have a talk.'

'C'est inutile,' he mutters. Then louder, 'Va-t'en.'

'You made a lot of enemies last night, my friend.'

With a shrug in his voice he tells him, 'C'est pas nouveau.'

He can hear the old man's laboured breathing. 'All the same I will remain here until you let me in.'

Damn it. Pulling on yesterday's underpants takes some time and a lot of pain. When he opens the door Arnaud is gazing up at him like a father disappointed by his errant son's behaviour.

He tells him straight, 'That bunch of halfwits were spoiling for a fight well before anything kicked off.' He shakes his head to indicate the pettiness of those bastards, the way their minor grievances take on such disproportionate importance. As if there wasn't so much more for them to worry about. Last night they'd been primed and pumped – looking for an excuse to take him on.

Arnaud clears a chair of its contents, sweeping everything onto the floor with no compunction before he sits down heavily on it. 'Is it unwise for you to alienate so many of your neighbours?' Slow to break eye contact, the old man rubs at an oil stain on his hand as he waits for a response.

'Yeah well, I wasn't born and raised in this…' He's heard the phrase *trou à rats* but decides not to use it. 'In this place,' he says, 'I will always be an outsider – un étranger. I'm never going to be one of your gang and, you know, that's more than fine by me.' He doesn't add that, by any measure, he's their superior – the real reason their communal resentment came to a head last night. 'A man's entitled to defend himself,' he says.

'This is true.' Arnaud sighs, his lined face looks grey in daylight. 'All the same you will need to watch your back from now on.' The old man taps the side of his nose. 'Like the good farmer you will need to mend some fences, my friend. Et tout de suite.'

He'd busted quite a few heads last night – this morning many of them will be in a sorrier state than he is and in no condition to do anything. 'Sod fences,' he says. Continuing the metaphor, he adds, 'They ought to be more concerned about what'll happen should some of those big bad wolves down in the valley decide to come prowling around up here. Perhaps you should remind them it will take more than fences to stop this place being overrun.'

'But this morning the people here are more concerned with the wolf who is dressed in a sheep's fleece,' Arnaud says, with that look in his wily old eye. Though his English may be imperfect, the implication is clear enough.

'Hoooowhoo!' he howls at the old man, who stubbornly refuses to smile. Having said his piece, Arnaud gets to his feet though he has some difficulty straightening up. 'Croyez-moi!' Arnaud demands waving a gnarled finger in his face and standing close enough for him to smell the garlic on his breath. They both know only too well the locals here have absurdly long memories when it comes to perceived injustice. 'Bienheureux les pacifiques,' the old man declares as he shuffles towards the door then closes it with some force.

Called many things in his time, he's never been accused of being a peacemaker.

When he probes the skin around his eyes, the resulting pain confirms he's sporting a couple of impressive shiners. In the old days he'd have laid an ice pack or a raw piece of steak on the bruises. If only.

Casting around for something to wear, he notices the t-shirt and fleece he had on last night are covered in blood stains. He'll need to soak them for a while to get that out. But for now his priority is finding something to dull the pain. He pours himself a slug of the local gut-rot. This village that calls itself a town would drive any sane man to drink. One thing's certain – he won't be going back to Benoit's bar any time soon. He's in no hurry to confront all those silent, disapproving stares. And besides, his knuckles are in no fit state to be rapped again. Better to let them stew – let them realise they need him far more than he needs them.

The booze is beginning to hit the spot. Hair of the dog and

all that. Pouring another couple of centimetres into the glass, his mind snags on something else that's been niggling at him. He shuts his eyes and tries to focus on what it might be.

Christ – someone just gave him a wakeup call on his satphone. Such calls are few and far between and yet he'd silenced it without a second thought. He might not be in great shape, but there's no sense passing up the opportunity of another extracurricular assignment.

Could the call have been from close to home? As far as he knows Fontaine is the only other person in this place with a functioning phone. If it was him who called earlier, it's not difficult to guess what he wanted to say. He's been on the receiving end of enough sermonising for one morning.

All the same, now his curiosity is aroused, he seizes the phone and scrutinises its log. Seems the call he'd silenced wasn't to his usual local number and hadn't come from anyone in his vicinity. Instead it was made to an alternative number he's only ever divulged to two people. He shakes his head in disbelief. As far as he's aware the dead don't get to make phone calls.

A tiny red light is flashing at the bottom of the screen to inform him the caller has left a voice message. Their ID is listed as "unknown". The duration of the message is under three seconds.

Passing a finger across his swollen lips, he hesitates for a moment before he finally selects play. There's a short pause. Then an electronic voice says: *New mark located 13:00 hours GMT yesterday. Update and terms to follow.*

Chapter Ten

Ash

'Yes!' Ash pumps his fist. Sitting in a swaying boat in one of the remotest parts of the world and using this one multifunctional device, he's been able to turn the tables and find a backdoor into the organisation's supposedly impenetrable system.

He scrolls through the latest updates for this sector. Jeez! His ebullience subsides. Might have been better not to know. Close to despair, he rubs at his forehead. He wasn't expecting a miracle, but all the same…

His self-imposed thirty seconds are up – time to shut down the link.

It's done.

There's a lot to get his head around. He takes a steadying breath while staring at the same spot on the deck, at those sturdy planks running parallel and true. Whoever built this boat intended it to last – possibly to outlive them.

When he checks on the girl, her head has dropped forward in sleep. How could someone begin to explain to a child what's been happening in the wider world, never mind the why of it? Given the injuries the kid's recently sustained, she's no stranger to the cruelty mankind is capable of.

He snorts at his own self-righteousness. Who's he trying to kid? In the beginning, he'd sought to justify his actions by claiming it was all about protecting civilians, upholding a better way of life… Ya-de, ya-de, ya… He shakes his head at how that all worked out.

The kid looks so peaceful, totally unaware of the risk he's just taken. Sure, he'd done his best to cover his tracks, but it's impossible to know whether his intrusion has been spotted by some eagle-eye and already flagged up.

Given that not all of the intel had been verified, that last report can't be relied on. While the device is out in the open, he might as well take a look at some of the unsecured sites still functioning.

The picture doesn't get any rosier. Various politicians are promising to take charge of the deteriorating situation. Given half a chance most "visionary" leaders tend to turn into ruthless despots. They promise the earth, a new beginning after they've won this last battle against the enemies of law and order. Faced with mayhem, everybody's crying out for a saviour with a noble gaze and that trust-me smile.

The worldwide web may be in tatters, but it's still managing to spew out more head-fuckery than a person can shake a gun at. Myriad new platforms have sprung up to pump out the same dark delusions and mad ravings – echo chambers with no escape route. One thing's certain – during his self-imposed sabbatical the same crazy shenanigans have continued unabated.

Enough. He shuts everything down and packs the field unit away. Everything fits neatly into its metamaterial box.

When he looks out to sea the tide is still running in the same direction, the stars above are where they've always been. Out here, surrounded by water and breathing only mildly polluted air, a man could convince himself nothing's changed.

And that's the crucial danger.

Shutting his eyes he tries to piece together the wider picture. Most of the planet has not only failed to come to its senses but seems more mired in violence and senseless slaughter than ever before. Worse, the remoter regions – those hitherto safe havens – are being dragged into the seemingly unstoppable flow of man-made shite.

The boat shudders and he opens his eyes to find the distinctive outline of Dumna Novus has just popped up on the horizon. Through his binoculars he can make out white waves breaking against its rocky outcrops. It looks different. At this hour, fishing boats could be heading home and yet not one light illuminates the jetty. Though it's early evening, and he's seeing it from his present low angle, the rest of the island also appears to be in darkness.

Suspicion crawls across his scalp. Something's far from right. He cuts the engine and allows the boat to drift. All he can hear is the rush of the wind spurring on the waves that run towards the shore.

From this distance, and with the moon as bright as it is, anyone with a pair of binoculars would be able to pick out his boat – *their* boat. Right now they're sitting ducks out here in open water.

He picks up the oars, slots them into the rowlocks then hesitates, unsure whether to row towards the island or straight on past it.

The absence of lights could be due to any number of factors. It's rained a lot recently so maybe, with a dwindling supply of solar energy, they're saving on power. He has fond memories of a rowdy drunken night, but since then they might all be reformed characters off early to their beds. The events he's just learned about are likely to have made them more cautious.

He could be getting spooked over nothing. Based on such flimsy evidence and his far from reliable instincts, if he gives this island a swerve, what then? He has a limited supply of fuel and drinking water on board. If he heads straight back to his home island, there's still the problem of his dwindling supplies and what he's going to do about the girl. Before they left he was convinced Dumna would offer her a chance at some kind of normal-ish future.

When he checks again, she's no longer asleep but sitting upright, staring at him as if perplexed by his indecision. He grins at her. 'Had a good sleep?' She turns her head towards the island and then back as if willing him to make up his mind one way or the other.

Damn it – considering the lack of alternatives, this place must be worth a shot.

After fumbling in one of the lockers, he finds some old oil rags to muffle the rowlocks before he dips the oars into the water and manoeuvres the bow to face the shore. Taking it steady, he scans the water for any obstacles or shadows lurking just beneath the surface.

The island is beginning to loom large. Over his shoulder he can see no visible lights and no clear landmarks to guide him to shore. He recalls an abandoned RNLI lookout post on the headland more or less directly above the jetty. Through binoculars he spots what's left of it silhouetted against the sky. He can't make out the jetty itself, but there's a definite gap between the rocks that has to be the mouth of the inlet.

He needs to glide in with the minimum amount of noise. Remembering the girl, he turns and beckons her forward. Keeping her feet spread for balance, she walks towards him. 'Okay, Lass, we need to be really, really quiet from now on,' he whispers.

He's about to remind her not to speak when, aware of the irony, he holds a finger across his lips. 'Shhh!' Her finger and thumb meet in a circle to form the "okay" sign he'd shown her earlier. 'Good girl.'

The brightness of the moon is a blessing and a curse. Moving with the incoming tide and needing only the occasional stroke with the oars, they drift into the narrow bay. Once they're closer he recognises the tiny harbour. To bring her in alongside the floating jetty he needs to navigate around a half dozen moored boats of various sizes. He puts a couple of fenders out. The air smells of rotting kelp with a hint of diesel fumes.

He scans for any movement ashore. All's quiet. Over his shoulder he lines up the bow. Another gentle stroke of the oar brings them near enough to throw a guide rope around an upright pole and pull hard until she's nudging the jetty. She fits right in alongside the other boats.

Hearing a cry he freezes. There's a series of answering calls from further away. He lets go of his breath. Not humans signalling, only a pair of short-eared owls getting acquainted.

What now? He can't recce the island with a small child in tow, but it can't be safe to leave her alone in the boat. Having secured the stern line to one of several iron rings, he ties the bow line to another. He picks up the girl and, after checking she still has both her boots, helps her onto the boardwalk before he jumps ashore.

She stands ridged, arms at her side, refusing to budge. He can feel her shivering as he carries her to the end of the dock. The moonlight brightens as they come to a small shack. The remnants of a poster are still visible on one side of it. He makes out what looks like a pod of leaping dolphins. Ah yes – this was the old pay booth from back when they used to run wildlife trips from here. Though the structure is dilapidated with its outer door hanging loose, there's a small bench along the back wall. She'll be safely out of sight inside.

He checks the wood's soundness before lowering her onto the seat. She's reluctant to let go of him. 'Stay here,' he says, pointing a finger as if instructing an errant dog. 'I'm going to fetch you a blanket.'

Back on deck he sheds the waterproof jacket that will restrict his movements. What he's wearing is sufficiently dark. Pity he shaved his beard off. He double-checks the safety catch before tucking his loaded handgun into the waistband at the back of his trousers. The metal lockers are bolted through the deck into a cross brace underneath. It's safer to leave his rifle and ammo inside one of them with his jacket lying on top.

Its stout padlock should thwart all but the most determined of raiders. Secured only by a couple of ropes, the boat itself is vulnerable but there's not a lot he can do about that.

He chooses his monocular not the bulkier binos. First off he re-scans the shoreline looking for movement and picking out only swaying vegetation.

When he gets back to the booth he finds the kid still sitting in the shadows where he'd left her. 'That's my girl.' Straight away he regrets using those words. 'You need to wait here for a bit, okay?' He drapes the blanket over her, tucks the longer edges around those skinny legs. 'I need to make sure everything's safe first. I'll be back as soon as I can, promise.' He has no right to make such a pledge when he can't be certain. How many times has she been lied to and let down in her short life? He can't make out her face or tell whether she'd signalled her compliance.

Should he blacken his face with mud? On balance that's not a good idea if he wants to appear trustworthy. He exhales. Okay, he's ready. 'Back soon, sweetheart,' he says, echoing his own mother from way back when she was alive.

Crouching to reduce the target area, he sets off at a pace. He remembers the pitted road that heads to the main set-tlement – an approach that would leave him too exposed. Instead, he bears right onto a lesser used dirt track that has to lead somewhere. After a couple of hundred metres the dark outline of what appears to be a regular house comes into view. No lights on inside, no smell of smoke lingering in the air on such a chilly night. The building's modest size suggests a limited number of occupants.

Getting closer he's able to make out a dozen or so wooden steps leading up to an open walkway and a door he assumes to be the main entrance. At ground level, and off to one side, a small gate leads around the back. Dark soil – recently culti-vated. In a hostile environment he'd advance from the rear, but there's no reason to believe the occupants here pose any threat.

Away from the harbour the offshore breeze has dropped leaving the air still and cold. Every plank groans under his weight as he makes his way up the steps. Reaching the front door, it occurs to him anyone in there will be spooked by a lone stranger rocking up at this hour. In their place he'd attack first, interrogate later. Pulling a gun on them won't exactly set the right tone. Then again, holding up his hands in surrender will leave him way too vulnerable.

He could just knock.

Okay, but then what's he going to say if someone answers? *Oh, hi there. Sorry to disturb you at this hour. You don't know me, but I've just arrived on this island, and I thought you wouldn't mind me waking you up so I can ask you if there's anything amiss around here.*

Hearing a creak down below, he spins around in combat stance. The girl is standing on the bottom step looking up at him. Surprised that he hadn't heard her approach, he stows his gun. Being caught out like that suggests his senses aren't as sharp as they once were.

Her presence changes everything. He tiptoes down the steps as quietly as the old timbers will allow before scooping her up and ducking into the walkway's shadow. Into her ear he whispers, 'I thought I told you to stay put.' He plants a hand over her mouth to stifle any protests. Her breath is hot against his palm.

All remains quiet. No one comes to the door, no tell-tale shadow looms through the gaps in the boards over their heads.

Once he's certain, he frees the girl and sets her back on her feet. She must be scared because she clings to his leg, effectively hobbling him. So much for doing this unencumbered.

He's irritated by her limpet grip, her disobedience. They've come all this way for her sake, trusting his hunch that some good-hearted folks here will be willing to take responsibility for her and free him of the obligation.

This after-dark foray was ill-judged in the first place. Now, with the kid by his side, he needs to change tactics. Better to wait it out at sea and make their approach in daylight.

The last time he rocked up here, the islanders were friendly enough and straightforward to negotiate with. Unless things have radically changed here, a visitor arriving in daylight accompanied by a small child is unlikely to be treated as a potential hostile.

He'll spin an appropriate sob-story about how he'd found her out at sea and alone in a small boat and assumed that whoever had been with her must have drowned. He might mention the possessions left on board, how, if not for the girl, it was a Mary Celeste situation. The tale of a helpless child abandoned in such dangerous circumstances should move the stoniest of hearts. True, the story's a bit short on details. Shaking his head, he'll say he has no idea who or what might have happened before he came across her. Always go with the truth when you can. The mystery of her origins should appeal to the more romantically inclined – if those sort still exist.

He's about to pick her up and head back to the boat when he hears the unmistakable sound of a rifle bolt being locked into the firing position.

Chapter Eleven

'Raise your hands.' A man's voice. 'Higher – where I can see them.'

'Okay, okay.' He squints into the narrow beam picking him out, then steps sideways to block the girl from the gunman's line of sight, hoping she has the sense to stay hidden back there.

'Now come out slowly.' Accent's not local. American? Canadian possibly? A good twenty-five metres away. Very tall, for sure. Can't make out his face beneath that headtorch. Rifle looks to be a vintage Lee-Enfield. Probably holds five rounds – more than enough.

'Now walk slowly toward that old telegraph pole over there.' The beam of his head-torch swings right to illuminate the pole. The man's circling around, keeping his back to the building. He wants him out in the open where he's an easier target.

Tall-guy waves the barrel to show he means business. Ash pictures himself helpless and tied to that pole, about to be shot in the head. He says, 'I sincerely apologise for startling you, sir.' To show willing he starts walking towards it. 'I mean you no harm.'

The gunman chortles. 'Yeah, well that's where you and me differ.' Cocky – likes playing the big man. He must be the guy on watch – "The Stag" they used to call them. Is he playing the villain, or seriously planning to use that thing?

He's taking smaller steps though not slow enough to piss the man off. The grass beneath his feet peters out as the ground turns to sand with the odd patch of scrub. 'There's no need for this,' he tells him. To suggest he's overreacting might come across as dismissive. He needs to show deference, acquiescence. 'Let me assure you, sir, I pose no threat to you or anyone else on this island.'

'Keep walking.'

Stumbling on purpose, he slows his pace further hoping to draw that rifle butt within reach. 'Look, I've only just arrived. My boat's tied up at the jetty in plain sight.'

Is this guy even listening?

'I thought I might trade a few things for some supplies same as I did the last time I was here.'

'What sort of things?'

Ash hesitates before answering, 'Some books.'

'Books!' Tall-guy gives a raucous laugh.

'Listen,' he says, 'if you or your friends aren't happy with me being here, I'll be on my way.' He clears his throat. 'I can see how you might think I was acting suspiciously back there, but I was only checking the lie of the land, so to speak. This was a peaceful community before, but, well, you hear rumours… So I thought I'd scout around a bit, make sure I wasn't about to walk into trouble.'

'Too late for that.' A line from some movie. Tall-guy could

be the local psycho getting his kicks by scaring the crap out of gullible strangers.

'If you could just lower your gun, sir, I'm sure we can come to some arrangement that's mutually beneficial.'

The man scoffs. 'You're in no position to bargain.'

He's almost reached the telegraph pole. In the moonlight he can see its old, loose wires have formed a kind of cat's cradle – or a net to snare the unwary.

Wind's got stronger now. Below, waves are pounding the shore. If he leaps off that edge, he'll probably be shot first. Either way, he'll smash into those rocks. Survive that, and he won't lie injured for long before he's washed out to sea.

Ash stops abruptly, hoping to lure the man close enough to grab that rifle and press his own gun to the bastard's skull. He gets ready for the poke in the back. Doesn't happen.

The bastard's been smart enough to keep his distance. Reaching the pole, he looks up at it – a monument to another era. Maybe it'll be the last thing he sees.

'Okay, now turn around.' He's staring down that barrel. With more of his face moonlit, he makes out the man's piebald hair and unkempt beard. Got to be in his late fifties. Possibly older. Still in decent physical shape.

His soon-to-be executioner says, 'You might want to close your eyes.'

First sign of weakness. 'Hold on a minute.' He dummies – raising his left hand to block that blinding light. 'I'm guessing you're the nightwatchman here. I'm also guessing your gang, or unit, or whatever you guys call it, will want a chance to interrogate me before deciding if I pose any kind of threat, or I've innocently arrived here. Shouldn't you let them decide?'

'I told you to close your damned eyes.'

'What – too squeamish to look me in the eye when you senselessly murder me?' Shaking his head he lets out a long breath. 'Look, if you're planning to shoot, you might as well get on with it.'

He's about to leap to one side when over the man's shoulders something moves. Fuck! The girl's emerged from her hiding place. She's standing a short distance behind the gunman. He daren't warn her or tell her to run. 'Get lost!' he yells, looking anywhere but in her direction.

'I guess Momma must have taught you never to curse.' Tall-guy's gutsy laugh causes the torch beam to bounce. Rifle's less manoeuvrable at close range… The light picks him out again. Staring into its centre, he shouts, 'Piss off!'

Smirk in his voice, Tall-guy says, 'Careful now or you'll hurt my feelings.'

This was her chance to get away but, maddeningly, she hasn't moved. He brought her here to what he hoped was safety, now she's likely to die alongside him.

The rifle's raised to shoulder height, aimed straight at him. Point blank – no way he can miss. The girl will stand a better chance if he can…

Wait.

Something's making Tall-guy adjust his stance. His head starts to jerk like he's got a tic. Nervous spasms? Tourette's? Instead of squeezing that trigger, he's hopping around. 'What the fuck?' Wiping at his eyes because sand is swirling up and around him like he's just stepped inside his own personal dust-devil. More and more of it rises up, pouring onto the top of his head and then cascading down over his face and into his open mouth. He rips off the torch, covers his face as he splutters and retches against the onslaught. His rifle hits the ground. Hands plastered over his mouth and nostrils, the man's staggering around, trying to outrun the sand-devil that's dogging him, clogging his limbs so he can't get away.

And yet the air around Ash is still breathable. His eyes dart towards the girl. To his relief she's unscathed. Instead of averting her eyes from the spectacle, she's staring intently at the writhing man, one arm outstretched as she points a tiny accusing finger at him.

There's a heavy thump when he falls. Tall-guy's legs and arms continue to thrash and kick as if locked in a stranglehold by an invisible opponent.

Finally, his movements begin to slow. His limbs give their last, reflex spasms and grow still. The sand that was swirling above him drops to cover his body from head to foot like a shroud. No point checking for a pulse since he's obviously dead.

With her thin arm back at her side, the girl steps forward. She peers blank-faced at the half-buried body. He looks from her to the human-shaped mound and back, while his brain struggles to make sense of what he's just witnessed.

He opens his mouth then closes it, finding no words.

Chapter Twelve

Guy

'Tying up a loose end,' is the only explanation offered. Not his job to reason why. The crypto figure mentioned gets and keeps his attention. As for the *how* – the voice tells him, 'We're relying on your usual ingenuity.' An electronic chuckle follows, as if this mission is no big ask. The nickname for these desk jockeys is nacho-men – skinny types talking big, fuelled by junk food while glued to their air-conditioned workstations.

Nacho signs off with, 'Immediate departure required. Intel updates as and when. One-way communications protocol from here on.'

He blows out his cheeks then slowly lets go of his breath. A sanctioned op – something he'd assumed he was over and done with. Tempting to think he's been chosen for his formidable reputation. The reality is, that with many fewer boots on the ground, they've been forced to bet on him and his "usual ingenuity" to find this particular needle in a vast haystack. Like one of those annoyingly persistent cicadas, he's about to surface – though making a lot less noise about it.

He surveys his cramped apartment with something approaching affection then gazes out at the rugged landscape beyond. Never home – though a place he's used to hanging his hat. He could still change his mind but knows he won't.

A roll of his shoulders catches on pain – especially down the left side. Elyna used to quote some Chinese saying about a thousand-mile journey starting with a single step. She'd give him a long look afterwards to show that this observation was meant to be profound.

Well then, breaking it down Chinese style, first step is to study the map. The update comes through showing his destination as a pulsating point in a vast sea of blue. A broken orange line – makes the journey appear easy. The readout informs him that, by this most direct route, distance to target is approximately 2,400 kilometres. Or a tad short of 1,500 miles. A theoretical pathway. It appears some ivory towers are still standing. Make that ivory bunkers.

He shakes his head remembering the once-upon-another-time when he might have caught a few connecting flights, taken a shortish boat ride – et voilà! Back then, even going about it the hard way – overland and by sea – he could probably have covered that distance inside 48 hours.

Better to banish that train of thought. The past is a lost land – concentrate on the present. Make that the future.

How to begin. He guides the cursor along an alternative red pathway that circumnavigates the many territories he'll need to avoid. It looks like some drunk's crazy meanderings. In reality, doing this alone will be no mean feat. There's also the little matter of getting across La Manche – a distance of some 18.2 nautical miles at its shortest point, 130 nmi at its widest. Assuming he manages to reach the English coast without drowning, he'll need to keep heading north through terrain he's unfamiliar with, until the landmass runs out. At this point he'll have to acquire a craft of some kind to cross another stretch of water before venturing into an archipelago made up of over 100 islands and, assuming his target stays put, a theoretical point where both the orange and red lines terminate.

Despite the many potential hazards, he's pumped up by the challenge. It's a relief of sorts to have his actions and goal decided for him. In many ways following orders takes the stress out of life.

Thinking through his brief, he whistles at that crypto figure. Since he's about to risk his life many times over, he ought to have demanded more clarification on the how and when of payment while he had the opportunity. Rookie mistake.

From here on, communications are strictly one-way – *from* them, never *to* them. The safest tactic, or so they claim. They'll track his progress through the hardware he'll be carrying.

His jaw and mouth are really painful from last night's fight. He feels along his teeth from front to back checking if any wobble. In spite of his neighbours' best efforts, all are present and correct. Those same locals will assume they've driven him out of town. A thought that would make him thump the table if his fists weren't so sore.

It's possible one or two people might regret his sudden dis-appearance – his expertise or, at a stretch, his company. Most will gloat, raise a glass and a santé to his departure. Likely adding a "Bon débarras!"

Out loud he mutters, 'And good riddance to you too.' He tries not to imagine how they'll crow over their apparent victory. Yeah well, from what he's witnessed and all the rumours he's been hearing, without him here to organise them into an effective fighting force, that smugness is likely to be short-lived.

Karma they call it.

High time he packed up and got going. He can't risk the burden of his heaviest rucksack. Fast and light is the order of the day. Though not too light. He's well versed in deciding what's essential and what he should leave behind.

He needs transport, though a vehicle will only get him as far as its fuel lasts. To get some peace, he'd silenced Arnaud's ancient pickup truck by removing the rotor arm before replacing the distributor cap. So far the old man's failed to smell a rat. If he puts it back together, he'll be able to hotwire the thing before Arnaud returns from tending his precious vines.

The last few weeks have seen a few incursions in the valley below. The safest route out is narrow and potholed but passable. Once he's left familiar territory behind, there'll be a lot of unknowns to deal with. Everyone's a potential enemy. Better to play the part of a naïve and foolhardy traveller.

He should clean and thoroughly check his rifle before disassembling it. Broken down into parts, it zips into the outer compartments of his pack. He'll take the rifle sling for situations where he needs quicker access to it. His trousers are loose enough to strap his handgun to his calf.

The way he comes across to strangers will be crucial if he's going to pull this off. To that end, he takes a moment to assess his reflection in the washroom mirror. With all its swelling and cuts, his face is almost unrecognisable. Someone once told him he had resting-assassin-face. At the time he'd pretended to take it as a joke not an unfortunate giveaway.

For everyday encounters he'll need to work on his charm. He nods and smiles at his reflection. Not a pretty sight. The cuts and bruises on his body will be hidden by his clothes, but, until they fade, his battered features will mark him out. Another reason to choose the road less travelled.

Minutes later he straightens up fully booted and ready for the off. Including the essential electronics, his pack is heavier than ideal. He hefts it onto his shoulders, telling himself the pain will ease once the bruising's gone down. Assuming he survives that long.

Never fond of goodbyes, he scribbles a note to Arnaud. *I won't be coming back.* Words with a finality that makes him pause. Picturing the old man's disappointed face, he shrugs off the guilt. *My remaining possessions are yours*, will have to serve as an apology, although a few books and stuff are hardly a fair trade for the man's beloved Toyota.

He signs off as *Guy* – not his true name but a serviceable nom de guerre.

Chapter Thirteen

Ash

Starting to sway, the girl then crumples to the ground. With her upturned face gilded by moonlight, she looks angelic once again. Her expression gives no hint that she might have just drowned a grown man in sand.

He crouches beside her, undoes her coat, lays a tentative hand on her chest and is relieved to feel its regular rise and fall. Only asleep. Exhausted, it seems.

On his feet again, he paces back and forth, doubting the veracity of what he'd witnessed only moments earlier. The adrenaline in his bloodstream is slow to subside. A familiar fight-or-flight high – though, this time, he'd managed neither.

Perhaps he's got this wrong, maybe the girl had nothing to do with that bastard's death. Shaking his head he tries to convince himself it could have been some rare, but natural phenomenon – a freak, highly-localised sandstorm which, by sheer good luck, had left the two of them unscathed before it subsided.

Ha! How likely is that?

Then again, how conceivable is it that a perfectly normal-looking child could have conjured up something so deadly? His brain keeps freeze-framing on her tiny finger raised against an armed man who would have shot them both without breaking into a sweat. The concentration on her face…

Before she'd drowned herself, the woman she was with described the girl as *an abomination*. Those exact words. Until a moment ago he'd dismissed this indictment as the ravings of an unhinged mind. What if it's true – what if that sleeping child is some kind of… Of Christ knows what? His vocabulary and imagination fail him.

He stops pacing and, keeping his eyes trained on her, retreats to a safer distance. To calm himself he takes a series of deep breaths until his heart rate begins to slow a little. His gaze travels to the sandy hump entombing the gunman. Will anyone shed a tear over the vicious bastard who'd been a nanosecond from shooting him?

Looking down that barrel he'd known for sure this was when and where his luck finally ran out. Certainty at long last. Until the girl appeared, he'd made his peace with death. Now part of him wishes the bloke had gone ahead and pulled the trigger, put him out of the misery of this never-ending struggle to stay alive.

He rubs at the unfamiliarity of his shaven face, registering the warm breath leaving his mouth, the growing stubble on his chin – a friction that confirms he's awake and what he'd seen was no hallucination.

A small, dark shape skims overhead and then circles back around. Not a micro-drone as he feared, but a pipistrelle feasting on insects. Roused, his thoughts turn to his immediate situation. Correction, *their* immediate situation. How long before someone comes to check on their dead nightwatchman?

By whatever freakish means, the two of them have survived. If they want to stay that way, they need to leave the island, and fast.

He approaches the girl with caution. As he towers over her, her eyes pop open and she stares up at him. He jumps back, an arctic prickle running down his spine. In the half-light she appears to be looking past – no *through* him.

What else is she capable of?

Steadying his voice, he tells her, 'We need to leave here.' She seems to understand, but, as she tries to stand up, she staggers like there's no strength in her legs. He's forced to catch her before she falls. She's trembling, her small hands icy on the back of his neck. How insubstantial she is – a far cry from the dangerous, unnatural creature of earlier.

Okay, what's his exit plan? Some kind of sensor or trail-cam must have picked him up and alerted the gunman. That same route is a no-go. Better to stick to the headland. He can make out a path of sorts – possibly an animal track – running through scrubby vegetation in the right direction.

Weighed down by the girl, he sets off at a pace, following the path's meanderings along the cliff edge. The only sound breaking the silence is the crashing waves below.

His foot snags on something. He lands with a thump. Winded, he'd taken the force of the fall, instinctively protecting the girl. He feels her weight leave him.

'You… okay?' Standing in front of him she nods while he's

getting his breath back. 'Christ, that was close.' He's on hands and knees. 'Couldn't see where I was going. Might be safer if I give you a piggyback. D'you know what that is?' She shakes her head.

Reluctantly he turns his back on her. 'Now put your hands around my neck.' He coughs. 'Not so tight.' Once she's loosened her grip, he threads his arms through her scrawny legs.

'Okay.' He straightens up. With her weight more evenly distributed, she's no heavier than a full pack.

Eventually they come to a viewpoint where he can get his bearings. His boat is swaying with the others on the moonlit sea. An innocent, serene, picture.

Picking his way from rock to rock, he manages to climb down to a ledge where he can lower the girl onto the concrete walkway leading to the jetty.

He jumps down beside her. From here on the closer they get, the more exposed they'll be. Through his monocular his boat comes into focus, still tied up securely where he left her. He runs the lens further along the shoreline looking for activity, any sign of hidden or approaching combatants. None he can see.

The tang of algae and brine hangs in the night air. He takes a breath before he picks the girl up and carries her towards the old pay booth. It's empty except for the blanket lying where she'd cast it off. He sets her down on the bench. This time he doesn't tuck her in. 'Wrap that round you,' he says. 'And stay here.'

There's no movement on board any of the moored boats. An offshore wind encourages him on. He draws his hand gun as he steps onto the floating jetty, alert for any sound. There's only the slap and sway of the tide against the old timbers.

Passing the other boats, he stops to scrutinise his. Wheelhouse empty. Deck's clear. Both the mooring ropes in place. Nothing appears to have been tampered with. Here goes.

He steps onto the deck anticipating an attack that doesn't come. Gun raised, he spins around to find himself aiming straight at the girl. 'Jeez, I could have shot you.'

She's standing on the jetty, one hand protruding from the blanket across her shoulders. Her finger points straight at him like a wordless accusation. He bows his head, lowers his eyelids accepting the sentence.

His hand twitches – no longer under his control. If she's about to make him turn his gun on himself, then so be it.

The weapon flies from his grip to clatter onto the deck. Shaking, he dare not pick it up. She walks towards the boat and, once alongside, holds out both arms in a silent instruction to help her onto the deck like nothing's happened. He's reluctant to touch her but has no choice in the matter.

Shocked to be still alive, he waits for his heart rate to steady before he begins to untie the mooring ropes.

The girl's in the stern already curled up between the lockers. Wrapped in the blanket – she's the very picture of innocent vulnerability.

Once he's on board, he fits both oars into the muffled rowlocks and with a few strokes they glide away, apparently free.

The accurate range of a standard rifle is around half a mile or so. With a more advanced weapon, in the right hands, it can be a mile or more. Reaching what he hopes is a safe distance, he starts the engine and takes her up to full speed. The fuel gauge is low. Once they're out of range, he sets a course for Ben Faoghla – the only land body they'll be able to reach before the HVO runs out.

His handgun is lying on the deck by the side of the wheelhouse. Bending down, he picks it up, half expecting it to be red hot or at least warm to the touch, but it's as cold as always. He stows it out of her sight in the cubby under the wheel.

As a kid he'd read a magazine article about secret experiments going on to prove people could move objects using only their minds. The Americans and Russians were said to be in a race to harness whatever military potential they envisaged this might have. There's a word for it. Tele something? Telekinesis – that's it. Excited, he'd shown the magazine to his grandfather, but the old man had scoffed, pointed out various laws of physics that meant it was complete nonsense. In science classes he'd learnt how objects that appear to be solid are actually made up of miniscule subatomic particles in constant motion. Maybe the girl can manipulate those restless particles to make things go in her desired direction? Before everything started to fall apart, doctors were inserting neural implants into brains so that paralysed people could move their artificial limbs and even type messages on a computer just by their thoughts.

Supposing those early experiments he'd read about had continued? Could those faceless "scientists" have succeeded in getting people to move things by telekinesis? Had they gone on to train them to manipulate objects in ways that went beyond mere parlour tricks?

Having such power at their fingertips would be a game changer. Who wouldn't pay for a piece of that action?

Chapter Fourteen

Ash pulls back on the throttle and the engine settles to a steady purr. If his boat was a pet, he'd pat her side and say something like, *Well done old girl, now you can take it a bit easier for a while.* Soothed by the sea air and starlit sky, he watches the bow slice through the dark water.

He's set a direct course for Ben Faoghla. He's not sure how to pronounce that last part. It sounds romantic. He conjures up a vision of mists and long-ago escaping royals. He can almost hear those mournful bagpipes. With that thought Ash sits back, tries to relax.

His mind won't settle. If they're about to encounter more hostiles, he needs to be better prepared.

Having no autopilot, he lashes the wheel so that, hands free, it should stay on course. Then he empties the sand from one boot at a time. Getting to his feet, the first thing he checks on is the girl. She's still asleep – as far as he's able to tell with her. Trying not to make a sound, he opens the lid of the spare-parts locker right next to her. She doesn't stir. Relieved, he lifts out his jacket before extracting the device again. Then he closes the lid, but this time those mutinous hinges give a plaintive groan. He expects her blue eyes to be staring up at him, but they remain shut.

He retreats a few metres, takes the field device out of its container and sets it up on the deck. Once it's powered up, he enters the island's name. A brief trawl of the threadbare net yields some out-of-date stuff about the island's rich wildlife and fauna, and various recommended hiking trails. He scoffs thinking of how folks back then exerted all that energy for no practical purpose.

The only helpful item he finds is a topographical model of Faoghla's landscape. He spins the schematic on its central axis. Big plus – he can take his pick of landing spots around the island. Major downside – that one high hill is only a few metres short of a mountain. Its summit will offer a three-sixty out to sea. It's a safe assumption someone is going to see them coming.

He can find no information about the current state of play. Since this island is now their only option, he needs to know what they'll be sailing into. Nothing ventured…

If his previous backdoor in had been discovered, they would have blocked further incursions by now. They can't have noticed anything yet because he's back in and scanning through the region's Defence Analysis Reports.

The first reference to Ben Faoghla is as brief as they come. *Estimated current population – 200.* And then, in bold, underneath: **Not known to be under N.S.L. control at this time.** This footnote refers to the so-called Northern Sea Lords – a regional militia who appear to be in the process of colonising the whole archipelago.

A link takes him to aerial infrared footage of a recent explosion to the north of Ben Faoghla. The analyst's addendum speculates that: "In an apparent attempt to prevent the island from being taken by outside forces, an explosion has destroyed the bridge linking B.F. and Laithaigh – one of the larger islands in the chain". The report doesn't stipulate how long this setback is likely to keep those "outside forces" at bay.

He exits, shuts the device down and puts it back in its metamaterial container. This time he hides it in a different locker.

Back in the wheelhouse he tries to fit the pieces together. That dead nightwatchman back on Dumna Nova could have been with the N.S.L. or another rival militia. Either way, their takeover of the island ought to have been flagged up. Had the locals put up a fight, or had they chosen to concede in the face of superior forces? Maybe the Sea Lords or their also-rans offered them protection against other marauders – the usual tactic of scumbag racketeers.

He shakes his head. It seems the all-seeing-eye has a few blind spots. The status update on Ben Faoghla had a dateline that was nine days ago. A hell of a lot could have happened there in the intervening time. Impossible to know the kind of reception they'll get when they rock up unannounced.

They should have stayed put on his island. True, his supplies were running out, but being so small and strategically irrelevant, it's unlikely to be of interest to anyone. He and the girl could have survived well enough there on salted lamb, rabbit, seabirds and fish with the odd root and berry thrown in.

The tide is slack and should remain so for the next couple

of hours. He cuts the engine while recalibrating. Their fuel's not going to last much longer. Once it's gone, he would need to summon the strength to row the rest of the way back to his island. Unfortunately, they would run out of food and fresh water long before they get there. Which means the only viable course of action is the current one. Not the most comforting of thoughts on which to take a nap.

When he wakes dawn is breaking on the eastern horizon. GPS confirms they haven't drifted far off course. His movements heavy with fatigue, he stretches and then gets to his feet. He must reek of sweat and brine. Above him the clouds are shot through with the pinks and golds of the impending sunrise.

When he gently shakes the girl, she wakes with a start. 'Almost morning,' he tells her by way of explanation.

Their sparce, wordless breakfast consists of hard biscuits soaked in a little of their precious water. He hesitates before using his knife to divide the last apple between them. Seeing no point in saving any, they finish the rest of the water. The girl grunts as she eats with enthusiasm. He'll say one thing for her – she's not a fussy eater.

Once it's fully light, he keeps a look out for Ben Faoghla. At first it's only a long blue streak on the horizon. As they get closer, that one hill emerges through the early sea mist. He grins. No bagpipe music.

Closer still, through his monocular he can make out a black and orange floating barrier laid out in a wide semi-circle across the mouth of the main harbour. Nature's warning colours and a formidable obstacle. There has to be a way to let friendly shipping in and out.

He keeps the engine running and its steady, determined note echoes across the water announcing their arrival. With the fuel gauge on zero, they're running on fumes.

There are glints at various points along the shore – the low sun bouncing off scopes. The girl is standing next to him in the wheelhouse. They'll both be visible. With luck, the islanders will take them for a father and his small child seeking refuge.

No going back now; nothing for it but to trust in the compassion and decency of their beholders.

A huge gamble.

Chapter Fifteen

Auvergne–Rhône–Alpes, France.

Guy

The words on the large roadside sign have been peppered by gunshot. Deciphering what remains, Guy gathers he's about to enter the Parc Naturel Régional des Volcans d'Auvergne. A smaller notice warns him against starting a wildfire.

According to his intel this is the safest route through in spite of the extra time it will take. Faced with a narrow, winding track he stops the truck. The silence unnerves him. Seems like a good time to assemble his rifle.

Once it's done, he lays it on the passenger seat next to him. He grins – it's riding shotgun. He puts his hunting jacket over it to hide it from prying eyes.

The road surface is breaking up, potholed and crumbling along many of the precipitous edges. He's forced to steer around near lethal water-carved channels and rockfalls.

At the first summit he's rewarded with a spectacular view across extinct volcanoes rising from deep river valleys. Millions of years ago this region would have looked like a moonscape. A few peaks have crater tops holding lakes that glimmer in the weak sunshine. It's a fine spring day, though a lot colder at altitude. At first he sees nothing but green, virgin terrain; then, through binoculars, he picks out a church tower on the distant horizon. No sign of human activity in the vicinity, although the dense woodland would make perfect cover.

A mob of griffon vultures circles overhead – unmistakable with their massive wingspans and distinctive bald heads. He's read that this is to help them regulate their temperature, but suspects it's so they don't get their precious feathers bloodied when ripping carcasses apart.

The way before him snakes down into a deep gorge, its bottom hidden by dense foliage. He sets off, telling himself to stay alert. Avoiding the many and varied obstacles in his path, he finally makes it all the way down to the valley floor. For a while the road runs parallel to an infant river, then plunges left into a steep-sided, dry ravine.

With the valley now behind him, he's steadily climbing. Rounding a blind corner, he's shocked to see that some distance up ahead, a blue family saloon is blocking the way, skewed sideways as if the driver swerved to avoid something.

He stops the truck. Through his binos the car looks to be a mid-twenties Megane. Windows all intact and closed. No passengers visible, though there is something on that steering wheel he can't quite make out due to the shine on the glass. No sign of accident damage, no bullet holes – nothing that explains its sideways skid.

One thing's for certain – to his left and right the valley's steep and rocky sides mean there's no way he can drive around it.

A classic ambush tactic.

So far he's made good progress, if he's forced to go all the way back he'll waste a lot more time and, more importantly, his precious fuel. Besides, he's already dismissed all the alternative routes as tantamount to suicide.

Once he steps out of the truck he'll be an easy target. Better to sit tight and wait for them to show their hand. He reaches across to the passenger seat and locates the rifle beneath his jacket. Nice and easy, he transfers the stock into his other hand and then, gun across his lap, he waits.

Five long minutes elapse.

Une Bouchage. Is that the French word for blockage? Or maybe that's more to do with constipation. He's pretty sure piège means trap.

Still no sign of hostiles to the front or rear. Clear up on both ridges. Nothing's happening in his mirrors.

Eight minutes and his patience is exhausted. He cracks the door at his side. When this elicits no response, he slides a leg, one shoulder and then the rest of his body out. Rifle raised, he uses the scope to home in on the various positions he'd hide if the situation was reversed. Rocks continue to be just rocks.

Crouching, he runs ten metres forward then dodges behind a young silver birch that gives less than adequate cover. Surely they would have opened fire by now.

Venturing further into the open, he progresses towards the car checking on both sides, his rifle veering through a series of one-eighties as he advances on the vehicle.

The smell hits him first – the unmistakable stink of corruption. He tries not to breathe it in. A greenish black hand lies across the steering wheel. The rest of the corpse is slumped down, head on their knees.

No other passengers. No visible wounds to the back of the skull. Short hair, mostly grey. No bloodstains anywhere. Not a mark on his clothing or the rest of the body. Bluebottles are buzzing around in there, so the chances are he's been dead for a while. What had stopped him walking away?

Could have died from natural causes. Maybe he'd chosen this route to escape pursuers, but death found him anyway. Wouldn't be the first time fear brought on a fatal heart attack or stroke.

Poor bastard.

The Megane is a petrol model. Push button start. Should he swap vehicles? No – the truck's a lot more robust over rough ground. And besides, he'd never get rid of that pong or the impression of that dead hand on the wheel.

All the same, one man's bad luck is another man's heaven-sent opportunity, assuming that man doesn't mind getting his hands dirty and blackening his soul more than it is already.

Bracing himself, he opens the driver's door. The stench is overwhelming. Stifling the urge to retch, he holds his breath and fumbles in the dead man's pockets until he finds a key fob.

'Sorry about this, mate,' he mutters to hide his revulsion as he manhandles the body then drags the corpse by his ankles out onto the roadside. From here on the smell of death will cling to him.

He walks around to the other side of the car to locate the

fuel cap. Like a fine wine uncorked, a heady sniff confirms what he'd been hoping. He searches for a whippy branch to use as a makeshift dipstick, breaking off a long willow spur. Crude, but it'll do the job. He feeds it in until it hits the bottom and then retracts it. Tank's more than half full. He chuckles. 'Guess I must be an optimist,' he says out loud.

He goes back to the truck and jumps up into its open back, looking for anything he can use. Before setting off he cleared out most of the old man's crap, but there's still that large tool-box bolted to the rear bed.

A stout combi lock protects it. Four digits required. After several unsuccessful guesses, he tries to imagine himself in Arnaud's worn leather boots. The old man is besotted with his four-year-old great granddaughter Elyna. "Mon trésor" he calls her, sounding like some Gallic Gollum. Arnaud had spent many hours carving her a creepy-looking, wooden doll for her birthday. That was roughly six months back – so around early October time. He estimates the month and year of the girl's birth and dials it in. When his first guess doesn't work, he tries the next month.

Open sesame! Inside, he finds the usual mix of tools and paraphernalia along with a narrow gauge hose and an empty petrol carrier. Not for the first time he suspects the old man wasn't above stealing fuel from his neighbours when they were asleep.

He drives the truck towards the Renault. Leaving room for manoeuvre, he parks up a short distance away.

After feeding the tubing into the car's fuel tank, he sucks on the end before dropping it into the petrol can at his feet.

While the fuel flows, he spits several times trying to rid his mouth of the taste. When the can's full, he pours its contents into the truck's tank then goes through the same procedure several more times. He stops just short of draining her dry.

When he springs the car's boot lid, he discovers a box of supplies. 'Merci bien, monsieur,' he says, as if he still had an appetite.

Nonetheless he transfers the food and water bottles to his truck before returning to the car.

The car's engine starts at the first touch. He winds down all the windows before putting her in reverse and wrestles her hard round. Once in drive, the car creeps forward. She sprays loose stones and rocks, but he keeps a steady pressure on the accelerator, steering up the side of the steep ravine as far as he dares. Leaving her in park, he jumps out to survey his handiwork.

Yep, he now has a clear passage through.

For a moment he imagines Poirot struggling to make sense of the corpse lying where he is, while his abandoned car is parked at a crazy angle up the bank. He shakes his head – it's not like anyone will bother to investigate.

A better man would use Arnaud's shovel to bury the dead man. As a mark of respect he might even tie two branches in the shape of a cross to mark his grave like they used to back in the Wild West. Or perhaps that only ever happened in the movies.

Either way, he's not that man.

Drawn here by the stench, the birds and foxes will find him soon enough. A sky burial they call it in other parts of the world. He may not be laid out with dignity on a mountain top but, resting where it is, the corpse is unlikely to pollute anyone's water supply.

Time he moved on. Fuelled up, the truck has a range of around 500 miles. Add to that the petrol in the carrier and, even by the circuitous route he's mapped out, it should be enough to get him to the Channel coast.

Chapter Sixteen

Ash

A shiver runs through him. He's read about some ancient part of the human brain that can sense an unseen enemy's gaze – a sensation that's kicked in big time. One thing's certain, both he and the boat are about to be searched. He needs to get rid of anything and everything that will contradict the story he's about to spin. With their destination growing larger every second, he can't put it off any longer.

He empties out most of the stuff in the lockers, wraps everything that might incriminate him in blankets then turns his back to hide what he's about to do from the invisible onlookers. The girl watches with interest as he drops his service-issue handgun and rifle over the side along with that precious field device.

It's all gone, the water deep enough for it all to sink without trace. Feeling the loss, he's tempted to mutter a few words over the spot. At least he still has the books.

A tap on his arm brings him back to the present. She's looking up at him as if about to comment on what he's done but, as always, she stays mute.

The mist has cleared to give a fine morning – clear skies overhead, the sea a polished gem. With the turquoise water lapping along those white sand beaches, he could be approaching some Caribbean island. Minus the palm trees. And ignoring the extreme difference in temperature.

As the early mist dissipates, Ben Faoghla's only hill/mountain resembles the peak of a sombrero. Through his monocular he watches a skua attempt to steal food from a gull that's not giving it up without a fight.

Movement draws his attention to some new activity at one end of the harbour's barrier. A large, black inflatable – a six-seater RIB – emerges from somewhere. Cutting through the water at speed, she's heading straight for them. Three of the four passengers are carrying assault rifles. Three against one and a half – some might call that overkill. They won't have factored the half in, won't imagine the small child alongside him poses any threat.

Now the mist's lifted, he can make out other buildings huddled behind the colourful cottages facing the quay. Black smoke is rising from somewhere to the rear of all those ice cream coloured facades. Could be a sign there's trouble in this paradise.

For the benefit of his unseen audience, he lowers the lens and plasters on his most convincing smile. He slides the engine into neutral and ushers the girl starboard ready to welcome their visitors.

Once the RIB is close enough, the pilot puts her in idle and raises a loud hailer. 'Identify yourself,' a tinny voice demands.

'My name's Ash,' he shouts against the sound of the

churned-up water and both engines. 'And this is my little girl.' Until now Lass has been the girl's placeholder name. He needs to christen her fast.

The four are dressed in dark civvies with camo accessories. The one with the loudhailer raises it again. 'Turn off your engine.' An order not a request.

He does as he's told. His boat drifts while the RIB skims on past to scribe a wide, white-water circle around them. Completing the loop, the pilot cuts the engine as they prepare to come alongside.

Resting one fatherly hand on the girl's shoulder he uses the other to give a friendly overhead wave. 'Hi there. I'm Ash and this is my daughter Isla.' A Scottish name. His accent will betray him as an outsider, but they might be more likely to help one of their own. 'Christ are we glad to see you. Our supplies have run out and our fuel's almost gone.' Like a desperate father would, he adds, 'Little Isla here is hungry and thirsty – aren't you, sweetheart? I thought – well, I'm hoping you'll help us.'

A stout man with an impressive red beard passes his gun to Loud-hailer-man and says, 'Stand back, I'm coming aboard.'

The only female – as hard faced as the rest – throws a rope up to Ash he's expected to secure. He ties it to a cleat on the side of his boat.

Redbeard climbs up onto the deck, a little out of breath from the effort. Since the man's not armed, "Isla" won't be tempted to disarm him.

'Keep yer hands where I can see them.'

Ash raises them a little higher.

'Yer boat's got no name or I.D.'

An apparent question. He answers with a shrug. 'Should I have hoisted the Jolly Roger?' His joke lands flat. Ash sobers his face. 'A sign of the times, I'm afraid.'

Redbeard lunges, pats him down with a thoroughness that's close to sexual harassment. Satisfied, his eyes shift to the girl and then, assuming her to be harmless, away to the empty wheelhouse and the deck. 'Just the two of you, is it?'

Ash nods, 'As you can see.'

'Ye've been acting suspicious. Dumping some things overboard.'

'Oh – you mean earlier?' Ash chuckles. 'That was nothing. I was getting rid of some rubbish – clearing the decks so to speak.'

Eyes everywhere, Redbeard walks a broad loop around him – his move in their dance. 'Yer inside our territorial waters.'

'Is that so?' They appear to have redrawn the map. Are they now under N.S.L. control? Alternatively, the locals may have drawn an imagined line around their territory – a safe circle that they hope will offer some sort of magical protection. He hides his scepticism with a nothing-to-see-here smile.

Hoping to initiate a rapport, he says, 'I didn't catch your name.'

A snort. 'I didnae give it.'

Hands still high, he takes a step closer to Redbeard. 'Listen, we were out of options. This island was, *is* in fact, the only dry land we could reach before we ran out of fuel.' He nods towards the other people on the RIB. 'I believe there used to be a maritime code of conduct – a protocol or understanding amongst seafarers to come to the aid of other seafarers in distress. So you see, my friend, I was hoping you guys still go along with that principle and won't mind helping us out. If not for my sake, then for little Isla's.'

'I'm not yer pal.' Those green-blue eyes aren't especially interested in him or the girl but continue to roam over his lockers with curiosity.

'Would you mind if I put my hands down now?' he says. 'The old biceps are beginning to ache a bit.'

Redbeard smirks. 'I wouldnae advise it.' He takes him at his word.

'Listen, if you and your colleagues would rather we didn't stick around, that's absolutely fine by me. All I need is a small amount of fuel and some basic supplies to keep us going and we'll gladly be on our way.'

The beard is subjected to a brief scrubbing. 'So, where are you two heading?'

'I doubt you've heard of Diurraus?'

'Aye, yer right there.'

'And why would you have? It's a tiny, insignificant island. Officially, it's uninhabited, but we've been managing to get by over there. Living off what nature provides and all that.' He nods the man's attention back to the kid. 'It's been just the two of us since her mother passed away, God rest her soul.'

He decides against crossing himself. Redbeard stares at Isla. Ash is ready to explain her silence is a symptom of trauma over losing her mother. For all he knows, it could be true.

A damned hard nut, Redbeard's expression makes it clear he's unmoved by Ash's tale of woe. Instead his lockers are given another onceover.

Time to change tactics. 'I'd been hoping to trade a few items for some supplies over on Dumna Nova,' he says. 'As it turned out, the situation there is very different from what it was the last time I called by.' Leaning in just a tad more, he lowers his voice as if sparing his daughter a painful reminder. 'They stole everything from us. Between you and me, we were damned lucky to escape from there with our lives.'

That's got him interested. 'So yer telling me they just let the two of you sail off intae the sunset?'

Ash frowns. 'No, not exactly. Look mate, it's actually quite a long story...'

'Like I said, *pal*, I'm no yer mate.'

'Okay, I get the message. I'm happy to tell you more about what happened to us over there. Maybe I can fill you and your colleagues in over breakfast? That's if you can spare us a little something...'

Redbeard thinks this over. Finally, he signals down to his gun-toting friends. 'These two are coming wi' us.'

They're not given a choice. 'Hang on a minute,' Ash says. 'What about my boat?'

'We'll be taking good care o' her, don't ye worry.' Redbeard catches something thrown over by the woman. Grin on his face, he says, 'Look behind ye, enough tae blind ye.' A bag is thrust over Ash's head plunging him into darkness.

Chapter Seventeen

Not the smallest chink of light. Ash inhales his own recycled breath along with the stale stench of the fabric. His cuffed hands sit useless in his lap. When the RIB takes off, his head jolts back, jarring his neck. The low mutterings of his captors are indecipherable above the noise of the engine.

This hasn't gone to plan. In every sense, he's going into this blind. Trussed up like a turkey, he's damned if he's prepared to sit back and welcome the festivities.

'Fuck this!' He tears at the hood. Many hands pin him down then wrestle him back into his seat. He kicks out but misses. A whack to the head sends him reeling. Then they tie something around his neck to keep the bag in place.

His training tells him he needs to calm down – save what breath he has. There's pressure on his arm and then the girl's tiny, cold fingers creep between his. It's been a while since another human sought his touch. He gives her hand a reassuring squeeze – a gesture he has no right to make.

Seating the two of them together might suggest a modicum of compassion. They could be buying his story. Or allowing them to stay together makes it easier to keep an eye on both at once.

'It'll be okay,' he tells her, the fight leaving him. He bends his head to whisper, 'Act normal.' His voice sounds close like he's descended too fast from high altitude.

Why tell her to act normal? What the hell constitutes normal these days? The stunt she pulled back on Dumna…

'Definitely not normal.' Was that out loud?

The RIB speeds up, thrusting him back. He's thrown left, then hard right. Kid could snatch their guns, make them hover overhead. A constellation of Kalashnikovs. Unholy trinity. He snorts. His ears are ringing. She might upend the RIB. Water would be freezing. Can't swim in cuffs.

Can't breathe. Out of air.

He's drowning.

'Fuck's sake… Too tight… He has tae breathe…' Untying the cord. 'Inhale. Aye, that's it. Big deep breath now.'

Sky's in a puddle between his boots. Surface is shuddering. Something's coming.

'Calm down!' Hand on his shoulder. That engine's still droning away. 'Another deep breath,' she says. 'All the way in. Aye. Now all the way out.'

'You teuchters are something else.' Redbeard. 'This isnae a fucking yoga class.'

'It's nae meant to be a lynching either.'

The hood's pulled down to his shoulders but not tied on this time. He's pushed back into his seat. They're changing direction. Slowing. The girl's back at his side, her tiny fingers cover his. He can't see through the bag, yet he can "see" everything in his mind's eye. She's gripping his hand.

A jarring thud. They must have docked. Outnumbered,

unarmed, and handcuffed, he might be incapacitated, but the girl isn't.

They manhandle him up onto the dockside. 'There ya go, little lass,' he hears an older man say. Her hand is quick to find his again.

'So, this is your latest catch.' New voice. Middle-aged. Posh. English or an English-educated Scot. Ash sees and yet doesn't see his iron grey hair, the tweed jacket stretched to cover his large gut. 'What's their story?'

'He claims to be a civilian,' the woman says. 'Just a regular da' and his wee lassie stranded at sea and asking for help.'

'All this is completely unnecessary.' Muffled, his own voice is striking the wrong notes. 'I'm not a threat to any of you.'

'Yes, well, that's for us to ascertain,' Posh-bloke says. 'I suggest you save your breath for later.'

'Ye cannae be too careful wi' this one.' Redbeard's voice. 'Could be a spy.'

Ash scoffs. 'No offense, but that's batshit crazy. I'm more than happy to explain exactly how and why we ended up here. If you could just take this ridiculous thing off my head…'

'Ridiculous or not,' the woman says, 'we're not taking any chances.'

'Might I suggest you handcuff your captives from behind in future,' Posh-bloke says. 'You'll find it's a more effective way of restricting their movements.'

A comms unit crackles. 'Be right there,' Posh-bloke says. Sounds like he's the one calling the shots. Some military training. NSL or leader of the freedom fighters? Hard to tell the difference – assuming there is any. Appalling acts have been carried out in the name of freedom. He should know.

'We'll take it from here,' Posh-bloke says. 'Robertson. Sin-clair. Accompany our guests to the old post office. Put them in the strong room. Once he's inside, you can remove his hood but make sure you keep those handcuffs on him.' He clears his throat. 'Off you go, lads. I'll be along shortly.'

'Wait – what about my boat?' Ash demands. 'What have you done with her?' In place of an answer, he gets a shove in the back.

They frogmarch him away. The street they're walking down is remarkably quiet. Gulls shriek overhead. The acrid smell of smoke infiltrates the hood. When the girl's hand slips from his, he's disorientated.

He notes the regular splosh of the tide against the harbour wall below, a few muted voices as they pass by. For all he knows they're being displayed to the locals – their latest show and tell. He'd wave if his hands were free. The girl is off to his left – he can hear her skipping along as if she's unbothered.

One of the guards lets go of his upper arm while the other steers him around to the right. The sound of their footsteps has altered. They're in a much narrower space, cobbles under-foot – probably a back alley. The other guard releases his arm and drops behind – single file necessary. The girl must have dropped further back.

Ash says, 'You know I may not be able to see, but it seems to me like the old elite are still the ones barking out the orders around here.'

'Aye, well, we dinnae need yer opinion,' the guard in front says.

'Hey, I'm just a blind observer here. Though, you know, I

was wondering how it makes you feel being ordered around like that?'

When Ash stumbles, the rear guard grabs his arm. 'Less talking, more walking – got that?'

Ash says, 'I would've thought that, what with you guys establishing your own independent territory and all, you might want to think about shaking the social order up a bit. Sounds to me like it could do with a radical rethink.'

'If I were you, pal,' Front-guard says, 'I'd learn tae keep my big trap shut.'

'Listen, I'm only pointing this out as an unbiased bystander. It's no business of mine if you people are happy being ordered around by the local laird or whoever that guy back there is. If you're content to be subservient – that's your choice. I'm just saying, in your position, I wouldn't be happy to be the underdogs.'

'Shut the fuck up.' Rear-guard pushes his back. When Ash stops dead he's shoved straight into Front-guard. Caught off balance, Front-guard stumbles. Ash grabs his pistol, pivots to make the man's body a shield. Finger through the trigger guard. Barrel end's found flesh.

'Hold it right there,' Rear-guard says. Panicked, unsteady voice.

Cuffs digging in, Ash is fighting to keep his two-handed grip on the gun. Faking confidence, he says, 'This is an interesting take on blind man's buff.'

'Bluff more like,' Front-guard says, in spite of the fact that the deadly end of his own gun is embedded in his back.

'Drop it now,' the other guard demands. 'Or I'll shoot the wee lassie here.'

Is she going to disarm him? Playing for time, Ash says, 'Seriously, you're prepared to shoot my daughter? An innocent child?'

'Aye. I might. I mean, I will if ye force my hand.'

'You'd commit cold blooded murder?' Ash lets that sink in. 'And what if I were to pull the trigger on your mate here? I don't know much about guns, but I imagine that, at this angle and this close it's likely to blow most of his arse off.'

'He's bluffing,' Front-guard says, not too sure about it. 'Nae father would take that risk.'

'Blaine Sinclair! I cannae believe my own eyes that yer pointing that dreadful thing at a wee lassie.' An older woman.

'Stay out of this, Mrs Galbraith. Please, just go inside.'

'Put that gun down right now, Blaine, ye hear me. Or so help me God I'll crack yer daft nut wi' this here poker.'

Ash shakes his head in disbelief. As Mexican standoffs go, this one's definitely not what he'd call normal.

Chapter Eighteen

Pas de Calais, France

Guy

According to a rusting road sign he's reached the Nord-Pas-de-Calais. Guy pulls the truck over and kills the engine. He scrambles up a low hill to get a view of the open terrain he's about to enter. Clouds are scudding east like they're in a hurry to get away. Much of the landscape looks to be productive farmland.

Due to its strategic position, it's a region that's been occupied and fought over repeatedly since ancient times and, in keeping with that fine tradition, is once again a battleground.

He's received very little information about the two opposing militia groups fighting to restore peace. Both are known by acronyms in which the letters FFA and L have been differently arranged. Whichever route he takes from here on he'll either be between or behind their lines.

He should make the distance on the remaining fuel. By truck he'll cover the ground faster but be way more conspicuous. Ditch it, and he's less likely to attract attention, though on foot it would take him many hours, if not days, to reach the coast.

He's been advised to head for the "recommended port" like he can simply rock up there and buy a ticket. He shakes his head – these analysts need to crawl out of their bunkers and pay a visit to the real world once in a while.

He studies the route Ground Intelligence have highlighted – a switchback hamster run to avoid the purple and grey "zones of action". Within the military these state-of-play schematics are widely referred to as *comics* due to their notorious inaccuracy. One young lieutenant in his unit was always complaining about driving "all around my arse" to avoid alleged enemy strongholds. Ironically, Lt Foster bought it inside what was meant to be a safe zone. A sniper's bullet blew her skull apart a week before her twenty-first birthday.

Guy exhales. This is no time to dwell on the past. When he listens he can hear birdsong, the low rumble of a plane passing overhead at altitude. Through binoculars he surveys the far ridge then checks out a herd of pale Charolais cattle – all grazing unconcerned. In the middle distance someone on a tractor is ploughing a field – turning pale green into exposed earth. A swarm of gulls are following its wake. He zooms in on a winding track that leads to a farmhouse where a line of washing is flapping, children's clothes hung out amongst the adult's. An unseen dog begins to bark. Another answers it, then runs out of enthusiasm and they both grow silent.

Still no sign of combatants or military action along the horizon. Near to his current position there's a junction with a lane which, according to the map, runs as straight as an arrow for a good fifteen miles in the right direction. Must have been built by the Romans. They weren't great believers in going around obstacles in their way.

Shattering the peace, he starts the engine. The wind ruffles his hair as he follows the meandering road downhill. About a mile further on he pulls over to scope out the cottage up ahead.

A bird shit splattered VW with flat tyres is parked outside suggesting it, along with the house, has been abandoned. Scrawny chickens scratching in the dirt are the only sign of life about the place.

Nonetheless as he drives past the house, he gets a feeling he's being watched. It's a relief to reach the junction with the Roman road without incident. He makes the turn unhindered.

It's a bumpy ride – in places the tarmac's been worn down to the road's stony origins. Within the lane's high sides he's relatively safe, but when it runs out he'll emerge into flat, open countryside. He'll be exposed for more than a mile before he hits a track running through a wooded valley. With a range upwards of 2 km, the scope of a military grade rifle would have no trouble picking him out. Or picking him off.

Assuming they don't shoot him on sight, he'll need a solid cover story. The boffs have suggested a touching yarn. Essentially, he's a concerned father visiting his sick daughter in Dieppe. Footnote: *option to make that Boulogne, Le Havre or Cherbourg as circumstances dictate.* A sad tale that's meant to persuade them to grant him safe passage, though he doubts anyone's that gullible these days.

The truck's suspension is being tested to the max. On the slightly smoother sections he can just hear the fading drone of that ploughing tractor. By tacit agreement and for the sake of food supplies, farmers are generally allowed to go about their business unhindered, unless or until their land becomes a field of conflict. He could throw a few bales into the back and pretend to be going to attend a calving cow. Having listened enough times to pissed up, complaining stockmen, he ought to be able to come up with the requisite bullshit.

It's a thought. Maybe more than a thought.

Rattling along in relative safety with the hedgerows clipping the wing mirrors on either side is giving him too much time to think. He can't help but remember his first visit to France – camping out on a foreign exchange trip not far from where he is now. They'd cooled off in the River Somme and, by some miracle, hadn't come down with E.coli. Gathered around smoky campfires they incinerated sausages and yet failed to warm up beans. The visit to the massed lines of white graves in a war cemetery hadn't impressed the skinny adolescent he was back then. Though he remembers how their history teacher, Mr Harris, had been moved to tears when he told them, "These men and women gave up their lives for us to live in peace". Quite a sugar-coating.

He brakes when a stoat runs straight across in front of him then watches it disappear into foliage on the other side. Was it waiting for that one opportunity to make a suicidal dash?

When the recent troubles – give that word a capital T – began, news outlets played things down by calling them *isolated riots*. Yet trouble kept bubbling up like farts in a bath.

Next, they described it as *civil unrest* – though there was nothing civil about it. The terminology moved on to *insurrection* before graduating to the more impressive sounding *regional uprisings* – words that, to him at least, conjure up a load of blokes brandishing their erections at each other. Which more or less sums up the scum who took to burning and looting with such enthusiasm. Cue the military – brought in to "keep the peace" because that's worked out so well for us in the past. Finding themselves in pitched battles against men in uniforms, the undisciplined rabble began to kit themselves out in army-surplus, though style-wise they failed to match the Hugo Boss sharpness of the Nazis many of them admired.

Once the insurgents turned on each other, the outnumbered armies of Europe decided to retreat to safe havens where, like grossly negligent parents, they've allowed them to fight it out amongst themselves.

Driving down an arrow straight road does get pretty monotonous after a while. Maybe that stoat was bored and wanted a bit of excitement in its life. Blinded by high hedges, he needs to stop and listen for gunfire or heavy manoeuvrings heading his way. He's also hot and thirsty. According to the most recent aerial images there should be some sort of structure coming up on his right. He approaches with caution.

Fifty metres further on he stops. Through binoculars he picks out a building that looks like an abandoned cattle shed. No sign of activity around or inside it. Half of the roof has fallen in.

He parks up under the covered section where the truck can't be spotted by helicopters or drones. Listening hard, nothing man-made is disturbing the peace. A low stack of straw bales is piled up against the more weather-tight side of the building offering the perfect place to rest. Some of the bales have unravelled but others are in better shape.

He sits down on one to take a long swig from his water bottle. Chewing on a protein bar, he surveys the bales then grins. Seems he's going with the farmer-with-calving-cow scenario after all.

Does he still reek of that corpse? Will the enemy sniff him out as an interloper? Funny if, in the end, he's betrayed by a dead man.

Around him nature is in the process of reclaiming her territory. The usual invasive weeds have sprung up through cracks in the concrete floor and wound themselves around and between the assorted junk that's been left here to rot.

He lies out on his makeshift straw bed. The sweet scent of blackthorn blossom is doing its best to lull him into submission. Exhausted, he shuts his eyes and drifts into sleep.

Thirty minutes later he's woken by his alarm. Long enough.

He drops the truck's tailgate and throws four of the more intact bales into the back. Remembering Arnaud, he crouches down to scoop up a handful of dusty earth then rub some of it into his palms and under his fingernails. His hands, at least, now look the part.

Chapter Nineteen

Ash

More voices – other people have emerged. 'What in hell's name's going on out here?' an older man demands. Good question.

It's taking all Ash's concentration to maintain his grip on the gun and the guard at the same time. Blinded by the bag, this could be a fever dream if the pain in his wrist wasn't all too real.

'Jeez, will you all just go back inside yer houses?' Blaine – the one whose pistol is aimed at the girl. Sounds like he might be about to lose his shit. 'Get tae – all of you!' he shouts. Gulls screech overhead – loud warning cries.

'I'm not standing by while ye threaten this wee lassie wi' that gun.' Older woman, Mrs Galbraith – the one brandishing the poker. 'I'm staying right here until the lot of ye come to yer senses.'

'I've done nothing wrong,' he tells these unseen arbitrators. 'Our boat was running out of fuel, that's all. We had barely enough to reach here. I was hoping you good people would help us. Instead they've made me their prisoner and now he's threatening to shoot my daughter.'

'Yer man here could be a spy,' Blaine shouts. 'If he's a regular fella like he claims tae be, how did he manage to grab Lewis's gun like that?'

'If ye handcuffed me and stuck a ruddy bag over my head, I'd dae the same if a could manage it,' Mrs Galbraith tells him.

'Handcuffing the fella and putting that thing over his head seems a wee bit of an overreaction by you laddies,' the older man says.

'The major wants him detained for questioning,' Blaine tells them.

'Interrogation, more like,' Ash cuts in.

'We're only following orders here,' Blaine says.

He scoffs. 'How many war crimes and atrocities have been committed by people *only following orders?*'

'That's rich, seeing how he's threatening tae shoot me in the back,' Lewis wails in his ear.

'Mr Campbell's right, you all need to stay calm.' A younger woman – softer accent. Edinburgh area? She sounds composed – used to taking charge. 'The three of you need to calm down. Then I want you to slowly lay your weapons on the ground.'

Ash says, 'I'd be more than happy to do that if I could *actually see* him doing the same thing.'

'Fella's got a point,' the old man says. 'If this was a poker game—'

'That's enough,' the younger woman says. 'Lewis, I suggest you take that bag off the man's head.'

'I willnae.'

'Right.' She sighs. 'Okay, let's suppose for a minute this man *is* a spy – what's he meant to be able to see right here that's not in every tourist photo of this island?'

'We're not tae take the bag off him till we get him intae the post office strong room,' Blaine says. 'Them's our orders.'

'Well that ship's upped anchor and sailed away intae the sunset.' Mrs Galbraith again.

'I cannae reach the bag wi' him holding on tae me,' Lewis says. 'If he lets me go…'

'I'm not falling for that.' He tightens his grip. 'That so-called major back at the harbour – the one giving the orders – he's not thinking straight. Ask yourselves this – would a spy take his young daughter along on a mission? In these troubled times, would he risk his own child's life by heading unprepared and unarmed straight for an island he knows nothing about? Doesn't even begin to add up, does it?'

'He's right,' the old man says. 'That disnae make sense. Pull that flaming bag off his head, will ye?'

'I cannae reach it,' Lewis says.

'Then I'll do it,' the younger woman says. 'Like I said, everybody needs to stay where they are and keep calm. I promise I won't try to grab the gun, okay?'

'Yeah, okay.' In any case, he can't hold onto it for much longer. 'I trust you,' he adds, though he doesn't.

Lewis sags. 'Aye alright, a suppose that'll work. Careful mind – don't go trusting the gadgie–'

His hair is pulled, the rough material scours his cheeks and then a brutal light blinds him. Half-seeing, he gulps in fresh air laced with smoke as everything comes into colour-drenched focus.

Isla's looking up at him, her expression calm yet curious – a tranquillity that must stem from the power at her fingertips. Blaine is holding her by the forearm. Military cut dark hair, a rash of angry spots colonising his pallid features, he's just an overgrown boy playing at being a soldier. The gun in his right hand twitches though everything about him says his heart's not really in the threat.

'Dinnae even think about it, Blaine Sinclair.' Mrs Galbraith raises her poker in warning. Stout with broad shoulders, she means business.

The younger woman is off to his left. Long, dark brown hair. A wide, sea-burnt face. Her pale grey eyes meet his with just a hint of amusement at their predicament. 'I'm Constable Reid.' She clears her throat. 'Catriona when not on duty.' Thirtyish. Tall. Open parka jacket bulking out her slim frame.

He nods. 'Good to meet you, Constable. I'm Ash and my daughter's called Isla.'

'A bonnie name.' The old man smiles at the girl, his wild white hair catching the light. His thick navy sweater is full of holes. 'Looks tae me like wee Isla and her da' here could hardly be mistaken for enemy spies by anyone except that bumped up eejit Aiken-Murray. And I'm nae convinced he was ever in the services.'

Reid gives him a sharp look before turning her attention to Blaine. 'As an officer of the law, I'm asking you both to slowly lay those guns down on the ground and then kick them over towards me.'

'This island's under martial law now,' Blaine tells her. 'Ye've nae jurisdiction here anymore.'

Mrs Galbraith waves her poker. 'In my book Catriona's the only one wi' a legitimate right tae represent the law around here.'

'I couldnae agree more,' the old man says. 'You need tae do what Cat says and lay down them weapons.'

All he can see of Lewis is his fair hair. 'Like I said before, I'll do just that providing Blaine does the same.'

'That's four out o' six for doing the right thing.' The old man's eyes twinkle.

Blaine shakes his head. 'The prisoner disnae count.'

'Seems to me we can all stand around arguing about this,' PC Reid nods towards a white-washed terraced cottage. 'Or, if you lay your guns down, and Mrs Galbraith lowers her poker, we can all go into mine for a cuppa tea and a chat.'

'I'm nae falling for all that cosy chat malarkey.' Blaine pulls his shoulders back. 'We've to carry out our orders. And right now you lot – including Constable Reid – are interfering wi' that duty.'

Lewis holds up a hand. 'It's nae yer arse that's on the line here.'

'Oh for pity's sake will ye not give it a rest wi' all this pumped up, macho posturing?' Mrs Galbraith shakes her poker. 'Ye need tae come tae yer senses right now, Blaine Sinclair, or so help me I'll crown ye wi' this.'

'Ye cannae give me orders,' he tells her. 'Yer no my teacher anymore.'

Blaine's pistol flies out of his hand and clatters onto the pavement at Reid's feet.

'What the…?' Blaine splutters. He turns on Mrs Galbraith. 'Ye just knocked that out of my hand.'

'I didnae.' She lowers her poker to half-mast.

'That there was an act o' sed... Erm, that was an act o' treason.'

'Sedition is the word ye're searching for – which is ridiculous,' Mrs Galbraith spits back. 'A didnae do a thing. Ye dropped it, and now, like always, yer looking tae put the blame on some bugger else.'

'Okay, enough with the bickering.' Reid is keeping her hands where he can see them. Blaine's gun remains on the ground at her feet. Focussing solely on him, she says, 'Your daughter is safe now, so I'm asking you to release Lewis and lay that gun down.'

The girl wrenches her arm free and skips over to stand at his side. All eyes, including hers, are on him.

Chapter Twenty

Reid hasn't yet seized the gun by her feet though she must be about to. Option one – push Lewis towards her, kick it out of her reach, and demand the guards uncuff him.

Cons – it'll blow his cover. Plus Isla's the wildcard. He doesn't doubt she'd disarmed Blaine a moment ago and might do the same to him. And he's still up against Major Paranoid-Bastard and his militia's superior firepower.

Option two – play nice. His story's won over these bystanders including the Constable. If they're going to escape this island, she could provide the means.

'Okay,' he says to himself as much as anybody. 'I'm putting my trust in you as an officer of the law.' Following this grand declaration, he releases Lewis and shoves him away. With a firmer grip on the Glock, he engages the safety before placing it on the ground and kicking it sideways towards Reid.

She stops it with her boot. Those grey eyes barely leave his as she stoops to retrieve both guns.

'I'm nae having this…' Blaine lunges at her, trips over nothing and face-plants onto the cobbles. 'Ooph!'

That must have hurt. Winded, he's immobile for several

seconds before he begins to cough and splutter. Ash steals a glance at Isla, but her face is a mask.

Both hands full, Reid nonetheless rests a foot on the boy's squirming back. 'Try that again and, so help me, I'll skelp that daft skull of yours.'

She steps back a few paces, checks the safety on Lewis's gun before tucking it into her front waistband. With practiced ease she adjusts her grip on Blaine's pistol – left hand supporting the right, legs wider apart for balance. 'This man and his daughter are now in my custody.' She points the muzzle at the boy soldiers. 'You got that?'

Lewis nods. 'Aye alright.' Short, fresh faced, his winter camos hanging loose, no way is he going to risk going up against her.

Mouth full of dirt and blood, Blaine's not capitulating as easily. Between laboured breaths, he mutters something about 'telling the major'. Rolling onto his side, he spits out, 'He willnae be pleased. Ye'll regret this, Catriona Reid.'

'Threatening an officer of the law is an arrestable offence. Consider yourself lucky I'm prepared to overlook it this time.' She points the gun at Lewis, 'You'd best help your friend onto his feet.'

The boy is quick to comply. Bent double and deflated in more ways than one, Blaine says, 'We'll be back wi' reinforcements.'

'Before you go…' Changing her grip, Reid frees her left hand. 'Give me the keys to the cuffs.' She waggles her fingers. 'Hurry up.'

Lewis does as he's told and drops them in her palm. 'Good lad.' She could be talking to a dog. 'Now fuck off both of you before I change my mind.'

'Them's our guns,' Blaine mutters leaning heavily on Lewis as he's led away. 'That's theft. Ye've nae heard the last o' this.'

To their backs Reid shouts, 'And tell *Mister* Aiken-Murray I'm the one who'll decide if this man poses a threat to our community or not.'

The five of them watch the two lads until they're out of sight around the corner. Mrs Galbraith shakes her head. 'Ye've gone and done it now, Cat. That major's nae going tae take this lying down. Soon as them laddies get back wi' their sorry tale, him and his wee army are gonna come looking for ye.'

'Annie's right.' The old man waves a knowing finger. 'Mark my words, lass, next thing ye'll be banged up in that post office strongroom along wi' these two. If I was ye, I'd lay low at least until Major High-and-mighty calms down a wee bit.'

Safety engaged, Reid tucks the second pistol into the back of her waistband. With her heavy jacket covering it, the weapon is less accessible. She shrugs. 'Something like this was going to happen sooner or later.' Nodding at him and Isla, she says, 'Right, you two are coming with me.'

Ash stands his ground. 'Where to?'

'You'll find out soon enough.'

Judging this as good a time as any, he holds out his wrists, 'Could you uncuff me first?' When she hesitates, he says, 'I took a risk when I put my trust in you just now.' He jangles the shackles. 'Handicapped like this I'm a liability. Hands free I could be an asset.'

'*An asset* is it?' As if still weighing the word on her tongue, she looks him up and down. 'You handled that gun like you knew what you were doing. Seems to me this ain't your first rodeo, Mr Ash.' A jocular remark to catch him off guard.

Two can play. He grins. 'Ash is actually my first name.'

'The second one being?'

'Immaterial right now.' He glances behind. A middle-aged, broad set man in stained overalls is standing next to the alleyway's other exit point. The way he's wiping the oil from his fingers suggests he's a civilian, but not whose side he might be about to take.

Ash says, 'Those two will be back mob-handed any minute now.'

'Is that so?' Reid seems to specialise in withering looks. 'Thank you for alerting me to that possibility, *Ash*.'

'He's right all the same,' the old man says. It's his turn to receive her death stare. 'What?' He chuckles. 'I'm just offering ye my opinion, hen. Take it or leave it.'

'Hmm.' She uncurls her hand to study the keys in her palm. No pushover, she's considering her options just as he would in her boots.

After a nod she unlocks his cuffs. Relieved, he rubs at his sore wrists. The five of them make an unlikely circle. 'Are ye alright, sweetheart?' Mrs Galbraith asks Isla, a soothing lilt to her voice; the poker in her hand forgotten. Under different circumstances she might have made a good choice of guardian for the child.

When Isla doesn't answer, he covers for her. 'I'm afraid she hasn't spoken since her mother died.' A truthful lie.

'Och, the poor wee mite.' Mrs Galbraith seems close to tears on her behalf. 'These are terrible times and no mistake.'

Head down, the old man nods his solemn agreement.

About to comment, Reid thinks better of it and clears her throat. 'We'd best be going.'

Glad to be out of those shackles, he rests a fatherly hand on Isla's bony shoulder. 'It's okay, sweetie. There's no need to be scared.' He squats to reduce their height difference. 'We're going to follow this nice lady who's called Catriona. And, for now, we're going to do exactly what she tells us to.'

He's shocked when she smiles up at him, the very vision of a devoted daughter. Her thumb and index finger meet to form the okay sign.

'God bless her,' Mrs Galbraith says. 'Ye're a brave wee lassie and no mistake.'

With a deep sigh the old man steps away, breaking the circle. 'Well, best o' luck tae all of you. Ye're going tae need it for sure,' he mutters, heading for an open door.

Behind them, the man in overalls is still wiping at his hands and in no hurry to move away. Mrs Galbraith's poker is on the rise as if she's about to defend the alleyway single handed. 'Would ye like us tae misdirect that major and his bunch o' bastards?'

'No point,' Reid tells her, eyeing up Overall-man. 'The two of you had best go back inside before they get here.'

She stuffs the handcuffs and keys into her jacket's capacious right pocket. Noticing him noticing, she says, 'And just so you know, Ash, I'm not convinced you're telling the whole truth.' She glances down at the pistol in her waistband as if to remind him of its presence. 'I'll be keeping a close eye on you.'

Chapter Twenty-One

Reid leads them down to the end of the alleyway, towards Overall-man. Close up he looks to be in his mid-forties, greying hair pulled back into a man-bun. Tattoos of Celtic symbols cover the visible part of his chest and terminate at his jawline. Physically, he's not in the best of shape.

A border collie has soundlessly materialised alongside him. The animal's cold blue eyes view Ash in an unfavourable light.

'Hi, Callum,' Reid says – an acknowledgment he presumes to be aimed at the human.

'Catriona.' Man and dog are reluctant to move aside. 'I see ye just sent them two laddies away wi' a flea in their ears,' he says with a nod.

'They'll be back soon enough.' She deploys a charming smile. 'Right now we need to avoid the cavalry.'

'Aye, ye will.' A grin softens his face. 'Why do I get the feeling ye're about tae ask me for a favour?'

'You know me too well.' Her chesty chuckle is more than a tad flirtatious. 'I'm wondering if maybe you could lend me a 4X4 – just for a wee while.'

Callum scoffs. 'I'll be happy tae *sell* ye one if ye've the means tae pay for it.'

Ash keeps checking their rear; they're sitting ducks here, and this little chat is taking way too long. Be quicker to steal the fucking thing and have done with it.

'You'll get it back,' she says. 'Now they've blown up the bridge there's only so far a person can run to on this island.'

'True enough.' He stuffs the oily rag into his pocket then, narrow-eyed he surveys the three of them with suspicion. 'I'm no in the habit o' lending out ma vehicles tae the polis.'

'Then how about to a friend?'

The dog is pressing itself against Reid's leg, hoping for some attention. Like she's got all the time in the world, she fondles one of its ears. Ignoring the man's objections, she reiterates, 'We need something that can cope over rough ground.'

With a squawk, a lesser black backed gull lands on the wall beside them. Head to one side, those yellow eyes stare unblinking at one and then the other. Callum scrubs at his wispy beard with grease-blackened fingernails. 'I've got an old Kawasaki Mule DXT round the back. Mind, I wouldnae guarantee she willnae break down on you. Top speed o' 30, if ye're lucky. I was in the middle o' servicing her for Dougie Fettes when he upped and died.'

At last they start to move away, but only as far as a nearby breaker's yard full of cars and trucks in various stages of decay and deconstruction. The same gull glides past them to perch on the roof of a vintage VW Golf that's been disembowelled. The bird opens its beak to issue a series of raucous told-you-so croaks.

They're approaching a shack that looks to be barely watertight. The Mule – a squat little Ute – is parked under the lean-to roof attached to the rear side. 'Dougie acquired her back when he used tae do a spot o' stalking for rich city types wanting a trophy kill.' He shakes his head. 'Seems another world away now.' After a moment of silent mourning, his chin comes up and he gives Isla a snaggle-tooth smile.

She smiles right back at him. The girl's learning from the best.

Ash surveys the vehicles around them. Given the state they're all in, none would be his choice for a quick getaway. The Mule is an open-sided workhorse. Aside from the windscreen, nothing shields its passengers from the elements or from any onlookers. Compact and olive green, she'll be less visible in woodland or if they're following a treeline.

Callum taps the fuel gauge. 'Still got the best part o' a full tank in her.'

'That seat's much too narrow for all three of us,' Ash points out.

Tapping the side of his nose, Callum says, 'True, but the rear bed here turns intae a second seat.' After engaging a lever, he lifts what is little more than an outsized rear shelf and drops a bench into place at its base. 'There ye go – now she's a four-seater.' He stands back, hands on hips, pleased to have achieved such a transformation.

'Perfect,' Reid says – not the adjective Ash would have chosen.

'Right then,' Callum says. 'I'll fetch the key. Won't be a tick.' His walk to his "office" could be a lot faster.

The acrid smell of smoke has grown stronger. Meanwhile, Reid jumps up into the driver's position and grips the wheel like she's practising. When Callum comes back with the key, she brazenly winks at him. 'I owe you one, Cal.'

The poor sap blushes.

Her tone changes. 'Okay then, what are we waiting for?'

Without being asked, Callum lifts Isla up onto the rear bench and makes sure her lap belt is secure. 'The ride will be a wee bit bumpy, lass, so ye might want tae hang on tae this strut here.' He grabs hold of it to demonstrate.

'You're a lifesaver, Callum,' Reid tells him.

'Mind how ye go,' he says, stepping back. Ash squeezes onto the bench seat next to Reid, their backsides and arms press up against each other. This close, it would be easy enough to reach around behind and grab that pistol. As if reading his thoughts, she gives him plenty of side-eye.

The Mule's engine starts on the first attempt. Reid revs it a few times and then allows it to idle – a regular purr that's encouraging. 'Sounds good,' she says.

'Aye, well, controls are straightforward enough,' he tells her. 'Aside from yon mountain, she'll take ye pretty much anyplace ye care tae go on the island and be quiet about it.'

'Hold on as tight as you can sweetheart,' Ash tells Isla.

With a lurch, they set off through the graveyard of cars and then turn left onto a piece of wasteland. When he glances behind, Isla is bouncing along but seemingly content.

It worries him that they're now on open moorland. The sea is just visible as a silver streak on the horizon.

A large smouldering fire is up ahead. They plunge into a bank of black smoke so thick it ought to obscure them from their pursuers for the time being. A toxic mix of chemicals catches in his throat.

'Callum's son, Aiden, sets fire to anything they can't resell,' Reid tells him. 'The neighbours keep making complaints, but he takes no notice. Lad's a bit of a pyromaniac, so I figure it's a better outlet for his urges than other alternatives.'

'Very pragmatic of you.' Eyes smarting, Ash grabs one of the struts as they emerge from the smoke and lunge towards a narrow, stony track between tumbledown stone walls. It's hard going. 'I assume you have some sort of plan in mind.'

Her long hair streaming away from her face, Reid pitches them sideways as they round a sharp bend. 'Now where would be the fun in that?'

Chapter Twenty-Two

La Côte de la Manche, France

Guy

The light's fading almost as fast as the fuel is running out. Guy veers off course to park Arnaud's truck along a wooded track that no longer leads anywhere. After climbing out, he pats her warm bonnet before abandoning her to the elements. Or human scavengers.

He's only a couple of miles short of his destination. On foot he should make it to the rendezvous point with time to spare. For now the wind has dropped and the darkening sky is mostly clear. That fickle moon should help him retrace his route back to the lane and from there out across the headland.

He straps his rifle into the carrier on the outside of his pack before shouldering it. He glances back at the truck one last time before breaking into a run.

It's easy to pick out the white tip of the monument against the now black sky. Closer, it resembles a towering, upside down V, its two prongs angled as if constant headwinds have blown the whole thing fractionally backwards. From his line of approach, it could be some artistic rendition of a giant tuning fork. Or a huge wishbone.

Under different circumstances this would be a perfect evening for a sea crossing. According to intel, showery weather is heading his way. Timing will be critical if he hopes to clear the coast without being spotted. Somewhere down below he can hear the waves dragging and then releasing the shingle like some snoring monster he'd better not wake.

He hangs well back from the monument. Whoever chose this particular meeting point is an idiot since it's a mere stone's throw from where light is spilling from a small chapel. He can hear voices inside. It's unlikely they're holding a religious service at this hour.

Sure enough, it's not long before there's a surge of noise and someone emerges from the building. Rifle slung over his shoulder, the soldier shouts and receives several vulgar adieus before he heads down a steep slope and out of sight.

Who the hell have they got working for Ground Intelligence these days? Any fool could have chosen a safer location along the 225 mile Channel coast. He shakes his head; he should have known better than to trust in any plan those guys come up with. There's still time to back out and make his own way.

Hearing a faint rustle, he draws the knife from his ankle as he spins around. A tall figure emerges from the shadows with both hands held high. 'Bonsoir.' The man keeps coming, his walk jaunty, overconfident. 'Je m'appelle Xavier,' he says breaking with protocol. Then, switching to English, 'You are expecting me.' It's not a question.

'Before you go any further, I believe you have a message for me.'

'Ah, yes – Aragorn sends his regards.' Section Controllers always assume the identity of fictional heroes. So-called-Xavier tilts his head to one side. 'May I lower my hands now?'

'D'accord.' Keeping the man in sight, he stoops to holster his knife. 'Keep your voice down,' he tells him.

The man's carrying a backpack. Coming closer, he whispers, 'I expect you have spotted our friends in the chapelle.' The Frenchman smells as unwashed as he is.

'Was it your idea to meet here?'

'It is appropriate, I think.' Xavier points to the monument. 'This is for l'Oiseau Blanc – the White Bird. The aeroplane who disappear here more than one hundred years ago. The pilots they try to fly from Paris to New York for the first time.' He waves a knowing finger at the structure. 'This is where their aeroplane is last seen.'

'You called it appropriate – why's that?'

The question earns a shrug. 'It is – was – not wise for Nungesser and Coli to attempt such a journey, but they do it anyway.'

'So,' Guy says, 'you seem to be suggesting that, since I'm unlikely to make it across the Channel, starting from here fulfils some sort of poetic notion of yours.'

'Perhaps this is so, no?' Xavier shrugs again. 'Also, here they keep only four, maybe five, soldiers to guard the beach. These men – sometimes they are women – they walk up and down la promenade.' Like some shadow puppeteer, his two fingers patrol the air back and forth several times. 'But soon they grow bored with this, and then they sit, and maybe go to sleep for a while.' He turns his fingers over to represent their unconscious state. 'Another thing – they do not patrol at this end of the beach now. It is not possible to pass because there was a – Boomph!' His hands mime an explosion. 'And many rocks fall down.'

'You're saying some sort of blast caused a rockfall that's now blocking this end of the beach?'

'Oui, oui. C'est le cas.' Xavier nods while chopping the air like a guillotine blade falling.

Such a landslide hasn't registered on any of the charts he's studied. If it exists, the explosion and subsequent rockfall must have occurred recently.

'The boat I find for you is at the beach. A very nice RIB. Good strong boat. Fast engine. Of course you cannot simply walk down the steps from here because…'

'It's after curfew and they'll shoot me on sight.'

'Exactement.' He holds up an index finger. 'But there is another way down to that part of the beach. I show you. We go down the rocks.' Two fingers begin a crawling motion.

'Hang on a minute – you want me to climb down a cliff I'm unfamiliar with in the dark?'

'This climb it is not so hard. We take an old piste that I know.'

'Piste? As in a ski run?'

'No, is more of a chemin – a path.' His two hands indicate a less than reassuring narrow gap. 'At the start it is easy. Do not worry, my friend, I will show you the best way. I have brought ropes for the last part.'

'I'm meant to abseil?' he scoffs. 'This just gets better and better.'

'For now we have the moon with us. And the many lights along la promenade so it is not so dark to see once the eyes are...'

'Adjusted.'

Xavier gives his shoulder a hearty slap. 'It will be okay.'

'A moment ago you compared my journey to some French bi-plane's fatal attempt to cross the Atlantic. Oh, and by the way, Alcock and Brown managed to pull that particular feat off first – and way back in June 1919.'

Xavier squeezes his shoulder. Is he usually this tactile or is he trying hard to appear trustworthy? 'I already get you a boat and he have enough fuel to cross La Manche.' His grip gets tighter. 'But the sea here she is capricieuse. Like a woman she is calm at one time and then... oh là là!'

Shaking his head, Xavier lets go of his shoulder so his hand can plunge up and down rollercoaster-style. Where in God's name did they find this clown?

Guy steps out of his range. 'Yeah, I get it – the tides and currents are unpredictable.'

Should he trust this man and his reckless plan? He's tempted by the prospect of a RIB that's fuelled up and ready to go a mere eighty metres or so below where they're standing. Figuring out an alternative way to get across the Channel will take more time and come with its own risks.

Bottom line – is he fool enough to embark on a dangerous climb in the dark guided by a man who, at best, is eccentric? Even if he makes it down to the beach in one piece, odds are he'll be shot.

What if he tests the water first, so to speak. If the descent proves too difficult, or he senses a trap, he can jettison Xavier and retreat. Although, once he's committed to something, accepting defeat is never an easy option.

The man's claim regarding the numbers patrolling this seafront does sort of make sense. With no natural harbour, only flat-bottomed craft can land on the beach below. Their commanders would concentrate their finite resources on defending nearby Dieppe and other major ports along the coast.

Undecided, he almost wishes reinforcements would emerge from the chapel to scupper this plan. However, aside from the raised voices inside the building, all remains quiet.

The soldier who just left has probably relieved someone down there from sentry duty. If so, that individual is making their way up here right now. The cloud cover has thinned but for how much longer?

'Okay then,' he says. 'Let's do this.'

The Frenchman grabs his arm. 'Between here and Angleterre there will be many who shoot if they see you.' He shakes his head. 'They take no prisoners, you understand me?'

Guy can't help but grin. 'Okay, thanks for the pep talk. If we're going to try this crazy plan of yours, we need to go before it's too late.'

Chapter Twenty-Three

Everything's gone quiet over in the chapel – too quiet for Guy's liking. The lights are casting a halo around the building. Those inside it are unlikely to believe in the doctrine of goodwill unto others. Perhaps they've all fallen asleep.

Or perhaps the two of them have been spotted.

'We go now,' Xavier whispers. Before he can grab the man's arm and advise caution, the Frenchman's off, skirting the chapel in an arc that's not nearly wide enough.

Guy doesn't move. Apart, if one of them is spotted the other still has a chance to escape. He checks again for any signs of nearby activity. With no contrary indications and with little option, he follows Xavier, keeping to a much greater distance as he skirts around the chapel.

His guide has upped his pace. Forging ahead, he can just make him out as he zigzags through the scrub and boulders. After that, he catches only momentary glimpses of the man's back but does his best to follow right up to the point where the ground gives way in front of him.

He reels back from the edge. Like some cartoon character, if he hadn't stopped dead, he might have continued running on air before reality and gravity kicked in.

Damn it – where the hell has his so-called guide disappeared to? He peers out into the surrounding darkness. 'Xavier,' he mutters. Getting no response he raises his voice a notch. 'Xavier – where the hell are you?' He half expects him to pop up from some hidey-hole and shout boo.

Fuck's sake – he's in no mood for this hide and seek in the dark.

There's nothing but open water before him. Out at sea he can distinguish the horizon line and then a few white horses – more like foals – rolling in towards the shore. He can't see the beach below – it must be hidden by the overhang. Getting his bearings, he makes out the top of the cliff face to his left, its chalky stone glowing white in the moonlight. It's likely to be more unstable since the explosion Xavier mentioned.

He retreats to what he hopes is safer ground. On the breeze he can smell ozone and possibly the coming rain – although that could be a trick of his imagination. Above him strands of cloud shroud the constellations. Ursa Major stands out. Leo could almost be chasing Cancer across the heavens. Like an incomplete puzzle, the missing stars bother him.

Motionless, he's drawn towards the void, is overtaken by a vertigo-like sensation that makes his head spin. He staggers backwards cursing his lack of sleep, the effects of raised adrenaline levels.

It's a shock when he backs into a boulder. He needs to press on while the moonlight holds, but without Xavier to show him the way he has no idea where to go next.

Peering at the rocks around him, he's able to make out a narrow but distinctive gap that has got to be the start of this downward path. 'Allez!' Xavier calls up to him, his voice merging with the gravelled hiss of the breaking waves.

Muttering a string of obscenities, Guy takes his time picking his way down the steep slope. Like some bulb about to go out, the moon is flickering on and off; now I'll show you the way, now I won't.

Some distance on, the path runs into pockets of scratchy vegetation and then becomes studded with loose stones. When he slips, his boot sends a small landslide skittering to oblivion.

While urging him on, Xavier remains just out of sight. 'Allez, allez! Dépêchez-vous !' Is he being rushed towards his death?

The sound of the breaking surf grows louder with each step. Unsure of his ground, Guy is contemplating turning around when he detects movement up ahead. From the darkness he's able to pick out the distinctive shape of someone's head and shoulders. Xavier – he hopes.

A pale, shield-shape face looms in front of him. Suspicion creeps across his skull. The figure must be standing on a ledge a short distance below. Next thing, they disappear. Could be crouching down ready to spring at him once he's reached their level. With the momentum behind him, he should be able to push them off the cliff if they try anything.

Friend or foe – there's one way to find out. He says, 'Is that you, Xavier?'

'But of course.' The Frenchman gives a prolonged chuckle as if he's enjoyed a great joke. For an instant the silver in his hair is highlighted.

'Why have you stopped?'

He chortles. 'Because, my friend, I am searching for the rings.'

The moon brightens the scene before him as Xavier straightens up. 'You see, here is one.' He's pointing at the rockface. 'And there is one more just there.'

'What the hell are you talking about?'

'The rings in the rocks. Two of them.' He stands up. 'Autre-fois ils descendaient en rappel ici.' He's excited, pleased with himself. Something about his pronunciation suggests he may not be French after all. Could be Dutch originally? 'Is from when they climb up and down the rock here before…' Xavier doesn't finish the sentence. Instead he's taking off his rucksack. Guy hears a zip run across.

'So you've located a couple of old pitons someone's left behind here,' he interprets. 'And at a wild guess, I assume you're planning to fix some ropes to them so I can abseil down the rest of the way.'

'Oui, oui. Vous voyez l'idée. Is good, I think.' He appears to be tying an overhand knot – otherwise known as the death knot. Before Guy can suggest a double fisherman's would be a lot more reliable, he ties another making it a double over-hand – most likely chosen because it will be much easier and quicker for him to undo it afterwards, leaving no trace.

'Is very strong.' Xavier grunts as he pulls on the rope he's fixed to one of the anchorage points. 'You see – is good.' He beckons him forward with enthusiasm.

So far this man has delivered on his promises. Then again, up to now he's been able to back out. Aside from the minor business of descending the cliff without falling to his death, what of the promised RIB? Will it really be ready and waiting for him at the water's edge or is that bullshit?

'They tell me you know 'ow to do this,' Xavier says, emptying the contents of his rucksack onto the rock in front of him. There's no safety helmet amongst the familiar climbing paraphernalia.

Hmm. He can recall plenty of examples where misplaced trust has led to

someone being killed. At the same time, this particular window of opportunity is about to close.

Guy jumps down onto the ledge. 'Leave the rest to me,' he says.

'Avec plaisir.' With a mock bow, Xavier offers up the ignition key. 'You will

need this, no?'

'Let's hope so.' Guy smiles at his own incompetence. 'Merci beaucoup.'

Xavier sweeps an arm sideways before stepping away.

After zipping the key into a side pocket on his pack, Guy inspects the anchor rings he will potentially be trusting his life to. He yanks one and then the other. Xavier's right – they are firmly bolted into the rockface, were intended as permanent fixtures back when permanence was a less abstract concept. Looks like they chose this precise spot to allow a straightforward walk off descent.

The knot he's tied is firm. He's relieved to see a harness amongst the various ropes and equipment in front of him. The weight of his pack will add additional strain. Using the headtorch will only make him an easier target.

Once he's strapped the harness around his waist, he selects a finer, shorter rope to tie a French prusik and then clip it in place. If there's a rockfall or he's forced to let go for any reason, it will grab the rope like an additional hand. He double checks to make sure the prusik can't reach the belay device then leans back to test the whole set up one last time.

It's all good.

The sky darkens as he prepares to retreat over the edge. A more superstitious man might regard this as ominous. Nothing ventured… 'Thanks a lot for all your help,' he remembers to say before he throws the rope over, not knowing if it will be long enough. For better or worse this is it.

The shadow of Xavier shrugs. 'Je vous en prie,' he mutters, like he's just served him a meal and not a lifeline.

Guy takes a couple more backward steps and then readies himself for yet another leap of faith.

Chapter Twenty-Four

Ash

Once they've left the billowing black smoke behind, he's able to see that they're skirting the lower slopes of the almost-mountain travelling in a north-easterly direction.

The Mule may be only about the size of a golf buggy, but it's proving impressively tenacious over rough terrain. At the wheel Reid is all concentration, handling the thing like a pro. 'So where does this lead?' he shouts into her ear.

While he's being thrown from side to side, all she says is, 'You'll see.' He's grateful that she'd extricated them from a sticky situation back there, but her lack of communication is starting to get to him.

The track they're following has been eroded in places, the going getting tougher all the time. Cursing under her breath, Reid is forced to slow to walking pace while navigating the deeper run-off ditches and avoiding some hefty boulders the rain must have brought down. Around every bend he expects to encounter a rockfall that will block their way. She ploughs on regardless. If it wasn't for her superior knowledge of the island, he'd be tempted to jump off and take his chances. Then again, where would he go? When he checks on Isla she's clinging on with both hands. He can't abandon her. Factoring her into the equation, there's no way the two of them could match this pace over this terrain on foot.

The route zigzags as they climb ever upwards; the higher they get, the more exposed they are. They reach an area dominated by loose shale with a couple of stunted heather bushes still clinging on. The stone walls on either side have petered out leaving a trail of diminishing marker stones that do nothing to screen them from any onlooker with a decent pair of binoculars.

He glances back the way they've come. No pursuers have emerged from the smoky mist hanging over the valley. Up here they should be out of rifle range.

Since this route is too steep and twisty for regular 4x4s, if he was in charge of the pursuit and guessed where they'd gone, he'd be searching for some point of intersection where he and his men could wait it out, ready to ambush them once they leave the mountainside. Reid is doing a good job at the wheel, but is she thinking far enough ahead?

He tries again. 'Where are we going?' seems a reasonable enough question though she doesn't deign to give an answer. His eyes fall to the key sticking out of the ignition.

Having made his decision, he waits until they reach a patch of level ground before he turns it. The engine splutters and dies. 'What the hell...?' Baffled, Reid throws up her arms. Before she tries to restart it, he grabs her hand. 'Just hold on a second.'

'*You!* It was you who turned the bloody engine off.' She shoves him away. 'What the hell are you playing at?' When he seizes her arm, she twists out of his grip and digs a sharp elbow into his gut.

'Jeez,' he says. 'Can't we discuss this in a more civilised way? This thing's not going to be able to take us much higher. In any case, there's nothing much up here as far as I can tell. I need to know what your plan is because, like it or not, we're all in this together.' He lowers his voice to a more conciliatory pitch. 'Perhaps you wouldn't mind explaining how we're going to stay under their radar.'

'Well now, Mr Ash Ash…' Her broad smile is unexpected and distracting to say the least. Next second he's staring down the barrel of that Glock once more. 'You're in no position to make demands,' she tells him, singing from the same hymn sheet as Tall-guy.

He grins at her. 'So I see.' She's drawn the gun from her front waistband, which still leaves the one currently nestling against her arse.

Like she's followed his train of thought and gotten well ahead, her eyes flick behind just before they meet his. 'Don't even think about it.'

His expression innocent, he says, 'About what?'

She gives a theatrical sigh. 'Since you obviously like to play games, let me remind you of the rules of this one. Number one, I'm the one calling the shots here. Period.'

'Ah, that explains why you're so cranky.'

Unamused, she nods towards Isla. 'If it wasn't for your little girl, I'd happily have stood by while they marched you off to that post office vault for questioning, forward slash interrogation.' Her grip on the Glock is solid. He glances back at Isla wondering if the gun is about to fly out of Reid's hands and tumble away down the mountainside. Her little face gives nothing away.

'You seem to have forgotten you're in my custody,' Reid says. 'Which means I expect you to sit tight and keep your fucking mouth shut.'

Holding up a hand, he tut-tuts. 'Such language, Constable Reid – and in front of a child.'

She shakes her head as she tucks the gun back into her waistband. When she turns the ignition key, it starts first time as if eager to get going after this pointless interlude.

Rounding the next bend, they plunge between dense patches of heather. He's afforded a spectacular view down the vertiginous slopes toward the sea. A smattering of black and brown cattle are grazing the lower pastures – such a peaceful, picturesque scene. And totally at odds with how recklessly Reid's driving. The woman seems determined to push this poor workhorse beyond any sensible limits.

Up ahead the way divides and at last she chooses the downward slope. 'Hold on tight!' Reid shouts. She skilfully avoids another rocky outcrop.

They're partway down a steep slope that runs close to the cliff's edge. The track they're on veers off, heading towards the drop. It must have continued straight on before a massive chunk of rock broke off and fell into the void. Close to sharing the same fate, the buggy comes to a halt a couple of metres from the brink.

He expects Reid to take a moment to re-evaluate. Instead, she releases the brake and, steering away from that sheer drop, plunges them helter-skelter downhill. Heather-clad slopes give way to open ground that's little more than exposed rock and moss. With nothing to grip to, the Mule is beginning to slip and slide.

'Reid, this is crazy,' he shouts against the sound of the crashing waves below them. 'Stop for Christ's sake.' In desperation he tries to stamp on the brake, but she kicks his foot away. 'Catriona, we'd be better off walking…' They lurch forward. She presses the brake but loses control and the bonnet bounces off the side of a boulder.

Having come to rest, the buggy begins to teeter. There's a moment when it seems to be making up its mind, and then it overbalances and lands with a metal-crunching thud over on its side. The two of them are thrown together as the UTE spins and graunches against the hard surface. Gaining momentum, they're now sliding towards that edge. Pinned under Reid, he's unable to stop their inexorable progress. He shuts his eyes, prepares for that moment of weightlessness before they smack into whatever lies in wait below.

Except… The Mule comes to a screeching, shuddering halt.

He dare not breathe. Reid is a groaning and cursing weight he can't free himself from. She's still gripping the useless steering wheel. He tries and fails to turn his head. 'Isla – are you okay?'

Silence.

'Isla!'

Like a mirage, her little face is staring at him through the crazed windscreen. She must have been thrown clear before they tipped over. The girl's hand reaches into the cab to pull on Reid's arm. Roused into action, Reid snaps the catch on her seatbelt and, coughing and spluttering and trampling over him, she hauls herself free then collapses. 'Holy Mary mother of God…'

All his limbs appear to be in working order. The Hail Marys continue as he crawls out of the prone vehicle onto solid ground. His legs are shaking. As he takes in gulps of air, he wonders if he's in freefall and this is his dying fantasy.

Isla is there in front of him, her pale eyes calm and yet curious. While he's bruised and bloodied, she appears unscathed with not a scratch on her.

It's an effort to smile. 'You okay?'

She nods.

The toppled Mule is balanced precariously, cantilevered over the drop with all four wheels on the wrong side. One wheel is still spinning. He watches as it loses momentum and comes to a halt. Without the weight of passengers, the slightest pressure on the wrong side of this fulcrum is likely to send the whole thing plunging over the edge.

Chapter Twenty-Five

Ash studies the veins and strata running through the rock under his feet while he waits for his heartbeat to return to something near normal. When he glances around, Isla is now perched on a boulder, both boots are still on, legs swinging free like she didn't just save all their lives.

If he hadn't witnessed it, he wouldn't have believed she could cause grains of sand to rise up and bury a man. Or send a pistol flying out of someone's grip. Halting the death-slide of a 900 kilo UTE including passengers is in a whole other league. Maybe he's wrong, maybe the Mule hit some obstacle that finally stopped it.

The girl seems to be mouthing something in time to the rhythm of those swinging legs, the regular thump-thump of her heels hitting stone. Is she singing under her breath? Or reciting a rhyme she's choosing not to voice out loud? Perhaps she can speak after all.

Reid is certainly not a fan of silence. Bent over, hands resting on her knees, those Hail Marys build to fever pitch. In an unlikely switch from the sacred to the profane, she then vents her frustration in a string of loud and highly imaginative swear words. Her anger echoes off the rocks like a witch's curse. Running out of steam and invention, as she straightens up, she bestows a final verdict on events. 'Shit! Shit and shit!'

'I almost did,' he says. 'It was a close run thing.'

She shakes her head. 'Ever the fucking wise guy.'

He runs a sobering hand down his face. Unable to resist, he says, 'I hesitate to remind you, but I was *wise-guy* enough to warn you about pushing that Mule too far and too fast.' He gives her an extended, told-you-so look.

She throws up her hands then turns her back on him. 'Okay, okay, mea culpa.'

Her words conjure an image of that suicidal woman, the way her head slowly disappeared under the water.

'I admit you were right,' Reid says, kicking at a stone.

He says, 'So, about this plan of yours…' She doesn't meet his eye. Planting his hands on the top of his head where they can do no harm, his jutting elbows go for the up-close-and-personal angle. 'Don't tell me you have no plan and you've driven us up this mountainside nearly to our deaths merely for the fun of it.'

Reid doesn't answer. Instead, she's staring at Isla. 'Your daughter seems remarkably calm all things considered.'

The fight goes out of him. He shrugs. 'Kids are pretty resilient.' Is she wondering at the girl's lucky escape? Fortunately, Reid soon becomes preoccupied with the blood soaking through a large tear in her jeans. 'Shit!' she repeats for good measure, clamping a hand over her wounded knee to stem the flow. After a cursory glance, he concludes her wound doesn't look too serious. A gentleman would show concern, offer her his handkerchief – not that he possesses one, or considers himself a gentleman.

Saving recriminations for later, he walks over to the stricken Mule looking for clues to explain why it stopped short of the edge and their mutually assured destruction. He runs a finger over one of the gouges it's carved out in the rockface. Lewis Gneiss if he's not mistaken and around three billion years old; the surface over which the Mule had travelled has been polished by the elements over many millennia. Hard to see how some sort of friction build up could have brought it to a halt.

Whatever – he's no physicist. The impact stalled the Mule's engine as it skidded out of control though he can't remember at what point it cut out. Before addressing the issue of how they might drag its dead weight back from the brink, he needs to decide whether it's salvageable.

A good proportion of the UTE's weight is on the wrong side of the precipice. Sucking his teeth, he runs a closer eye over the bent and twisted metal in front of him, then sniffs. He can smell escaping diesel. It's coming from underneath the battered rear seat. If it had a petrol engine, he'd be more worried that moving it might create potential sparks.

They must have used up a fair amount of diesel already. Even supposing they could figure out a way to drag the whole thing onto solid ground, the process would cost them time and energy. Perhaps the leak can be stemmed if they get it upright. And after that the engine might not start. If it does, how far are they likely to get on what's left of the fuel? All that would come before the near impossible task of squeezing themselves into that mangled cab.

Whatever Reid has to say on the matter, his mind's made up. All the same it seems wrong to leave the Mule balanced on a knife edge. He's tempted to give gravity a hand to preclude any further discussion.

Facing the steep slope in front of them, he tries to pick out a viable route down. He's distracted by the glint from an object lying on a patch of moss around thirty metres away. Is it what he thinks it is? He doesn't react. Doesn't turn around. He listens for Reid's footsteps but hears only her mutterings, seabirds squawking, the waves breaking against the stony shore below.

Reassured, he saunters over and stoops to pick up the gun. It looks to be undamaged. He turns it around, weighs it in his palm. Does Reid still have the other Glock or did the crash send it over the edge? In their current predicament, a handgun is of little use. But there again, the balance of power has shifted.

After checking the safety is on, he stuffs it into the back of his waistband. He can feel its icy touch against his skin. When he turns around Reid is staring straight at him. 'What have you got there?'

'Nothing.' Like some guilty kid, he shows her his empty hands. Those grey eyes seem to see right through him. To distract her, he asks, 'How's the leg?'

They both stare at her knee. She's bandaged it with a strip of pale blue material she must have torn from the bottom of her t-shirt. 'It's okay,' she tells him. The bandage is soaked. 'Anyway the bleeding's stopped.'

She looks over at the Mule. 'I noticed you checking it out. So what's the prognosis?'

'Even if we could drag it back from the edge, it's a goner. And it's leaking fuel, so...'

'I guessed as much,' Reid says. Uncharacteristically, she seems prepared to take his word for it. Did she see him pick up the gun? She comes to stand alongside him. 'We're damned lucky to be alive.'

The two of them are silent until, pointing to something in the distance, she says, 'We need to head for that barn down there. Next to that wee geo.' By geo she must mean inlet. Reid shields her eyes with her hand. 'You can't really see either from here.'

She's right – he can't. 'Anyway,' she says, 'this friend of mine keeps an offshore racing boat in a barn down there. It's not very big, but its hull is sound. Rory's just replaced the rotten floor, so she's good to go.'

'You're planning to steal your friend's boat, Constable?'

She shrugs. 'Needs must. I've helped him out in the past, so he should be fine with me borrowing it for a bit. If it bothers you, I'll leave him an IOU.'

Should he mention that she'd "borrowed" the stricken UTE from another friend on the false promise of its safe return? Instead he says, 'I assume this Rory bloke has an outboard?'

'Yeah – a 90 horsepower Yamaha in full working order. He's even fitted a go-fast propeller which should come into its own at high speed – or so he tells me.'

'Right – then you *did* have a plan.'

She snorts. 'You seriously imagined I'd risk life and limb without one?' His bullshit detector suggests she's making at least some of this up on the hoof.

A look of sadness on her face, she says, 'This island's become divided like never before. Aiken-Murray regards me as a threat to his authority. The man's all puffed up like a sheep with the bloat. He's been itching for an excuse to discredit me.'

Until this moment he hasn't thought about what she's risked to help them. 'I'm really sorry I dragged you into this, Catriona.'

'Yeah, well, it was bound to come to a head soon. Besides, what's done is done. If we'd used regular roads, there'd be plenty willing to blab to the major's men.'

'Pity it's all smashed up,' she says, surveying the Mule. 'Shame to leave the poor thing like that. I was planning to park it up once we'd reached that main road down there. See that flock of sheep – just past that field there's a footpath that will take us the last couple of miles to Rory's barn.'

He can make out a few tiny sheep though, from a distance, they could be maggots. 'It's a bloody long way,' he says. 'Going to be a fair old slog especially with Isla in tow.' He glances down at her injured leg but decides not to mention it.

'That was why I was pushing the Mule so hard.' Nodding towards the wreck, she says, 'I feel bad. Callum's not going to be a happy bunny.' The UTE creaks like it might decide to overbalance any moment. She says, 'Why don't we do the decent thing?'

'You mean send it over the edge?'

Hands in her pockets, she shrugs. 'It's the logical thing to do. Covers our tracks and should get Callum off the hook if anyone traces it. He can tell them it was stolen.'

He grins. 'I'd suggest you might want to say a few words

before we send it to its watery grave, but you've already expressed your feelings with some force.'

Chapter Twenty-Six

With the girl on his back, Ash needs to concentrate on every step. They've come a fair way down but there's still a long way to go. It's late afternoon and the temperature is dropping. While he waits for Reid to catch up, he sets Isla on her feet. Her skinny body and mismatched, inadequate clothes must seem like a poor reflection on him as a father figure.

She wanders off while he scans the spectacular vista searching for any sign of their pursuers. Some distance below, a boxy, off-white vehicle is winding its way along the contours. Possibly a vintage Land Rover, though without a scope he can't be certain. No other vehicles in sight.

Reid is taking her time as she negotiates the trickier sections of the slope, protecting her uninjured leg; suffering in silence as he would in her situation. When she reaches him, he draws her attention to the vehicle. 'I'm hoping that's just some farmer going about his business.' They watch it pull in. Someone gets out to open the gate before driving into a field. Satisfied that whoever it is poses no threat, he asks, 'So, what do we do after we steal your mate's boat? Sail off into the sunset – dot, dot, dot?'

'Not exactly,' she says.

'I'm guessing you've never been much of a team player.' Aiming to provoke, he adds, 'Is that why you ended up here?'

Eyes fixed on the landscape below, she says, 'That's none of your business.'

He tries again. 'Where are we heading afterwards? I doubt there's some haven where life is so harmonious all newcomers are welcome, where nature's bounty is rich and the lucky inhabitants live laid back, peaceful lives ad nauseum.'

She doesn't take the bait. A black and white dog leaps out of the 4x4 and sprints off to round up the widely distributed sheep. He says, 'Call me sceptical but I don't imagine such a place exists in this hemisphere. Or in the southern one for that matter. If it did once upon a time, I'm 99.9 percent certain it's now been well and truly fucked.'

Isla is poking a stick into pockets of drying mud. 'Your daughter must get lonely,' Reid says, apropos nothing.

Down below, the dog's gathered the flock into a tight knot and is driving them into another field – onto the fresh pasture that's always more appealing. 'I get that you're not the sharing kind, Catriona,' he says. 'But I do need to know what your plan is.'

She thinks about this for longer than is reasonable. Eventually she says, 'A few years ago some friends of mine – well, more like acquaintances really – they set up a commune on one of the abandoned islands. The last survivors of the original crofters were evacuated in the 1950s. Thanks to climate change, the weather's less harsh there these days. The group have restored a few of the old crofters' houses and they've renamed the island Pailteas – after the Gaelic word for abundance.'

He smothers his amusement. 'Right – so now everything's fine and dandy over on Phallus.'

'Pailteas,' she says, with no hint of amusement. 'Last time I heard they were doing okay. Very few people know about the colony, and, for obvious reasons, it needs to stay that way.'

'My lips are sealed.'

He drops his grin when she turns to glare at him. 'Make sure they stay that way. Pailteas is off the NSL's radar – for now at least.'

'Okay, so that's where we're heading.' He tries to sound upbeat though he can't imagine they'll be greeted by open arms and smiling faces.

Shaking her head, she says, '*We* are going nowhere. Assuming we launch Rory's boat before we're detained, I plan to sail back to the harbour. I doubt they'll have anticipated that. Fortunately, I still have the necessary access codes. We then moor his boat well away from the main port. Like I said, I'm only planning to borrow it.'

'And after that?'

'Let's assume your boat's been impounded. They don't tend to guard that area at night. My pass should lift the barriers. We refuel your boat from the police supply, then head for Pailteas where you will drop me off.' She throws her arms out wide. 'After that you're free to go about whatever nefarious business brought you here in the first place.'

Before he can respond, she holds up a hand and, staring him in the eye, says, 'Believe me, I don't want to know.'

'Okay,' he says. 'Then I guess we'd better crack on.'

Dusk is already gathering as they reach the valley floor. Isla might not weigh much, but his back is feeling the strain from carrying her most of the way down. 'You can walk for a bit,' he tells her. She doesn't protest but catches his hand, swinging his arm as she skips beside him like an affectionate daughter might.

The road's smooth and level surface is a welcome relief. Reid soon overtakes them, her head darting towards the slightest noise, while Isla alternates between trotting and splashing in the larger puddles. Ignoring the nighttime moochings of the local wildlife, his ears are tuned for the sound of approaching vehicles. When the cat-like call of a long-eared owl startles Isla, a sensation akin to an electric current runs from her hand up his own arm. Like he's touched a live wire, he lets go.

Before he can analyse what happened, Reid points his attention to a single storey building silhouetted against the darkening sky. The perfect ambush site. With no light spilling from it, the place appears abandoned. No sign of any vehicles parked outside.

Reid holds a finger to her lips. Isla plays along as the three of them creep closer to what looks like a typical 1980s bungalow with its windows boarded up. The only movement is in the swaying vegetation that's grown up around it. When it was built, such an isolated spot so close to the sea would have been desirable. The fact that they protected the windows suggests the owners hoped to return some day. Amongst the graffiti tags and symbols daubed along the building's blank face, the words **FUCK THE NSL** stand out. The same sentiment is repeated several more times at different angles. He couldn't have put it better.

Ash swoops Isla up, lugging her underarm as if it's an extension of the game. No one springs out from the shadows as they pass by. He carries the wriggling girl a further fifty metres until the words *put me down* enter his head as if she'd spoken out loud. Back on her feet, her cold little hand seeks his, but he doesn't take it.

A shiver runs through him. Had he imagined her voice or was that another of her magic tricks?

They've reached the start of the footpath. Above them the moon has risen, its reflection caught here and there in puddles. Further along, the track's surface turns to a fine gravel of crushed shells crunching underfoot. They skirt around a wide, swaying machair – the shoreline habitat unique to the archipelago. All's quiet now, but in a month or so it will be full of migratory waders.

His senses are saturated by the sounds and smells of the marshland. He hears flowing water some time before a stream emerges. It runs alongside the path and then feeds into a wider pool.

Ash takes off his boots and rolls up his jeans. The water's so cold he catches his breath. Wading in further, he stirs up the sediment as he tests its depth. When he beckons for Isla to join him, she refuses. Instead, she pulls off her boots, perches on a rock and dangles her feet, crying out when her bare toes reach the icy water. If she's capable of making such a sound, she ought to be physically able to speak. Her little feet are unmarked in spite of her lack of socks.

'Having fun?' Reid's voice brims with disapproval.

He cups his hands under the feeder stream and tests it for

salt before quenching his thirst. When he wades over to Isla, she slurps from his hands. He fetches her more until, with a giggle, she opens her mouth and lets it dribble down her chin. Watching her childish antics, he finds himself chuckling.

'Can I offer you a drink Catriona?' he asks.

She scoffs. 'No, thanks. Some dead animal could be lying upstream.'

'Tastes pretty pure to me.'

'I'd rather not risk it when there's a tap in the barn.' She might have mentioned that before.

'Where's the fun in that?' he says, echoing her earlier words.

Looking around, Reid says, 'We should press on before the light goes.' He drags his socks over his wet feet, hasn't finished fastening his boot laces before she's sets off at a pace. Switching allegiance, Isla pulls on her boots and, catching up, trots alongside her.

He can hear the regular sigh of the tide. The view opens up and Reid stops to get her bearings. The first stars are visible, the horizon a sparkling streak. He can just make out a stout, squarish building perched above the inlet.

They set off towards it, while he hangs back until he's certain there's no one else around. He catches up with them on the slipway leading to the barn. Small fragments in its granite blocks are catching the dying light.

Reid keys in the padlock's code. On the second attempt, it springs apart, and the chain falls slack allowing her to open one of a pair of wide wooden doors. The hinges give a long, weary groan. The three of them blindly file inside. Once she's closed the door, Reid flicks a switch and a couple of swaying lights reveal the wooden rafters above. Rory's boat is sitting on a trailer with its outboard engine already attached. He smells paint – her hull's been freshly sprayed in white. Not the ideal choice for a covert op. A series of high windows run along one elevation allowing the tell-tale light to shine out into the surrounding darkness like a homing beacon.

Chapter Twenty-Seven

Guy

Maybe dangling over a cliff isn't the ideal time to wonder why the hell he's putting himself through all this. Guy takes a steadying breath. 'Focus,' he mutters, leaning back as he begins the long walk down the near vertical rock face.

He takes it easy, controlling precisely how much rope he releases. The offshore wind is tugging at his hair, reminding him of the added danger of making this descent without a helmet. In the absence of light, his other senses are working overtime. He smells brine and rotting kelp, is aware of the off-balancing weight of his backpack, the roughness of the rope running through his hands while below there is only an unseen void filled with the sound of water colliding with rock.

Has Xavier allowed enough rope to reach the bottom? The knots he'd remembered to tie near the end of both lines will warn him only when it's about to run out. He can't judge how far he still has to go, or whether he's lowering himself onto the beach. He could end up stranded on those rocks or dunked in the sea like a giant teabag; but for now there is only the next step and the one after that.

After making good progress, his lower boot fails to connect with anything solid. He tries again and fails before concluding that he must be about to step off an overhang. Provide a man with enough rope and he'll find himself hanging in mid-air above the sea in total darkness.

Releasing a lot more of the rope this time, he swings backwards hoping the corresponding forward momentum will be enough to put his feet and not his head in touch with the rockface again. His first attempt leaves him dangling. Given a bit more rope, his outstretched boots finally make contact with the cliff.

The recent explosion and its subsequent landslide may have exposed some jagged edges that could begin to gnaw away at his only means of support. Picking up his pace, he lowers himself step by step, metre by metre until the knot runs through his hand.

The ground has to be close – he thinks he can feel a fine spray from the incoming tide on his face. Dangling from the very end of the rope, the toe of his boot runs across a surface that feels like pebbles. Christ, talk about cutting it fine – Xavier might have allowed a bit for error. He lets go of the rope and lands feet apart on shingle. At this point a religious man might praise God for his deliverance; he's more inclined to call it the luck of the devil.

He can't reach enough of the rope to give it the two sharp tugs they'd agreed. All the same, Xavier will be able to tell it's gone slack. Once he's hauled it back up, there'll be no trace of him ever being here.

Though he doesn't see the rope disappear, he senses its absence. 'No going back now,' he whispers to no one. He looks up at the sky, hoping the moon will play ball and help him locate the boat he was promised. Finding the damned thing is just the start; he'll need to launch it from the beach singlehanded and then make his way across the perilous currents of the English Channel without being spotted and fired on by any one of the hostile forces fighting for control of the shipping lanes; not to mention both heavily guarded shorelines.

'Don't get ahead of yourself,' he mutters. Pebbles scrunch and shift under his weight. The sound of his footsteps should be masked by the tide dragging shingle from the shore.

He stops to take off his backpack and unzips the pocket containing his old-tech watch. A quick glance at its luminous face confirms the time. High tide is fast approaching. He stuffs it back in then rummages around for his headtorch. The soldiers guarding this stretch of the coast will shoot at any unidentified light on the beach. He straps it to his head for use only in extremis.

Xavier will have dragged the RIB clear of the high tide mark. A few more paces confirm his initial impression that the beach is shelving steeply. He walks down the slope to meet the incoming tide, its lacey, white edges barely visible.

The landslide has blocked off everything to his left. He climbs a short distance back up the beach. Facing the cliffs, he turns the other way and continues along the same contour in what he hopes is a straight line. Fifty metres or so further on he's able to make out a few darker patches amongst the shingle. They turn out to be a group of rocks and then, lying alongside them, what looks to be the promised RIB.

Caught in a beam of light, he drops to the ground. Its origin is not a searchlight but the moon. He curses it for choosing this moment to make an appearance. Easy now to pick out against the shingle, the RIB is around six – make that seven metres long. Is she tough enough to withstand the rigors of the crossing?

Xavier has tied her to one of the rocks. He'd had the foresight to leave her with her bow facing the sea, which means that gravity and the uneven weight distribution should make dragging her down to the water a hell of a lot easier.

He waits for the clouds to snuff out the moonlight again before he dares to move. Hand over hand, he feels his way along one side of the RIB towards the stern. She seems sturdy, dependable – though that's about to be tested to the max. The angled propellor shaft is jutting out. His fingers travel up its length to the outboard motor. He rocks the whole thing back and forth to check that the shaft has been locked in the up position and can't drop down onto the beach like an anchor.

His searching hands locate the fuel tank just below the motor. A good size – it probably holds around 50 litres. He shakes it, listening for the slop of petrol, but it's impossible to hear anything above the sighing of the sea. He was promised a full tank and so far the Frenchman has been good to his word. On half throttle, and excluding all the many variables, there should be enough in there to reach the English coast before dawn.

Checking for any weakness, he works his way by touch towards the bow. His fingers grasp a long, wet rope which he traces to a carabiner protruding from the front anchorage point. He drops his backpack onto the shingle. It takes him a moment to locate the side pocket containing the ignition key. Stretching further in to reach the controls, he slots the key into the ignition, sighs with relief when it fits. He turns it a half notch, just enough for the tiny red ignition light to come on – a good indication that her battery's not dead. After groping around the deck, he picks up what turns out to be a wooden paddle – a vital piece of equipment if he hopes to slip away from shore under the noses of the military.

Having completed these rudimentary checks, he takes a moment to think things through. For the last eighteen months he's carved out a living of sorts in France and now he's about to leave the country that gave him sanctuary. Surviving such a hazardous voyage in this small, untested craft, is not nearly the end of it. Is he crazy to have agreed to this mission? Only a foolhardy idiot with a death wish would take a risk like this. Somewhere he'd heard, or maybe read, that there are two kinds of people: the wise who know they're fools, and fools who think they're wise. Guy shrugs. He could be either. Or both. Meanwhile, the tide is about to turn while he's standing around philosophising in the pitch black.

He stows his backpack and then his dry boots and socks at the back of the boat. The shingle digs into his bare feet as he locates the rope and, after a struggle, untethers the boat. He ties a loop in the end before wrapping the rope around his waist. With one hand through the loop, he takes a breath mustering what remains of his strength to haul her down the sloping beach and onto the water.

Chapter Twenty-Eight

Ash

Adrenaline is still coursing through his body when Reid smiles up at him and says, 'Fancy a cuppa?' Unbelievable! She goes over to the barn's makeshift kitchen, fills a kettle at the sink and plugs it in before tossing a teabag into one of two mugs. Noticing his expression, she says, 'Or a coffee? Instant only, I'm afraid.'

What sort of parallel universe has he stepped into? He shakes his head in a manner he hopes will convey both his incredulity and disapproval. Reid seems not to notice. As she waits for the water to boil, she works her way along the shelf above the sink removing the lids of various cannisters and peering inside.

'Looking for something in particular?' he asks.

'Yeah.' She grins. 'Rory's stash. Of snacks that is – I already know where he keeps his drugs.' She frowns her disappointment with the contents so far. 'Just how many screws does one man need?'

He can't help but smirk. 'I wouldn't want to put a limit on it.'

Chuckling, she pours the boiled water into the mug. 'Okay,' Reid says, 'while that's brewing, I'm going to use the facilities.' She opens a door he hadn't spotted, walks inside, and shuts it behind her. He's left calculating how long it's been since he used an electric kettle, or a plumbed-in toilet for that matter.

There's a small pot of gold paint lying on the workbench beside him. Someone, presumably Rory, must have used it to write the words WHITE KNUCKLE along both sides of the newly sprayed boat. Has the lettering had time to dry?

Before he can test it, he hears a flush and then running water. Reid re-emerges wiping her wet hands on the back of her trousers. She says, 'Your lassie might be needing a pee.'

Isla has always seemed happy enough to squat outside. Reid beckons her over. 'The toilet's just in there, sweetheart.'

At first Isla hesitates, then seems to cotton on and goes inside and shuts the door. Hearing a bolt run across worries him.

He watches Reid dunk a teabag, open a small fridge and takes out what looks to be a jug of fresh milk.

He jerks his thumb towards the sea like some hitchhiker from another age. 'We really should get going.'

'And we will,' she says, 'just as soon as I've finished my tea.' Is this a power play? 'Maybe your daughter might like one to warm her up?' she says, reminding him of the hot chocolate he'd made for the kid after he found her on the beach.

While Reid's sipping tea, he checks out the rest of the barn. Two full sized buoyancy aids are hanging on the back wall.

The toilet flushes. Did Isla just figure out how it works? More likely she was raised someplace with fully functioning plumbing. She comes out shaking her damp hands; someone must have taught her basic hygiene. When Reid picks up the spare mug and points to it, Isla frowns and shakes her head.

He unhooks both survival vests and hands one to Reid before approaching the girl. 'I'd like to put this on you in case you fall into the sea,' he says, hoping she'll acquiesce. He'd rather not experience her unique style of resistance. 'It'll keep you from drowning.' He wishes he hadn't said that.

'Women and children first, eh,' Reid remarks. 'How very gallant of you.' Right now he could do without her sarcasm. After giving the floatation device a cursory glance, she hands it back to him. 'I'll take my chances.'

Isla is more cooperative. The PFD is way too big for her, but she lets him slip it over her head and double tie the straps around her tiny waist.

After prising the lid off the final tin, Reid yells, 'Bingo!' She sniffs its contents. 'Mmm. Fiona, Rory's mum, still bakes a different batch of biscuits every Sunday.'

'Really? Doesn't she struggle to get hold of the ingredients this far from civilisation?'

'Civilisation – now there's a thorny concept.' Reid holds the tin out to Isla, 'You get first pick.' The girl doesn't seem to comprehend what she's being asked to do. Reid turns on him and in broad Scots says, 'Dinnae tell me this wee lassie hasnae had a homemade shortie?'

Not knowing the answer, he equivocates, 'There are worse deprivations.'

Golden and crumbly, the shortbread looks way more ap-petising than the hardtack biscuits he's accustomed to. After her usual sniff test, Isla takes a bite. She chews it with a look of wonder on her face.

'How about you, Ash.' Reid picks up a biscuit and waves it in the air as she walks towards him with the tin. 'Can I tempt you?'

Her flirtatiousness seems out of character. 'I'll save it for later,' he says, taking one and stowing it in his top pocket.

A first-aid kit hangs on the wall next to the workbench. He picks it up and shows it to Reid. 'You might want to see to that cut of yours before we go.' He stops short of mentioning that infected wounds are often the number one cause of death in combat situations.

Without giving it a glance, she says, 'I checked it when I was in the loo and it's fine.'

He shrugs. 'Your funeral.'

Prowling around checking the exterior of the boat, he notices a small paddle stowed to one side of the deck. The instrument panel includes a radio, sensors for depth, speed and wind direction plus a compass and GPS. The latter will more than likely be unavailable – and in any case ill advised. Though the boat's well equipped, a scope would have been handy. Failing that, binoculars.

The two of them are still munching biscuits. His patience exhausted, Ash strides over to the doorway. 'Sod this,' he mutters killing the lights.

'What the hell…' Ignoring Reid's protests, he lifts the latch and peers through the gap between the doors. No lights out there. No movement. No extraneous noise above Reid's complaints.

Satisfied they're not about to be ambushed, he opens both doors as wide as they'll go, ready to wheel the boat onto the slipway.

He takes a long look out to sea. There are no other boats in the vicinity, only the moon's reflection in the gentle waves running towards the shore. There's enough light to launch her with ease. Once they're at sea the moonlight will be a problem – White Knuckle might as well be renamed Sitting Duck.

By the time he's winched the trailer back up the slope and into the barn, Reid is at the helm. Isla is perched on the back bench. The boat rocks when he climbs in, his wet trousers dripping seawater onto the newly varnished deck. Though she was built for speed, someone hasn't skimped on interior comfort – they're cocooned by plump, white pleather upholstery. Relegated to the role of passenger, his contoured seat would be a lot more comfortable if the business end of the Glock wasn't sticking into his arse.

Reid starts the engine. Keeping the throttle at a steady 750 RPM produces a low rumble that must carry across the inlet. She steers straight out to sea. Once they're in open water, she yells, 'Hang on!' then pushes the throttle forwards. The racer lives up to her name, rearing up as it slices through the waves at an impressive speed. In the half light, he can see Isla is smiling despite the bumpy ride.

'I thought we were going to pootle quietly around the coast to the harbour,' he shouts above the noise of engine, wind, and waves.

He has to lean in to catch Reid's reply, 'We'll keep our distance for the time being.'

He shouts louder, 'Yeah, but now the bridge has been blown up, there's bound to be night patrols between here and the other islands. A white boat creating a wake like this will soon get their attention. They could have spotted us already. I'd much rather run into Major Aitken-Disaster and his band of merry men than a fully armed NSL patrol unit.'

Above the noise, she yells, 'Then I suggest you keep your eyes peeled.'

Isla taps him on the shoulder. 'Don't worry, sweetheart,' he shouts, 'I'm sure Constable Reid wouldn't dream of risking our lives again just to prove she's got the biggest cajónes.'

The girl's prodding becomes insistent. He spins around. 'What is it?' Isla's on her feet and struggling to keep her balance as she jabs her finger towards a spot roughly north-north-east of their current position.

He stares into the darkness. Though he can't make out another craft, given the girl's extraordinary abilities, he'd be a fool not to heed her warning.

'Bandits at two o'clock!' he shouts.

'Where?' Reid throttles back. 'I can't see anything.'

Not prepared to argue the point, he grabs the wheel and steers them hard left towards the shore.

Chapter Twenty-Nine

'Are you out of your mind?' Reid is on her feet trying to wrestle back control of the wheel. The boat is zigzagging all over the place. 'Let go dammit!' she yells in his ear. 'You're crazy – there's nothing out there.'

'Trust me, there is.' He fends off her interference with one arm, while trying to keep them heading towards the shore. 'I have exceptional vision,' he says, which sounds lame even to him.

Unable to match his brute strength, Reid's forced to let go. 'Have it your way.' She holds up both hands in apparent submission.

He pulls back on the throttle.

'What are you doing now?' She shakes her head. 'Why the fuck are you slowing down? If you're right about them being onto us, this thing goes like shit off a shovel. Why don't we try outrunning them instead of wallowing here waiting to be picked up?'

Trying to sound like he knows what he's doing, he lowers his voice. 'Because, Catriona, they might not have seen us yet.'

She gives a deep throated growl of exasperation. 'Bullshit!

If you spotted them, their tech would certainly have picked us up.'

'Then maybe they'll assume we're just a family out on some pleasure jaunt. Either way, if we go easy and don't create too much of a wake, we might be able to chug around to the harbour unmolested.'

'Grrrh!' Unable to voice her frustration, she flops down into the passenger seat leaving him to set the boat on a heading that will take them a lot closer to the shore.

When he looks back at Isla, she gives him the thumbs up – not a sign he knew she was familiar with. Now he thinks about it, there's always been something imperious in her manner.

They're gliding almost soundlessly through the dark water; under different circumstances this slow, night cruise in moonlight beneath a perfect array of stars would be a delight.

But Reid isn't done arguing. 'Do you seriously imagine the guys in an NSL patrol boat are in the habit of shrugging their shoulders and giving other seafarers the benefit of the doubt? I haven't had any direct dealings with them yet, but I'm pretty sure that's not how they operate.' She throws her hands up. 'I've no idea where you've sprung from Mr Ash Ash, and I don't want to know, but I don't imagine you've just crawled out from under a giant stone. And it certainly wasn't from some isolated religious order.'

He says, 'I'm quite sure the Sea Lords never ignore a genuine threat, but if they run across a couple with a young child in a pimped up, brilliant white, offshore racer, they're not going to immediately jump to the conclusion we're a covert unit trying to infiltrate their defences. I mean, come on…'

Her guffaw is way too loud – like she's trying to attract their attention for the hell of it. She says, 'Ah yes, the NSL are renowned for being a sentimental lot. In fact, if it looks like they might be about to board us, maybe we should lean in for a long, lingering kiss. That'll get them all teary-eyed and soppy, and eager to wave us happily on our merry way.'

To piss her off some more, he nods. 'You know, that's not a bad idea. I'm game if you are.'

'Arrgh!' With that, she goes quiet.

When they're nearer to the shore, he stands up to lean further forward – now for the tricky bit. He keeps a steady eye on the depth readings while scanning for white water breaking around unseen rocks.

In the corner of his eye there's movement. Isla is tapping Reid's arm. Half turning around, Reid asks, 'What's up, sweetheart?'

Why would the girl warn her and not him? After checking repeatedly, he can make out nothing but open water around them. Isla must still be trying to get Reid's attention because again she asks, 'What's the matter?'

He checks ahead, then to the starboard and port sides. Nothing. Clear off the stern, so far. He shifts his attention to the various sensor readings before risking another glance behind. Wait – is it his imagination or is there a pale wave running against the tide in the far distance? It could be the leading edge of a bow wave. If so, they're still a long way back.

Seconds later, he's more convinced. 'Hold on tight,' he says, 'I think we might have company off our stern.'

Before he can thrust the throttle forward, Reid stays his

hand, 'Wait! There's a sea cave just over there on our port side. Trust me, I know it well. Give me the helm and I'll steer us inside.'

'But if they follow us, we'll be trapped.'

'Or they might just sail on past unaware of our existence.' When he hesitates, she says, 'Well?' He looks back at Isla. As far as he can tell her thumb is in the neutral position; her expression blank as if to say, *Up to you this time.*

Damn it. There's an awkward moment of close bodily contact as they trade places. Once she's back behind the wheel, Reid steers hard towards the shore. Soon the pale rock of the sea cliff is looming up at them. In fact, they appear to be on a collision course with it. 'Are you sure you know what you're doing?' he shouts over the sound of the breaking waves. 'It's not too late to back out.'

'Shush!' she snaps. 'I need to concentrate.' She slows her right down. When it looks like they're about to smash into the rocks, he instinctively braces for impact. At the last second, Reid steers hard to the right and they sail in through a narrow opening.

They're engulfed by complete darkness. Reid kills the engine. The smell of spent fuel hangs in the cave's dank and silent air.

He lets out his breath. 'Shit, you certainly cut that last bit fine.'

'Nonsense. Didn't I tell you I knew exactly what I was doing?'

He can afford to chuckle. 'I'll never doubt you again.'

'Ha!'

'I won't ask how you knew about this place. I assume it involved some youthful liaison you'd rather not talk about.'

'I wish,' she says. 'A few years back this cave was being used by a drug gang to stash their gear before we got a tipoff and arrested the lot of them. Back then I was part of a team of five, and not a lone voice crying in the wilderness.'

He's noticed before her habit of making light of something that's heartfelt. 'In any case,' she says, 'the gang's overlords soon found other routes and other willing victims to do their bidding.'

'You did what you could,' he tells her. 'There are way too many heads, on way too many snakes, to cut them all off.' On that note they fall silent.

Once his eyes grow accustomed, he's just able to pick out their shadows against the overhanging rock.

They wait. Isla's cold little hand finds his. 'It'll be okay,' he whispers, forgetting for a moment that she's anything other than a small child. If they were alone, he'd suggest that now would be a good time for her to tip the balance in their favour.

He swallows hard. Beside him, Reid's breathing grows louder.

At first he hears only the slap of displaced water against the sides of the boat. It's not long before the distinctive sound of an outboard engine drifts inside.

Chapter Thirty

The English Channel

Guy

The night's as black as they come. He's long since lost sight of the French coast.

Guy breathes on his hands to warm them as he huddles behind the boat's spray shield. His waterproof jacket is protecting him from the relentless rain, but his trousers and boots are soaked through.

Shading its light with his hand, he checks the screen hoping to make better sense of the nautical charts they've sent through. The same download contains a mass of information about shipping lanes, tidal ranges, depth of shoal patches, submerged rock formations, submerged wrecks, buoyed channels either partially or fully intact, lighthouse and coastline identification, and so on and so on.

The RIB is being tossed around a fair bit. If his stomach wasn't growlingly empty, he might even succumb to nausea. The current sea conditions are classified as 4 – "moderate", though they've warned him that, within the next few hours, this could change to 5 – "rough", in which case he can expect waves of between two and a half and four metres high. Presumably, they decided to share this information with him on the forewarned-is-forearmed principle. Up to four metres! What the hell's he meant to do about that? Waves half that size are likely to wipe him out.

On all his previous ops, a journey like this would have involved a much bigger boat with someone more experienced at the helm, someone who knew what to do, or not to do, when the going gets "rough". On this crossing his main tactics so far can be summarised as: *try not to be seen*; *avoid other shipping*; and *look out for anything hard sticking out of the water.*

Current readings show he's still a worryingly long way from the English coast. A ping alerts him to the latest on-the-ground intel over there. According to this update, there's been a "significant" build-up of forces around all of England's south coast ports. It doesn't tell him *why* they're on high alert – that would be on a need-to-know basis. Seems they're happy to keep a lone operative in a tiny fucking boat in the middle of the English Channel in ignorance.

One thing's certain – he can't risk rocking up at any of the obvious landing spots. Meanwhile he's at the mercy of the elements in what is little more than an oversized bathtub.

Sod that!

He takes a closer look at the charts – zooms in on the East Sussex coast. Between Newhaven to the west, and the Seven Sisters cliffs to the east, there's a river outlet with a shelved beach on either side. Cuckmere Haven – a name that conjures up smugglers and makes him want to utter several ooh-aarghs afterwards. Previously a nature reserve, it promises to be a quiet spot with a navigable passage to shore. The only nearby houses – a row of cliff-edge, coastguard cottages – are marked as *abandoned due to coastal erosion.*

He enters the coordinates and sets a course for the smuggler's bay. On his screen, what he'd hoped would be a straight line trajectory has a number of significant kinks to it. He's meant to take it on trust that these time consuming deviations are essential for his survival.

While he's been preoccupied, a row of lights has popped up off his port bow She's a large ship. Backtracking her movements, the A I suggests she's heading down to Bordeaux. No available intel on ownership, origin, or cargo. An officially sanctioned shipment. Her crew won't be concerned about an insignificant blip heading off in the opposite direction.

While maintaining his present course, he keeps one eye on the Bordeaux-bound ship and the other on the weather and tries damned hard to avoid the many and varied hazards lurking beneath the heaving waters around him. With so many threats to weigh up, it's going to be a bloody long night.

Against the odds he's within sight of the English coast. The rain is still hammering down with sea conditions deteriorating fast. To outrun the gale that's hard on his heels, he'll need to make land soon. The demands of the crossing have left him wrung out – he could sleep for a week though he'd settle for a couple of undisturbed hours somewhere warm and dry.

He's able to make out lights and identify the more obvious

landmarks along the headland. All give him visual confirmation of his current position. He's close enough to be able to pick out the chalk-white faces of the Seven Sisters Cliffs.

That's the good news; the bad is he seems to have picked up a tail. His screen categorises her as a class 11 craft. Way bigger than the RIB, she's unlikely to be out fishing or running contraband in these conditions.

And she's definitely aping his movements. When he turns to starboard, she does the same. When he makes a course correction, she follows suit.

Bollocks!

Having shown their hand, his pursuers accelerate towards him. The distance between them is shrinking fast.

He can see Beachy Head. The pirate's beach is roughly seven km further along the coast. There's a dark stretch of land beyond with no visible lights, which has to be it. His screen concurs. Wind lashed, it's hard to make out the tiny, pulsating dot that's guiding him towards the mouth of the Cuckmere river.

When he thrusts the throttle forward, the other boat increases its speed. He steers the RIB closer to the shore until he's able to pick out white water breaking against the steeply shelved beach on either side of the river outlet.

He turns hard to starboard as he lines her up. At maximum throttle, he aims straight for the gap, keeping up speed for as long as he dares before he cuts the engine and lifts the propeller out of the water.

Momentum propels the RIB on into the shallower river outlet. Meeting the full force of the outflowing water, she slows down, glides towards the riverbank where she comes to a final shuddering halt.

He grabs his backpack and leaps overboard. His boots land in a deep layer of silt. To his left is the promised cover – a thicket of overgrown bushes hugging the track that will take him inland. The mud and shingle underfoot slows him down as he makes a run for it.

A burst of gunfire lights up the darkness. He dives into a mass of thorny bushes as a second round pings off the earth hitting the vegetation around him.

They've stopped firing. A quick glance confirms his pursuer's boat is idling just off shore, its lights blazing. They must be weighing up the chances of running aground if they advance any closer. He'll be visible through their infrared scopes, but the rolling motion of the incoming waves is making it hard for them to target him with any accuracy. His trousers are torn, his skin cut and scratched by briars. Nature's drawn the first blood.

No point in hanging around while they make up their minds. Head down, he breaks cover, running at full tilt. Bullets pepper the earth as he dives for shelter again.

Firing's stopped. Snagged by hawthorns, it takes him a moment to register the warm trickle of blood seeping through his trousers. A searing pain overwhelms him as his sticky fingers locate the open wound in his thigh.

Chapter Thirty-One

Ash

The Glock is still tucked into the back of his waistband. They'll be heavily armed on that patrol boat. Brandishing a weapon means they're more likely to shoot you on sight. Better to keep his powder dry for now. Reid must be thinking the same.

In any case, the hum of the other boat's engine is fading. Ash is beginning to relax, then he hears it manoeuvring, growing louder again. Shit – it's heading back. Have their sensors detected this place – this tell-tale void in what should be solid rock?

He squeezes Isla's freezing cold hand. Outside the entrance a powerful light is now bouncing along the surface of the water sending refracted rays dancing in intricate patterns on the stone above their heads.

He's startled by a flash that illuminates the three of them. Then it's gone. With that sweeping searchlight likely to discover the cave any second, they're trapped. Three sitting ducks.

Isla's hand begins to grow warm, then positively hot. Before he can let go, a burning wave travels up his wrist through his arm and into his chest where his heart is pounding. A scalding sensation climbs the back of his neck then spreads out across his scalp, raising every hair. His whole body thrums with the vibrations from the other boat's engine. The noise grows louder, deafening…

Then inexplicably, it accelerates away. Rocked by its departing wake, they're plunged into a deeper darkness.

With the heat in his body dowsed, he can breathe freely again. Those tiny fingers have grown cold. He drops her hand to check first his chest and then his neck where he finds his heart is still pulsing.

Silence envelopes the cave. The occasional flicker on the surface of the water reaches them like a storm that's passed over.

'Jeez that was so close.' Reid's voice echoes around the cavern. 'They were right there! I mean… I can't believe they managed to miss this place.'

He rubs his damp forehead. What just happened? When he goes to speak, an odd croak comes out. Reid nudges him. 'You okay, Ash?'

'Yeah,' he manages. No point mentioning how a moment ago he had some sort of coronary episode. In high stress situations, he's always kept it together, now the danger's passed, he might lose it.

The water around them grows calmer though its gentle rocking is far from soothing. 'I doubt they were the major's lot,' Reid says. 'They don't tend to venture offshore after dark.' For her this was simply a lucky escape – end of. She gives a loud snort. 'Whoever they were, or are, it sounded like they're heading around to the harbour.' Her sigh is all relief. 'Guess we should stay here for a bit. If they're an NSL patrol, I doubt they'll venture ashore unless they have backup.'

Reid's moved on, while he's still reeling.

'Can't hear any other boats out there,' she says. 'You?'

'What? Sorry.'

'Can you hear anything? If they're a lone patrol, they'll bugger off back to wherever they came from.'

It's so dark he might be inside one of those sensory-deprivation, floatation chambers Smithson used to swear by. Not that it did him much good in the end. Could a small child really be the source of that much power?

'You're unusually quiet,' she says. 'Any tactical suggestions? Or thoughts you'd like to share about what we do next?'

'We wait,' is all he's capable of right now. The regular drip off to his left could be a steady radar ping.

'Then we agree.' She sniggers. 'That's got to be a first.'

He shrinks back when she touches his chest. She says, 'When was the last time you ate? I'm guessing it was a while ago. Have you still got that biscuit in your pocket? I'm not one to advise a grown man—'

'Then don't.'

'Okay. Have it your way. I'm just saying...'

Maybe she's right? Could his light-headedness, this weird feeling of detachment, be partly down to lack of food?

He locates the shortbread biscuit he'd stowed away. Crushed against his chest, it has more or less disintegrated. He grabs a handful of dry crumbs and swallows them. Their buttery sweetness makes him gag. Ignoring this reflex, he hoovers up the rest.

A distant flicker lights up the cave for a split second. 'That particular storm seems to have missed us,' Reid says, 'And will you look at that – your wee one's fallen asleep, bless her. Kids, eh?' After a pause, she says, 'I suppose she's too young to understand what just happened. Or nearly did.'

He waits for the next drip. Then the one after. Through the cave entrance he can see slivers of light on the water beyond.

Reid's silence doesn't last. 'Earlier today we almost went over that cliff in the Mule. And now, by the skin of our teeth, we've just escaped a patrol boat. I mean, what are the odds?'

The shortbread will have reached his stomach by now. He waits for his blood sugar level to rise, for everything to snap back into focus. 'Can't rely on luck,' he mutters, more to himself than her.

'Ever the optimist.'

Something clatters onto the deck. Next thing, they're beginning to move. He hears the oar running through water as they glide towards the cave's narrow opening.

He grabs the end of it. 'It's too soon,' he tells her.

'You're kidding.' She wrestles it back again. 'We've waited bloody ages. Besides, I'm only taking a wee peek.' They're being buffeted by the tide. The moon is shining through broken clouds, highlighting the spray breaking against the rocks.

Reid says, 'Can't see any boats out there. How about you with that superior eyesight of yours?'

'Nothing,' he admits. 'They could be further around the coast.'

'True, but we can't afford to wait around all night.' He hears the click as she stows the oar. 'I think we should go for it.'

'What if we run straight into their trap?'

The silhouette of her head turns towards him. 'I had you down as a risk taker, Ash-Ash, now you sound like my great aunty Bessie. "Ye cannae be too careful…" was one of her favourite sayings. Never went more than a ten-mile radius from home. *There be dragons* pretty much summed it up for her.'

He shrugs. 'Given the unrest–'

'Ah but this was way back. In those days, the only civil unrest they had to worry about was when Celtic were playing Rangers.'

Tonight the craters on the moon are easy to pick out. He says, 'We should leave it a bit longer.'

'In the end Bessie choked to death on the bone of a fish she'd caught and cooked herself.'

Irritation is clearing his head. 'So, the moral of your story is that caution won't stop you dying.'

'Something like that.'

'And on that basis, you think we should risk our lives – including Isla's – because hanging around is getting boring.'

He hears her long exhale. 'No, Ash. I'm saying that since you and I agree there's no sign of any more boats, and this night won't last for ever, I think we should proceed with caution while staying close to the cover of the cliffs. Any sign of a patrol boat, we kill the engine and sit tight until, hopefully, they bugger off again.'

'Okay.'

'What – just like that, you're agreeing?'

'No, but I've listened carefully to your reasoning and have been persuaded by your logic.'

Reid laughs out loud. 'Said no man ever in the history of the universe.'

He can't help but chuckle. 'Seems to me, Catriona, you've been mixing with the wrong type of men.'

'Which makes you the right sort, does it?' Not waiting for an answer, she turns on the ignition. They're in a bright white boat on a moonlit night in hostile waters. The engine may only be at a quarter throttle but, amplified by the cave's acoustics and carried across the water, it's advertising their presence for miles around.

Chapter Thirty-Two

East Sussex, England

Guy

He's losing blood. Feels like a lot. Breathing hard, one hand clamped over his wound, he hobbles up the track keeping close to the cover of the thicket. Any second he expects to hear the thud of hurrying feet or gunfire as they shoot him in the back. He stumbles on, panting through the pain. Each step puts more distance between him and his pursuers.

The path takes him wide of the floodplain before it curves back towards the river. He can't see the water yet, but the gurgling's getting louder. If they were going to hunt him down on foot, they ought to have caught up with him by now. Must have decided he couldn't have survived that hail of bullets.

With that thought he stops to catch his breath. The rain has eased off – a break before the next onslaught. Leaning on a fencepost, he struggles out of his backpack. It takes him a while to ease the boot from his foot. Hard to keep his balance while he takes off his sock. It's too short to tie around his thigh. He sets his jaw to stop the scream as he stuffs it into the wound. 'Fuck!'

Teeth clenched, he increases the pressure then uses a strap from his rifle carrier to hold the sock in place, tightening it as much as he's able to tolerate.

Breathing through the agony, he distracts himself by dismantling his rifle. Eject the magazine. Unscrew the suppressor. Remove the hand-guard. Unscrew the barrel. Fold the stock in half.

Okay that's done. Now he needs to rearrange the kit, stow the gun's components in the backpack's outer pockets and secure them.

What next? Out loud, he tells himself, 'Assess the situation.'

He peers out at the darkened countryside, tries to concentrate only on the emerging contours of the South Downs against the skyline, the pale surface of the road sweeping around the headland.

The sound of an engine rouses him. Still some way off. Approaching from the Eastbourne direction, its headlights strafe the wider landscape. Civilian or military – can't tell yet. Fortunately, he's a safe distance from the road it's on.

He shoves his bare foot back into his boot. Crouching makes him gasp. He ties the laces tighter hoping his heel won't be rubbed raw.

Delving into his pack, he locates his binoculars. As the vehicle gets closer its lights illuminate the bridge. The track he's on crosses the same bridge. If there's a roadblock on it, there'll be no viable way around it.

Focusing in, from its size and shape he's pretty sure it's an old Ford Fiesta. A knackered one – its death-rattle audible for miles. Only a civilian would drive a pile of crap like that. Engine mountings could be shot, though it sounds like something more serious. Terminal probably.

The car stutters and rattles as it crosses the bridge unhindered leaving only clouds of exhaust fumes in its wake. No roadblock. Given the elevated alert level, why no military presence on such a strategic crossing?

He gropes for the remains of his last protein bar and bites off a large chunk. Chewing, he raises his binoculars and continues to watch the Fiesta. It forks right at the next junction onto a single track road. Some 300 metres along this it turns onto a rough track that winds uphill. After struggling up a steep incline, the car pulls up outside what looks like a farmhouse. The driver kills the lights. No sign of any other buildings around it.

Switching to infra-red, he watches a glowing figure climb out of the driver's side and head towards the house. Seconds later, a ground floor window is momentarily lit up before a blackout blind comes down.

Interesting. He's been briefed about the political and social turmoil in the disunited United Kingdom. If he hadn't witnessed this arrival, he would have assumed that house was one of the many abandoned dwellings along this coastal stretch.

His parched mouth reminds him of the fluids he's lost. One hand pressed on his makeshift bandage, he stumbles towards the riverbank. Adopting a semi-prone position, he's able to scoop up water and gulp it down. He can taste what the French call the terroir – the lingering taint of chalky soil.

Having eased himself onto his feet, he makes his way back to his previous vantage point. The sock's probably picked up some mud, but it seems to have stemmed the bleeding.

He listens for the tell-tale sound of overhead drones. All's quiet. And no other vehicles in sight or approaching. When he checks the bridge for concealed personnel, a large fox emerges on its far side. Unconcerned, it trots across the structure before disappearing into the scrub beyond.

He stows his binoculars wishing he'd packed a first-aid kit. His original plan was to head north after crossing the bridge, keeping away from major roads. He straightens up, hoicks the weighty pack onto his shoulders. Time to go. Lightheaded and struggling to put one foot in front of the other, he won't get far, and he knows it.

In his professional career he's survived where others haven't due to his ability to think on his feet. As the saying goes: Improvise, adapt, overcome. Struggling just to stay upright, he needs a more immediate goal.

It can't be more than a mile or so from the bridge to that house. He ought to be able to make it. Chances are the Fiesta driver is alone in there, though it's a safe bet they'll be armed.

He stumbles on. Beside him the river is quickening as it's funnelled past the concrete struts supporting the bridge. Up ahead he makes out a steep flight of steps leading up to its surface.

Mind over his rapidly failing matter, he hauls himself up by the handrail one step at a time until he reaches the top. With both feet planted on the bridge, he's the king of the castle. Exposed, struggling to breathe, he leans against the side barrier.

Around him all is silent except for the unstoppable rush of the river. Should a vehicle come along, there's no hiding place. Fighting the urge to give up, he sets off along the main road keeping well into the verge.

A huge black object is coming straight towards him. Snorting, it takes on the shape of the devil come to claim him, before it morphs into a lumbering cow. A small herd is following on its heels.

He waits for all the animals to pass him by. The wet road is littered with fresh cowpats that make him slip and slide. They'll be able to smell him coming.

It takes him an age to reach the turnoff. Further along it, he remembers to bear left. From here he counts down the metreage before turning onto the track. Rough and pitted with potholes, it's no wonder that Fiesta's suspension is shot to bits. His hand pressed to his thigh, he staggers through puddles up and around the final bend to find himself confronted by the Fiesta. Reaching it is a triumph. He leans against it, runs a hand over its mosaic of dents and rust with something close to affection.

Now what?

Option One – steal the car. It has four wheels and is old enough to be hotwired. Any attempt to start the engine, will immediately alert the owner within, though it might take them a moment to believe anyone would want to steal it. If his luck holds, he'll get away before they get a shot at him. The car might be knackered, but it's probably got more left in its tank than he has.

Option Two – break into the house. No sign of movement

in there. No noise. Assuming Fiesta-dude is alone, chances are he's asleep. There are no other vehicles around. If some hidden surveillance equipment has picked him up, Fiesta-man would have emerged by now.

He drops his backpack onto the car's bonnet and takes out his pistol, weighing it in his hand to get used to the feel of it before he releases the safety catch. After considering other options, he leaves his pack where it is before stumbling towards the house.

Under normal circumstances he would circle around the back and force a window. Given the state of his thigh, there's no way he could soundlessly climb inside. A better option is to shoot the front door lock and storm in. Not exactly subtle, but it has the element of surprise.

His strength fading, he staggers towards the front door. When he leans against it, it gives way. What the fuck! He's heard how trusting country folk used to leave their front doors unlocked, but that was way back when the world was sane. Well, somewhat saner. Fiesta-dude's lack of caution is bizarre. A sign of madness? Or it's deliberate – a trap. Or he's left it unlocked to continue the illusion that the place is abandoned. Very clever.

Whatever the reason, he's too committed now to back out. When he opens the door wider, a soft light frames a narrow passageway. He steps across the threshold. The smell of woodsmoke is the first thing that hits him. The next is a blow from behind that sends him sprawling onto the hard floor.

His pistol falls from his grasp. Pain overwhelms him. That scream could be his. Winded, he's staring at a worn pair of slippers. The cold barrel of a gun is pressed to the back of his head. 'Who the fuck are you?' a woman's voice demands.

Chapter Thirty-Three

Ash

White Knuckle is chugging along at low throttle with Reid at her helm. Against all odds, they've managed to sail unmolested around much of the island's north-east coast. The last shreds of cloud have been blown away, leaving them worryingly exposed, but they can't outrun the moonlight.

When he checks the back seat, Isla appears to be sound asleep, but then, with her, appearance is always deceptive.

Catriona's long dark hair is streaming out behind, the moon highlighting the contours of her face. The woman looks ethereal – and far too good for the likes of him. The illusion is shattered when she speaks. 'We've been fucking lucky so far.'

'Shh!' He holds up crossed fingers. 'Don't jinx it.'

'Don't tell me you're superstitious? Seriously?'

'I believe it was Roosevelt who pointed out that the good luck of the early bird depends on the bad luck of the worm.'

She steers a few degrees further to port. 'Then let's hope we're the birds in this scenario.'

They've rounded the last kink in the headland and now the

harbour bay is within sight. He can just make out the cluster of buildings that constitutes the main settlement. The church stands slightly apart, its bell tower sporting a flag – probably a token of Ben Faoghla's newly declared independence. He'd admire their stand against their would-be oppressors if it hadn't allowed a band of incompetent thugs and adolescents to rule the roost.

The floating barrier is still deployed across the harbour, a row of lights marking its top edge as it curves away to their left. The intermittent orange and black sections are doubled in its watery reflection like some giant snake's poison warning. He can see the radar masts and raised cabins of the islanders' boats sheltering behind it.

They're making their approach from an oblique angle. The quiet throb of their engine will be travelling across the water to any ears that might be listening, but it's too soon to cut the engine.

He nods towards the formidable obstacle they appear to be heading straight for. 'I didn't like to bring this up earlier,' he says, 'but how exactly do you plan to get past that beastie?'

'The barrier, you mean?' She's grinning. 'I don't.'

'Okay.' He throws up his hands. 'Then how are we meant to get ashore?'

Her 'Shhh!' silences him. The barrier is growing ever closer.

Without warning, Reid turns the wheel hard to port. And now they're heading for a row of substantial wooden fenders put there to protect boats from the harbour's high granite walls. 'Trust me,' she says. He's tempted to shut his eyes.

They make the turn, the boat's bumpers grazing the fenders.

Reid steers them into a narrow, unmarked channel. 'When the barrier's deployed, they leave this wee exit open for locals.' She shuts off the engine. As they begin to drift, she grabs the paddle and steers them almost silently into the harbour.

They've emerged alongside an unlit area at the far end of the dock. Reid manoeuvres them into a vacant berth between two larger boats. White Knuckle's stern drifts in nicely. 'That was impressive,' he tells her.

'I thought so too,' she whispers.

After lassoing the stern cleat, he ties the line off in two figures of eight. He's about to jump ashore to secure the bow line when he freezes at the sound of far off voices. 'Don't panic,' Reid whispers. 'That'll be the major's men.' Having been held captive by those vicious bastards, this is less than reassuring.

Her shrug suggests their proximity isn't a problem. 'The senior officers force the youngsters to do the night patrols. Being wet behind the ears with too little training and no imagination, the lads and lassies who are meant to be on the lookout for invaders assume the barrier will do the job. Which leaves them free to get pissed and play cards.' She nods towards a dimly lit building some distance away. 'And it's a lot warmer in that old salt house than out here patrolling the dockside.'

'You can always rely on the irrepressible hedonism of the young.' He's chuckling as he leaps ashore. Mindful of the tide, he leans back to take off a little slack before securing the bow line.

Reid nods towards the back seat. 'Seems a shame to wake the wee sleeping beauty.' Isla's pale little face is the picture of unperturbed innocence.

'Time to wake up, sweetheart.' As he brushes the hair from her forehead, she opens her eyes and stares at him unseeing. Then she smiles.

'I hate to interrupt this touching daddy-daughter moment,' Reid says, 'but we really need to get going.'

Isla stands up. The floatation device she'd been wearing earlier is now lying on the deck at her feet. 'Okay, Houdini,' he says, 'You'll be needing this later.' When he tries to put it on her, she steps back shaking her head, her face defiant.

'Okay, have it your way,' he says.

Isla grins.

'Great parenting,' Reid says, unimpressed.

He picks the kid up and sets her down on the dockside. The two of them follow Reid through a maze of creaking derelict cranes and winches to a rusty shipping container. Isla's cold hand finds his. There's an echoing metallic scrape as Reid opens a door cut into one end of the container. She ushers them inside. Shutting the door produces a long, haunted-house style groan.

'Welcome to my office.' Reid locks the door before switching on a small lamp. Spreading her arms wide, she adds, 'The last word in minimalism.'

There's only one door and no windows apart from a tiny skylight set into the roof. 'More like the last word in claustrophobia,' he mutters. A beaten up door that must serve as a desk sits on top of piled-up concrete blocks. Its surface is littered with papers and the components of a computer system that belongs in a museum. The only other furnishings are two hard chairs that have seen better days, a strip of rubber matting and a large whiteboard. Rubbing at the stubble on his chin, he says, 'I like what you've done to the place – that whole post-apocalyptic vibe.'

She smirks back at him. 'Since I'm the only police officer left on the island, the major and his mob decided to commandeer our old headquarters along with all the decent tech.'

Various notes and diagrams are scrawled across the whiteboard. It's hard to get an impression of the local criminal activities from the various arrows leading to and from initialled boxes. It's an interesting, if indecipherable, illustration of Constable Reid's working methods.

Isla jumps up onto one of the chairs. Staring down at the floor, she begins to wave her legs in overlapping circles. Although they have no laces, those black ankle boots of hers look like something from the Victorian era.

'You didn't bring us in here to admire the décor,' he says. 'I thought the plan was to liberate my boat and get the hell out of here fast.'

'I am about to do just that,' she says. 'Meanwhile, you two need to stay in here, out of sight.'

She's about to leave when he grabs her arm. 'Look, I get that you like to do things your way, but I'm sure it'll be a whole lot quicker if you let me help.'

'I'll manage.' She shakes off his grip. 'You can help by staying here out of sight while I locate your boat and refuel it. If they spot me, I'll pull rank, convince them I'm following an important lead or some other nonsense. That lot are probably naïve or drunk enough to swallow any excuse.'

Sidestepping him, she takes a fleece jacket from a hook by

the door and goes over to hang it around Isla's shoulders. 'This should keep you a wee bit warmer,' she tells her. Isla strokes the garment like it's a cat.

He surveys the metal box they're in. Reid unlocks the door then reaches to unhook a further set of keys. He blocks her exit. 'You're not planning to lock us in?'

'If you'd rather I didn't that's fine.' She jangles the bunch. 'I need these to unlock some of the smaller barriers.' Meeting his eye, her expression changes. 'Still don't trust me, do you?'

He's slow to step aside. As Reid opens the door a shaft of light leaps out – it could be an arrow pointing straight at them. 'I'll be back as soon as I can.' There's another spooky groan as she closes the door behind her.

He looks up at the skylight and then at the lamp. It would be safer to extinguish the light, but there's no way he's prepared to wait it out in complete darkness inside this steel mausoleum.

Chapter Thirty-Four

Though he's dog tired, Ash alternates between pacing and listening at the door. What the hell's keeping Reid? If she's managed to locate and liberate his boat without a hitch, wouldn't she be back by now? He has to consider the possibility she's been detained.

Or, given her somewhat laissez-faire attitude to ownership, maybe she's "borrowed" his boat and is now on her way to Phallus or whatever that damned island is called.

Or maybe, everything went according to plan, but she's decided to nip back home to retrieve some of her things – the sort of sentimental or practical stuff that, when it comes down to it, most people aren't willing to leave behind.

Hmm.

It's almost *too* quiet out there. He puts his hand on the Glock tucked into the back of his waistband. If Reid doesn't appear soon, he might just crack the door a few centimetres and take a peek out there.

On his next pass, he decides to check out Reid's desk once again. He looks at her empty, white mug – no decoration, no perky slogan. There's a vintage perpetual calendar that could be some family heirloom. Funny how she hasn't mentioned her family once. Or a lover for that matter. Could she have gone to say goodbye to loved ones? Or a loved one?

He stops pacing to stare up at the whiteboard and the bigger picture it could offer. Reid's hard-to-decipher notes are her attempt to make sense of what's been happening on this island. A psychologist might suggest all those intersecting lines represent the web of her thoughts. Or possibly a graphic illustration of the way she's been reined in since Major-Pain-in-the-Arse and his adolescent army took over as the enforcers of law and order.

Lost inside the bulk of Reid's jacket, Isla is swinging the drooping ends of the sleeves as if lending them a life of their own. In spite of the circumstances, she has a big smile on her face.

After more pacing, he's back at Reid's desk. It bothers him that she hasn't updated that calendar in nearly two weeks. He's heard that on a few of these islands they keep to traditions from the Julian calendar instead of the "modern" Gregorian one. Back in the eighteenth century, outrage over those eleven "lost" days caused unrest because the rioters believed the change of date meant they would die eleven days earlier than they were destined to. Insurrection stoked by ignorance and misinformation – it has a familiar ring to it.

Where's that bloody woman got to? If she doesn't hurry, it'll be getting light by the time they leave here. Propelled by uncertainty and inaction, in a few strides he's at the door again.

From across the room Isla shoots him a look that says, *don't open it*. She's taken off her coat to thread her skinny arms through the sleeves of Reid's more substantial jacket. When she stands up, it's skimming her ankles. Like him, she's been staring at the whiteboard and now she's angling her head this way and that as she walks towards it. He goes over to stand beside her. Is she able to make better sense of it than he can?

He picks up a marker, flips it end to end, over and over. On impulse, he uncaps it to draw a circle in one of the few empty spaces on the board. Aware Isla is watching him, he turns it into a smiley face.

She giggles like any normal kid might. He pulls an exaggerated pout at her reaction before drawing a grumpy face next to the smiling one. Giggling again, Isla tries and fails to ape his grumpy expression.

He offers her the pen. 'Your turn.' Her face drops. She hesitates before taking it, bunching the sleeves up to free her small hands. On tiptoes, she reaches up to draw a tiny circle then gives it two dots for eyes and a diagonal slash for a mouth. Is this a clue to Reid's state of mind? Or maybe her own?

That slanting mouth could represent anything from scepticism to annoyance. It certainly has a stern expression. He skews his own mouth sideways trying to match the emoji's. Isla's half-stifled giggle makes him laugh out loud.

Abruptly, she stops laughing and plants a finger across her lips. She adds a stick body to Stern-face. Alongside this figure she sketches a large 3-D box. Her sense of perspective is impressive. Inside the box she draws a couple more stick people – one a lot bigger than the other. It doesn't take a genius to work out this is meant to be the two of them.

There's a clang outside. Pointing to Stern-face, he whispers, 'Is that Catriona?'

Isla shakes her head. She draws a broken line from Stern's foot around the outside edges of the rectangle and back again. According to her diagram, someone who's not too happy is circling the shipping container.

He takes out his gun hoping she'll allow him to hang onto it this time. Isla ducks under the desk. He creeps towards the door then flattens himself against the back wall, ready to pounce. Seconds later the handle begins to move. There's an ominous creak as the door opens. Colder air rushes in to ruffle the papers on Reid's desk. Through the slit by the hinges, he watches a tall, hooded figure, who is definitely not Reid, hesitate on the threshold. He wills them on, eager to press his Glock to their head and demand some answers.

Instead of stepping inside, Stern-face melts back into the darkness, leaving the door wide open and light spilling out into the dockyard beyond.

What the? Did they sense a trap? Or hear his close breathing behind the door? Whatever – the shipping container is now the equivalent of a rat trap with the two of them its live bait.

He needs to warn Reid. Ear to the gap, he holds his breath and listens. All he can hear is the creaking of wind-tugged metal, the sea lapping against the harbour wall. He looks over at Isla and pats the air down, hoping this time she'll follow orders and stay hidden. If Reid is about to walk into an ambush, doing nothing is not an option.

Adopting a two-handed grip on the pistol, he nudges the door with his elbow so it will swing shut. It groans as it gathers momentum. His boot stops it centimetres from closing. All the industrial machinery out there could hide a small army. The moon's still shining; random metal edges are catching the light but nothing else. No discernible movement – but then there wouldn't be. If he turns off the lamp before he steps out, he'll betray their presence. Leave it on and he'll be silhouetted in the open doorway – the easiest of targets.

When he checks, Isla is still crouched underneath the desk. For her sake the light should stay on. Stern's retreat could be down to the girl and her awe-inspiring voodoo. Being incapable or unwilling to talk, he can't quiz her about that or anything else. If the normal rules of cause and effect can't be relied on, it's hard to figure out what to do next.

One thing's for certain, a child shouldn't be fighting his battles. He needs to deal with the situation his way. Gun raised, he prepares to take his chances with whoever and whatever might be waiting for him out there. Guardian angels don't tend to protect men like him. Nor should they.

Chapter Thirty-five

Guy

Spreadeagled at the woman's feet, his head reeling, Guy shuts his eyes on an overload of pain. If she's going to shoot him, now would be as good a time as any.

'Hey, mister.' Something hard pokes him in the back. He opens one eye. She's jerking a shotgun barrel near his face. 'Wake up, you fucker.'

He'd rather not. 'Now on your feet.' The slippers back off a little. Tartan trousers – is he hallucinating? 'Slowly does it.'

If he could summon the breath, he'd chuckle. 'To be honest… with you…' He would make a feeble effort to get up but knows everything will remain where it is. 'I'm not sure I can… after the crack on the head you just gave me.'

'You've injured your leg.' Not a question. She's noticed the strap – or the blood on her floor.

'Duh.'

'Badly?'

'Well not goodly for sure.' With both eyes open, the worn brick floor comes into focus. He manages to transfer some of his weight onto his forearms. Wooden furniture, an open dresser. Feels like he's time-travelled to the rural England of the 1930s.

'I told you to stand up.'

Pushing with the other knee leaves him in an ungainly position. 'I don't suppose you could lend me a hand here?'

'Fucking nerve of the man.' Is she talking to him or is someone else in the house? One slipper propels a wooden chair towards him. 'Use that.' Gripping it like a lifeline, he pulls himself partway upright. She says, 'You'd better sit on that thing before you fall.'

Clenching not just his teeth, he does as he's told.

Raising his head makes the room spin. When the merry-go-round begins to settle, he takes in her baggy, plaid pyjamas, cropped dark hair, shadowy features. She could be anything from thirty to fifty. She has a firm grip on that shotgun.

'Sorry for barging in here like that.' His handgun has come to rest under a sturdy table. Unreachable.

She nods towards it. 'You forgot to mention the armed part. Nice gun by the way. I'm guessing a service issue Glock.' Her accent hovers somewhere in the mid-Atlantic. 'You military?'

'Not exactly.' He touches the egg-shaped lump on the back of his head and winces.

A long sigh issues from the far corner of the room like some disappointed parent has been watching him. Pads clicking on the hard floor, a tall, wiry-haired dog steps out of the shadows. Not a threat – it's trembling from head to foot. To establish rapport, he says, 'Your dog seems a little nervous.'

'He's terrified of guns. And strangers. Guess what – you

ticked both boxes.' The animal's dark eyes are sizing him up.

'Not much of a guard dog then.'

'Depends on your perspective.' Keeping him in her sights, the woman begins to circle the table. 'He alerted me when he heard you sneaking around out front.'

A harsher light goes on. Squinting, he says, 'This probably isn't my best angle.' While his attention was elsewhere, the quivering dog has ventured closer like it's playing grandmother's footsteps. Those red-rimmed eyes are glued to him. 'What breed is he?'

'He's himself. Guess you could call him mixed heritage, like me. Not that anyone bothers with such niceties of language these days.'

The scaredy-cat dog is startled when a log shifts in the open fire. 'Looks to me like he's part wolfhound.' He clears his throat. 'With maybe a soupçon of collie.' She doesn't respond. 'What's his name?'

'None of your fucking business.' She kicks the pistol into the open then has to stoop to pick it up. In the process she has to juggle both guns – a vulnerable moment if he had the strength to do anything about it.

'My name's Guy, by the way.' Smiling increases the pain in his skull. 'Guy Lambert.' He opts for the English pronunciation.

'Yeah and mine's Cinderella.' She circles back to stow the shotgun in an otherwise empty gunrack behind the front door. Noticing him paying attention, she grins. 'To save you the effort – it's not loaded. I ran out of cartridges a while back.'

Holding the pistol like a pro, she comes towards him then

stands alongside the dog, eyeing him up. There's an upward sweep to her dark eyes. Fortyish. Attractive, if she wasn't aiming a gun at him. She nods. 'Pull down your trousers.'

'Not sure I'm in the mood right now.'

She scoffs. 'Don't flatter yourself. I want to look at your thigh.'

Not a bad suggestion. He follows orders. Sans sock, his exposed wound is a mess of torn flesh and semi-congealed blood.

'Got yourself a nasty-looking bullet wound there,' she says, indicating with the barrel like he might not have noticed.

'It's just a scratch.'

She shakes her head slowly. 'Needs cleaning up if you plan to avoid sepsis and, or, gangrene. I can never remember which one rots your flesh, and which one is the fatal blood infection.'

Hoping to appeal to her softer side, assuming there is one, he says, 'Maybe you could help me to clean the wound up a bit. It wouldn't hurt to pour some alcohol over it.'

She scoffs again. 'Let's get this straight – armed and in the dead of night you come sniffing around my car, then decide to break into my house, and now you sit there leaking blood and expecting me, because I happen to be female, to take pity on you and waste my precious whisky disinfecting a bullet wound you self-evidently deserve.'

'When you put it like that…'

The throbbing in his head has become a steady ache. Keeping her distance, she pulls out a chair and sits down opposite him. She switches to a one-hand grip. 'How would you put it, *Guy*?' It sounds like an invitation to plead for his life. Her dog is frowning. Only the truth is going to cut it here.

'What can I say? I was out of options.' Hardly a compelling argument. 'Look, if you're expecting me to sit here trying to justify my continued existence, you'll have a very long wait.'

'That's the first honest thing you've said.'

'Shit – I must be slipping. Put it down to that whack on the head.'

She looks different when she cracks a smile. 'If I were to ask what brings you here, would you tell me the truth?'

He pulls a face. 'What do you think?'

'What if I tie you to that chair and poke something hard and pointy into that *scratch* of yours?'

'You'd be wasting your time. Believe me, many before you have tried and failed.'

'Right – so that would make you a pretty tough guy, Guy Lambert.'

'Not especially. I'm just aware that divulging details of a mission is tantamount to signing my own death warrant.'

'Interesting.' She taps a finger against her lips. 'You know, it's possible you and I are operating on the same side.'

'I agree – that's a distinct possibility.' His wound is far from clean – highly likely to become infected. 'The problem here, Cinders, is that in order to find out if that might be true, at least one of us will need to blab. Since it's not going to be me, that just leaves you.'

She wags her free finger at him, windshield-wiper style. 'Well it's not gonna be me. I'm on home territory here – always an advantage. Plus, I'm uninjured. Oh, and then there's the small detail that I happen to be the person holding this gun. I make that a full house.'

'For now.'

'Fighting talk from a man who couldn't fight his way out of a cardboard carton right now.'

The dog gives a long, bored sigh as he lowers himself to the floor. Head resting on his front paws, he looks up at them with a weary expression.

'Then again, we could be on opposite sides,' she says. 'In which case, I should shoot you now and bury your body out back.'

'Ah, but you wouldn't want to do anything so rash. Besides, that whole shallow grave thing – it's a bit of a cliché, don't you think? And what if it turns out you've terminated a fellow agent and thwarted their vital mission?'

'Thwarted – now there's a word.' She grins. 'I guess that would look kinda bad on my resumé.'

'Exactly.' He points to his thigh. 'Meanwhile, if you happen to have some painkillers…'

She peers at his wound then sucks her teeth. 'Needs cleaning up and quite a bit of stitching. Pity there isn't a functioning hospital in fifty miles or more.'

'In that case, and I'm sorry to press you, could you rustle up a bowl of water, some antiseptic and maybe a needle and thread, just to stop me, you know, dying by default on your watch?'

Chapter Thirty-Six

Ash

Ash hesitates. Should he leave Isla alone and unprotected? Then again, she may be a small child but she's not exactly defenceless.

Stepping outside, he kicks the door shut behind him, extinguishing the light. That resounding clank could be a cracked bell struck. Seconds out. Gun raised, he checks to his left then his right as he weaves through the forest of discarded shipping junk. He takes care to avoid stepping on anything that might give him away. The moon is reflected in shards of broken glass and random seawater puddles; it casts menacing shadows at each turn. He swings the Glock one way then the other trying to cover every angle an assailant might come at him from. The wind is constant, whipping his hair and whistling through every small gap. Clanging metal provides the lyrics.

He's beginning to think his fears are unfounded when, some way ahead, the shadow line of an old wheelhouse thickens. Ash ducks behind a pile of oil drums to check the other quadrants for signs of movement. Nothing.

The major's men would patrol in the open, not lurk amongst dockyard scrap. With his line of sight compromised, he listens for clues that he's got company – which is near impossible against so much background noise.

Keeping low, he creeps closer to the wheelhouse then dodges behind a toppled forklift. From this new angle he's able to scope out that shadow. If someone had been there, they've moved on. It could have been a fox or a feral dog that's since slunk away. Rationalising can't shake the sensation that he's being watched.

Movement! A darting figure. Hard on their tail, he skirts around the skeletal remains of a boat. He hears a heavy thud, a howl of pain, then grunts and clatters of an ongoing struggle. Following the sound effects, he's confronted by two figures wrestling on the ground.

The writhing stops. One has managed to get the other in an armlock, pinning them face-down in the dirt. It takes him a moment to recognise Reid as the person on top with her knee pressed to her opponent's arse. If the loser doesn't hold still, they're going to dislocate that shoulder.

He clears his throat. 'Nice moves, Constable.'

Her head jerks sideways. 'Don't just stand there,' she says, breathing hard, 'Give me a hand with our friend here.'

Choosing the easy way, Ash flashes his gun, the muzzle close enough to get attention. 'On your feet. Any sudden movements and I'll shoot you in the leg. Got that?' His answer is a spluttering nod.

Backing off, he checks for any companions then nods to Reid. 'All clear.' She releases her hold and the two of them step back to allow the bastard space to stand up.

He or she takes their time about it. On their feet, they skulk alongside the picked-clean carcass of the boat. The hostile's hood has slipped to reveal a military-style buzz cut. Gesturing with the Glock, Ash says, 'Come closer – into the light where we can see you.'

Rubbing his shoulder, the youth steps forward. He's wearing camo kit beneath the hoodie. His head finally comes up. 'Blaine fucking Sinclair!' Reid balls her fists like she's about to hit him again for pleasure. 'Why were you following me, you wee shit?' She spits the words into his acne-ravaged face.

Give the lad his due, he meets her eye. 'I kenned ye would come back here sooner or later.' Cocky little bastard is evidently pleased with himself. 'I tried yer office, then scoped out yer cottage. When I saw ye come out o' yer house, I followed ye.'

A few metres away a shiny metal suitcase lies on the ground with a head-sized dent on one side. Ash smothers a grin. 'What do you want me to do with him?' Remembering their earlier standoff, he'd shove a bag over the boy's head if he had one to hand. Sounding serious, he says, 'Give me the nod, Catriona, and I'll shoot him and dump his body in the sea.'

'Yer havering,' Blaine says. 'Ye wouldnae dare.'

Reid snorts. 'Tempting, but maybe we should just take him back to my office.' She goes over to retrieve her suitcase. After wiping off some mud, she runs a hand over the damaged section then holds it up in front of Blaine. 'Look what you made me do.'

It's a pleasure to wave the business end of his gun at the boy. 'Start moving.' Then, in a stage whisper, 'How are we going to stop him squealing like a stuck pig?'

'We'll tie the bawbag up and lock him in my office.' Half under her breath, she adds, 'Hardly anyone comes down this way. Like outer space – no one will hear him scream.'

The boy won't budge. 'Ye cannae dae that, Constable Reid, it's unlawful detention.'

His temper rising, Ash says, 'Oh that's rich coming from you.'

'Aye, well, I'm an official protector o' this island. And besides, what if I'm stuck in that fecking container for days?'

'He's got a point.' She rubs at her chin. 'You know, the lad's got me wondering how long people can survive without food or water.'

'Let's see, Blaine here is young and reasonably fit, so my guess is maybe a few days. I did hear of someone lasting a week, but that's exceptional.' He glances at her. 'If he cooperates, we might consider leaving him something to drink.'

'Aye, and maybe a bite or two tae eat,' Blaine says. 'And if ye could leave the door open a wee bit so anyone who comes by will hear me hollering.'

'Then you'd better start moving,' she says, 'while I'm still in a receptive frame of mind.'

The boy does as he's told. Reaching the container, the three of them troop inside. Isla has come out from under the desk and is standing in front of the whiteboard. She's been doodling on the bottom of it, the sleeves of Reid's jacket rolled up to free her hands. Unfazed by their reappearance with Blaine in tow, her pale eyes take in this development like she'd known of the outcome all along.

He grabs the shoulder of the boy's hoodie, leads him to the

chair by the desk and shoves him down into it. Reid rustles up a pair of handcuffs from somewhere.

The fight's gone out of Blaine. He offers little resistance when Catriona pins his arms back. Having secured one wrist, she threads the connecting chain through the spindles of the chairback before locking the other cuff. His eyes follow her as she hangs the key on a nail by the door.

'Ye promised to fetch me a drink,' he whines.

She picks up a mug and, with a distinct lack of caution, disappears outside. Thirty seconds later she comes back, strides over to the desk and plonks it down in front of him spilling more than a drop. The boy leans forward to examine its contents. 'It's rainwater not saltwater,' she tells him. 'I normally boil it.'

'Aye, it looks a wee bit cloudy tae me.'

'Please yourself. Drink it or leave it.' Done with him, she turns away. 'We should go.'

'Wait!' Blaine cries. 'Ye promised me something tae eat if I did what ye told me tae.'

'I promised no such thing.' Reid shrugs. 'If I'd any snacks in this place, the rats would soon sniff them out.'

'Rats – there's fecking rats in here?'

'Lucky for you, they're fussy about the company they keep.' Seeing his horrified expression, hers softens a little. 'They tend to be shy when the light's on.' She picks up the desk calendar then, changing her mind, puts it back where it was.

'We'll leave the light on,' Ash tells him.

When he picks up Isla's old coat, the girl looks at it with distain and vigorously shakes her head. This could be her way of shedding some bad memories. Since she seems adamant, he drops it again.

Before they leave he runs an eye over Isla's drawings. They feature boats, cottages and lots of stick figures. Are they simply random childish scribbles or clues about what's going to happen? Before he can ask her, Reid waves her battered case. 'We should go.'

Swamped by Reid's adult-sized jacket, Isla walks towards the door. 'Wait a sec,' he says. 'It's cold and windy out there, let me zip the front of it up.' This time she doesn't object.

Before Reid opens the door he steps sideways to block their exit. 'Let me go first. You two wait here while I make sure we're not about to walk into trouble.'

Reid grins. 'Look at you being all gallant again.' A man could grow tired of her sarcasm. 'Be quick about it,' she adds, like he's some underling.

The wind almost rips the door out of his hands. It's a battle to close it as he mutters under his breath about what a nightmare boss Reid would make. Once he's certain there's no one out there, he beckons them to follow.

Having wrestled the door shut, Reid locks it and places the key on the ground just in front. 'I doubt it'll hold for long if Blaine puts his shoulder into it.'

She's about to stride off when he grabs her free arm. 'We've left the boy handcuffed to a chair in a locked shipping container, Catriona. He might be a jumped up little prat, but what if he can't get free and no one hears him calling out?'

'It seems you have a conscience after all, Ash-Ash.' She rotates her arm to throw off his grip then, looking down at his gun, calmly redirects the barrel. 'That chair's actually quite rickety. Once he starts thrashing around trying to free himself, the spindles will probably give way. Failing that, there's always Stewie Robertson.'

'Explain.'

'Stewie is a lonely old man who sometimes drops by.' Mimicking him, she adds, '"He likes a wee chat now'n again".'

Ash looks at Isla hoping for a sign from her that Blaine's going to be fine, but her hands remain in her pockets and, though the sky is growing lighter by the minute, it's still too dark to read her expression.

'Better get a move on,' Reid says. 'We need to be well away from these shores before daybreak.' She strides off with Isla running to keep pace with her.

He holds back. The boy could already be kicking up a racket in there, but he can't hear him above the wind-blown cacophony.

Ash picks up the key, weighs it in his palm and then, hoping he won't regret it, he unlocks the door.

Chapter Thirty-Seven

Reid leads the way through the wind-whipped scrapyard. They come to a high chain-link fence and follow it along until they reach an equally high gate. She taps in a six-figure code and waits. At first nothing happens and then the rickety structure groans as it begins to lift. They hurry underneath before it changes its mind and guillotines them.

Once out in the open, the force of the gale pushes against them. Reid forges ahead, her body sheltering Isla from the wind's full impact.

He pauses for a moment to take in the bigger picture. Clouds are racing across the sky, the coming dawn a mere glow beneath the horizon. The harbour's dominant feature is that floating barrier – a writhing black and orange snare that seems to have taken on a life of its own. To his right, a granite breakwater stretches out into the choppy water to form the eastern boundary to the harbour, the lapping sea almost level with the narrow walkway along the top. Boats of various sizes are moored alongside it. High tide – one factor in their favour.

Her long hair blowing around Medusa-style, Reid is making straight for the breakwater. Close on her heels and bulked out by the jacket with her head bent low against the gale, Isla could be her fairer mini-me. Once they step out on the walkway, they'll be visible from every angle. Looking around, he sees only restless water, curious gulls and empty, lolling boats.

The paving being wet and slippery, Reid has taken hold of Isla's hand and is leading her along it, anchoring her so she doesn't get blown into the water. The two of them are silhouetted against the new day's light, like some vintage footage he might be watching. He tucks the gun into his waistband and strides after them in the style of a man simply out for a spot of early morning fishing with his family.

Having walked past all the other craft, they're waiting for him alongside the last boat. The closer he gets the more certain he is that it's his. And in the ideal location for a quick getaway. On closer inspection there's no sign of damage to her hull, no water sloshing around her deck. She appears to be unscathed in spite of her recent spell in captivity.

He pats her familiar gunwales with something close to pride. 'I see you've already become acquainted.'

'We have indeed.' Reid dips her head. 'She's fully refuelled and good to go.'

'You've done a great job.'

She gives him a long look. 'It's safe to assume they've removed whatever you might have had stowed away.'

He shrugs off the inference. Watching the boat tugging against her moorings, he says, 'She may not be much to look at, but she's stout and dependable.'

Reid guffaws. 'Sounds like you're introducing a girlfriend.'

'Touch wood…' He knocks reinforced fibreglass. 'We've weathered many a storm together and come out the other end pretty much in one piece. As pathetic as this may sound, it's a partnership that's lasted longer than any of my others.'

Isla lets go of Catriona's hand to slip her fingers through his. With a nod towards the girl, Reid asks, 'What about her late mother?'

To make light of his gaff, he chuckles. 'Ah but what you have to remember is I'm the undisputed master of this boat, whereas, in my personal experience, women aren't so easily persuaded into doing what you want them to.'

'I see.' After another glance at Isla, she lowers her voice. 'You told me her mother passed away. It sounds more like she left you,' is said like a true police officer.

'In a manner of speaking both are true.' To hide any tells her trained eye might pick up, he looks away. 'Isla's mother committed suicide.'

'I'm so sorry.' Reid is nonplussed and for once shame faced.

They need to go but, swinging her suitcase, she takes a step back, less certain of her ground. She turns to gaze inland where the mountain's peak is beginning to emerge out of darkness.

He gives her a minute. 'Second thoughts?' he asks. 'Not too late to change your mind. I mean, I can't get away from this place soon enough, but for you it's different. This is your home, Catriona.'

'*Was* my home.' She looks out to sea. 'Nothing's how it used to be here.' A long sigh. 'Your arrival – how they were treating you and little Isla – I suppose that was the final straw. With every day that passes, Major Fuckwit and his sheep-like followers become more dictatorial, and more ruthless.' She shakes her head while surveying the sleeping village. 'The way our so-called defenders treat strangers, or anyone who doesn't immediately bend to their will – well, it's become just as brutish as the behaviour of the bastards they're meant to be protecting this island from. Like Nietzsche said: "He who fights with monsters might take care lest he thereby become a monster".'

He completes the quote. '"For when you gaze long into the abyss, the abyss gazes also into you".'

They both fall silent. Reid could be shedding a tear – with her wild hair shrouding her face, he can't tell. 'It was only a matter of time before they came for me,' she says. 'Helping you escape their clutches has marked me down as their enemy.' She sniffs. 'Anyway, I'd rather not stick around to find out what happens next.'

She keeps trying and failing to tuck her errant hair behind her ears. He touches her arm. 'I totally get that you want a new beginning somewhere else, but, to me, you don't seem the type to run away from a fight.'

'True if it's a fair fight, but not one I can't possibly win. Whichever way it goes with the NSL, life on this island will soon be unrecognisable.' She gives a sad smile. 'I've learnt the hard way to know when to quit. And I'm not afraid of starting over.'

Standing on a narrow walkway with nowhere else to go is not the ideal time or place to quiz her about what brought her to this isolated community in the first instance.

'If you're sure this is what you want…'

Her head comes up. 'Nice try Ash-Ash, but you agreed to drop me off on Pailteas before you disappear off wherever you plan to go next. Don't go thinking you can renege on the deal at the last minute.'

He squeezes her shoulder. 'Okay, then Phallus it is.'

She drops her suitcase onto the deck. 'You know these small fishing boats all look pretty much the same, so it took me a while to be certain this one was yours. Then I figured it had to be the one with no sign of any fishing gear and no name or distinguishing marks.'

He shrugs. 'Given the present state of play, anonymity has many advantages.'

'For some more than others, I imagine.' A twitch of a grin.

Alluding to her more than himself, he says, 'Having a past doesn't mean you can't make a future.' Then, embarrassed, 'Christ, listen to me – that sounded like some line from a psyche eval.'

'A psychological evaluation – so you *were* in the military.' The police officer is back.

'I guess you'd already figured that out, Catriona.' It's time to break the truth-spell. 'Enough!' he says. 'Now, all aboard that's going aboard.'

Even though they're in sheltered waters, the boat is rocking around a fair bit. Reid lifts Isla onto the boat and then jumps in herself. The kid goes to the same spot as before between the lockers. She crouches down out of the wind and hidden from view.

He unties the mooring ropes. Studying the scurrying clouds, Reid says, 'It'll be heavy going once we clear the harbour.' She's making a beeline for the wheelhouse. 'Since this place is deserted, I think we should risk running the engine.'

Rope in hand, he leaps on board. 'Oh no you don't. My boat, my helm.' He nudges her aside.

'You need a harbour pilot.'

'I'm more than happy for you to call the tune, provided I'm the one doing the dancing.'

'Aye, aye, Captain.' She gives him a mock salute. 'Can I humbly suggest we chug out nice and slowly so, if any of the major's men spot us, they'll assume we're off after an early catch.'

'Roger that.' The engine starts first time. He has no trouble manoeuvring her away from the breakwater on low throttle. Reid dictates the heading, fingers flexing as she itches to take the wheel. 'Another ten degrees to port.' She's finally managed to trap her wayward hair inside her collar.

He follows her instructions. Narrowing his eyes against the brightness of the rising sun, he steers blindly towards the harbour wall, hoping the entrance to the channel will reveal itself soon.

Raising his voice, Ash shares a thought, 'You know, they say the best way to catch a fish is to let him think he's escaping.'

Chapter Thirty-Eight

Guy

He exhales. 'Jeez, that really hurt,' – a major fucking under-statement. At least he hadn't passed out. The water in the bowl she'd brought him could be wine – a full-bodied red. Miraculously, the bullet had missed all major blood vessels as it tore through his flesh, leaving no fragments behind to fester.

Cinders had laid out what he needed on the table then stepped back as he dealt with it, jeans around his ankles. Arms folded, she'd watched, looked to be enjoying his ordeal.

Staring up at him with those mournful eyes, her dog is showing more empathy while his hostess seems disappointed, 'Just a flesh wound,' her verdict.

'*Just!*' He uses a cloth scrap to stem the renewed bleeding. Kid's material covered in cartoon dinosaurs – a surreal touch.

Now there's *just* the small matter of closing the gaping hole in his thigh. He takes a breather to summon up the blood. 'Hate to bother you,' he says, 'but could you thread this needle? My hand's still a bit shaky.' He holds it up as proof. 'I can do the rest myself.'

Sighing, she unfolds her arms. 'I wasn't planning to offer.' She chooses the black thread. 'Along with home baking, craftwork's never really been my thing.'

'So how come you have all this?'

'Previous occupant's. Guessing her kid was into dinosaurs.' She sucks the end of the cotton before passing it through the tiny gap on the first attempt. He decides not to ask what happened to the woman and her child; at this stage in the proceedings, it's better not to trigger a response.

A blue stegosaurus is now wallowing in its bloodbath. He asks a more innocuous question, 'Why did you choose this material?'

She shrugs, 'These offcuts happened to be in the drawer next to her sewing kit.' Then, pulling a face, 'Were you looking for some symbolism?' Her laugh could freeze a man solid. 'At a stretch, I guess you could say that in the great unfolding of history, our kind will eventually become extinct. Then peace will reign over the lands once more and the meek will finally inherit the earth. Strange how The Good Book doesn't give any indication of timescale.' She lays the threaded needle down in front of him. 'Maybe it needs another asteroid to hit.'

'You had a religious upbringing,' he says.

'Yeah, well spotted. All that early indoctrination,' she taps her temple, 'gets lodged in here like some parasitic brain worm.'

'The Church could use that as a recruiting slogan.'

She peers at his wound. 'You're stalling. When you burst in here, you didn't strike me as someone in the habit of putting things off, Guy Lambert.' In a faux French accent, she says, 'Or should that be Gee Lambér? I imagine Gee would be less squeamish. Plus stoïque?'

'Or a nut job who would revel in a spot of self-inflicted pain.' He sighs. 'I'm not–'

'Not what? Not the tough guy you pretend to be?'

'Not in the habit of stalling.' He picks up the needle, checks the length of the thread, doubles it up, ties a knot in the end, then clamps his jaw ready for the next bout of prolonged agony.

It's done. His thigh looks like something Frankenstein might have cobbled together on an off night. At least the bleeding's almost stopped. He drops the bloodied stegosaurus into the bowl before laying a pristine velociraptor over the wound, holding it in place with the final strip of material which he ties around his thigh as tightly as he can without cutting off the blood supply to his lower leg. When he pulls up his muddy jeans, the tail of a pink brontosaurus is visible through the tear in the denim.

Exhaustion is making his head swim. 'I'm all in,' he tells her. 'Need to lie down for a bit.'

'Well, you're certainly not going to be sharing my bed.' She flashes his gun to remind him who's boss. 'Or Flint's, for that matter.'

'Ah, so that's his name.' Grinning, he taps his good thigh to call the dog nearer. 'Here boy. Here Flint.'

The hound backs away. 'He may be a nervous wreck, but he's no pushover.' She nods towards an internal door. 'There's a couch through there – if you manage to get that far.' Since he's manifestly no longer a threat, she turns her back to climb the stairs with the dog following hard on her heels.

'Goodnight,' he shouts after them.

No reply.

Gripping the table edge, he manages to straighten up but, as soon as he puts weight on his injured leg, it sets off a whole other level of agony. He tries to hobble across the room but it's too much, the door too far to reach. Curbing his ambition, he stumbles towards the dwindling fire and its residual warmth. In spite of the hard bricks, he curls up next to the hearth and surrenders to the many blessings of unconsciousness.

Footsteps overhead. Cold, pitch black at first then slivers of light around the blinds. So stiff he doubts he can move. His mouth's a desert. Above him he can hear someone rifling through stuff. Doors are being opened, drawers yanked out, their contents skittering across the floorboards.

Is some intruder ransacking the place? No, the dog's quiet for a start. It has to be her, Sinister Cinders, frantically searching for something. Whatever it is, she's seriously pissed off. And, lest he forgets, newly armed.

Though the fire has burnt out, he can just make out logs piled up alongside it. A poker would be easier to wield.

The rest of his gear should still be in his backpack which ought to be lying where he left it on the bonnet of that knackered Fiesta. Unless she'd noticed and had snuck out there while he was asleep to steal the rest of his possessions. He wouldn't put anything past that woman.

Her car continues to bother him. Why would a covert operative – friendly or otherwise – choose to drive a wreck like that? Maybe that's the point – maybe it's a clever wheeze to throw off suspicion. Who'd pay attention to a lone, forty-something, slightly built woman driving a car so ostensibly on its last legs and with only Fainthearted Flint riding shotgun?

Careful not to make a sound, he uncurls his legs, wiggles his toes and then rotates his feet to restore the circulation. On the second attempt he manages to stand up. His thigh muscles spasm as pain overtakes him in waves. He breathes through it, registering a level well below the agony it was. Last night she'd goaded him about his lack of stoicism, comparing him with her notion of his braver French alter-ego. Maybe he should try channelling Gee Lambér? Mind over matter and all that. He allows himself a moment to get used to bearing his weight along with his character defects.

Directly above him, Cinders is cursing about something – throwing out expletives in English interspersed with cries of 'Ssi-bal-nom!' and 'Geh-Saekki!' in Korean. An object hits the wall hard and smashes. Guess she's not a happy bunny this morning.

His searching gaze comes to rest on a shadowy object leant up against the hearth. He bends down, closing his mind to the pain this movement generates as he seizes the poker. Straightening up, he swipes at the air in front of him. 'En guarde,' he mutters under his breath. Now he's armed, though admittedly with a crude weapon that would be useless against a handgun. All the same, it's something.

Now for his next hurdle – getting to the front door and opening it without alerting her, or, more likely, the dog. What then? Leaning on the table, he shuts his eyes to marshal his thoughts.

Plan A: Make a run for it. Okay, make that a hobble. Once outside, grab his rucksack and disappear into the undergrowth – assuming he can find sufficient cover nearby. Odds of success – not brilliant.

There's a loud thud overhead. 'Gae-Sae-Ggi!' Then, 'Joj-Dwaesseo!!' Ah – now that one means penis. Roughly translated, ATM things aren't looking favourable for our heroine.

Plan B: Once outside – big caveat – silently open the car door, climb in, hot wire the engine – which will need to start first time – and drive off into the sunrise before Psycho-Cindy has a chance to shoot him dead with his own gun. Odds of success – thirty percent would be pushing it.

Which just leaves plan C – stay put and allow her to call the shots.

Hmm. From his observations, Cinders is not someone brimming with the milk of human kindness. Then again, neither is he.

More crashing and banging from above. His mum used to tell him that lightning was only God rearranging his furniture up there. Cinders sounds like she's tearing it apart. To say she's woken up on the wrong side of the bed is an understatement. No wonder her dog's a nervous wreck. How long before she decides to vent all that anger on him? Assuming he's lucky enough to survive the next few hours, it's hard to relish the prospect of becoming that bitch's bitch.

A banshee cry from above. 'Ssi-bal!' she screams, echoing his thoughts as he limps towards the door.

Chapter Thirty-Nine

Ash

Behind scuttering clouds, the sky is streaked red by the rising sun – shepherd's warning according to that old saying. He braces himself as they head into stronger wind. The growing swell is already bucking the boat while, under Reid's instructions, he navigates the narrow channel leading to open water and unfettered waves.

A blunt crack splits the air. Ash ducks as more bullets ricochet off the harbour wall and smash holes in the wooden fenders.

'Fuck!' Reid's hit the deck. 'They're firing at us.'

'No shit!' He stays at the helm. When he checks, Isla's still crouched in the stern, protected in part by the aft lockers. With no possibility of taking evasive action, he ramps the engine up to full throttle and heads straight for the gap and the relative safety of the open sea.

Bullets are slicing through the water, pinging off the harbour wall. Semi-automatic. Probably a Kalashnikov – notoriously inaccurate. Maximum range 800 metres. Effective range 350. Best course of action – try to outrun the bastard.

Isla's first in the line of fire though she appears unfazed. When he checks again her eyes are shut and those thin arms are raised like she's appealing to the gods, or conjuring up an invisible shield, because something is deflecting the bullets streaking through the water on both sides of the boat.

'Isla, stay down.' On her hands and knees Catriona is crawling along the deck towards the girl and about to break her concentration. Or encounter her wrath.

'Leave her be,' he shouts. 'She'll be fine.' But of course Reid ignores him.

The boat's bouncing off each wave, slowing Reid's progress. More bullets glide through the water to port and starboard like a shoal of miniature dolphins swimming alongside them.

Then the firing stops.

In the hiatus, they clear the confines of the harbour at last. Meanwhile Reid has managed to reach Isla. She's pulled her into a protective embrace. When he looks back to the shore-line, there are no more bright flashes. He can just make out the line of figures staring after them. Damn it – Blaine must have raised the alarm. His fault for taking pity on the little weasel and unlocking that container. This was payback for his weakness.

A glance over his shoulder confirms there's no boat in hot pursuit. In case the major's troops change their minds, he takes evasive measures, turning the wheel randomly to the left and then to the right while simultaneously trying to put the greatest distance between them and the shore.

When he next looks back, those figures have merged into the shadowy harbourside. 'I doubt they'll bother to pursue us,' he shouts above the engine and the pounding waves. 'They'll assume the NSL will do their dirty work for them.'

Reid looks up but, for once, doesn't venture an opinion. She's still hugging Isla, the girl's head snuggled into her chest. An outsider might be touched by this motherly embrace.

Perhaps that's the answer – maybe Reid might be prepared to take the girl on. In silent rebuke, her eyes meet his. *What sort of a father...*

He shrugs, offering no defence to her unspoken accusation. Having established his unsuitability as a parent, perhaps she'll be more easily persuaded that she'd make a much better job of it. And why shouldn't he hand over a responsibility he'd never asked for in the first place? What just happened illustrates the folly of allowing sentiment to guide your actions.

He turns his attention back to the control panel and sets a course for Pailteas – a small speck to aim for in this vast, turbulent sea. He hangs on tight as the boat shudders while wave after wave launches her bow into the air. With so much spray hitting the windshield, it's near impossible to see anything but the next one looming. Each time the bow rises he throttles back ready to increase power as soon as it drops again.

At a top speed of around 15 knots and in a calm sea, they could probably reach their destination in around three hours; in the current sea conditions it will take far longer and in the process use up far too much of her precious fuel.

Okay, so what's plan B? Even at this rate of progress, they can't be more than half an hour from Papar Beag which isn't much out of their way and uninhabited. Even more compelling – it has a sheltered, almost circular bay where they could drop anchor and wait out the worst of this storm. Since he's the one at the helm, and his erstwhile navigator is giving him the silent treatment, he makes an executive decision and changes course.

He can almost feel Reid's reproachful eyes boring into the back of his head. Why should he feel an iota of guilt for not running this change of plan past her?

Again he eases back on the throttle and waits for the bow to drop. Reid's one suitcase is stowed in the locker to his left, its contents amounting to all her worldly possessions. Unlike him, she has a lot to lose.

Acquaintances that's how she'd described the small community living on the island they're ultimately heading for. The word suggests a certain distance, untried and unproven loyalties she's nonetheless prepared to bet her whole future on. As soon as he's dropped her, and possibly the girl, off on Pailteas and sailed away, she, or they, will in effect be stranded there. According to Catriona, the founding members have established some sort of Brave New World, but once they have nowhere else to run to, she could discover those *acquaintances* of hers have created something less than idyllic. He could maybe stick around for a day or so just to satisfy his curiosity.

But at the end of the day, it's not his problem. He pats the wheel, preferring to put his trust in more dependable objects even in the present sea conditions. Solitude's always a safer bet. Sartre was right about hell being other people and their never ending judgment.

A lot more seawater is coming over the sides and sloshing around on deck. Before long he'll have to start the bilge pumps.

Once the bow begins to drop he increases her speed. It's the same sequence as each new wave bears down on them – rinse and fucking repeat.

When he next checks on his passengers, Isla's still snuggling up to Reid while she, sensing his gaze, looks up at him and then sharply away. The pair of them must be soaked through and freezing. 'You're welcome to join me in the wheelhouse,' he shouts over his shoulder. 'It's a lot drier over here.'

For both their sakes he hopes the Pailteaseans, or what-ever they've chosen to christen themselves, will live up to the woman's lofty expectations in a way that, face it, someone like him never could.

Chapter Forty

Guy

It's a beautiful, fresh, birdsong morning. Better still, his back-pack is resting on the Fiesta's bonnet exactly where he'd left it. Doing his best to ignore the pain in his thigh, he's reached the driver's door when there's a shout from behind. 'Hey, Bad-Guy!' He freezes. 'Where d'you think you're off to?'

Without turning around, he yells back, 'I'm about to take a piss al fresco.'

'So, despite that injured leg of yours, you decided not to use the downstairs bathroom?'

When he turns around, Cinders is leaning out of an upstairs window with the gun pointing right at him.

'Force of habit.' He shrugs. 'Besides, I didn't want to risk disturbing you since you're obviously a little, um…' *Mad* might not be the best choice, he opts for, '*Upset* about something at the moment.'

'Funny, because it looks to me like you were planning to steal my car.'

His broad smile might not be fooling her. Spreading his

arms wide, he says, 'No key. And besides, do I look like the sort of man who would sneak out at the crack of dawn without saying goodbye to a lady?'

'Hell yes!' Smirking, confident she's holding not just his gun but all the cards, she nods towards the Fiesta. 'What's in the bag, Wise-Guy?'

'What, in that old thing?'

'Yep.'

'Oh, just one or two odds and ends.'

'Like what?'

'Let's see now – there's my dirty clothes, a few energy bars and a change of underwear, which, unfortunately, is long overdue.' He's shrugging too often. 'Nothing of value,' he adds. 'Regrettably.'

'Think I'll be the judge of that.' She waves the gun motioning him towards the house. 'Bring it inside.'

Leaning against the roof of the car, he picks up his pack and then puts it down again. 'It's too heavy.' He really needs to stop shrugging. 'Not sure I've got the strength to carry it. But as you're so interested in what's in it, why don't you come out here and take a peek for yourself?'

'Think I'll do just that.' She hesitates like she's sensing a setup, then narrowing her eyes, she says, 'One wrong move and I won't hesitate to shoot you.'

'Understood.' He managed to keep his shoulders down that time.

As soon as she disappears from sight, he walks around the car then ducks behind it, pulling his backpack down with him. The stitches in his thigh are straining fit to burst as he shuffles along until his feet are hidden from her line of sight by the back wheels. Working quickly, he takes his knife out of a side pocket and manages to stuff it up his sleeve seconds before he hears the front door open.

The side mirror offers only an angled view of the surrounding countryside – all of it peaceful and deserted. A periscope would be handy. He listens hard for her approaching footsteps.

Of course her damned dog sniffs him out straight away, his wagging tail beating the side of the car like a come-hither drum. Seems they're the best of friends all of a sudden. When he tries to push him away, the stupid animal won't fuck off.

'So now we're playing peekaboo are we?' Her voice grows louder and angrier. 'This is tedious. I'm not in the mood for your stupid games. Before I count to five, you'd better show yourself or I'll start firing.

One.

Two.'

Since the dog won't leave him alone, maybe he can use him as a shield – assuming Cinders is fond enough of her pet not to risk shooting him.

'Three.'

They're about to find out. Before she makes it four, he shouts, 'I'm down here. My leg just gave out on me.'

Leading with the Glock, she strides around to his side of the vehicle then looms over him and her slobbery dog. 'Seems you've made a conquest, Fall-Guy,' she says. 'I'm disappointed in this mutt. It's not like him to root for the underdog.'

Her expression mutates from less-than-amused to seriously pissed off. 'On your feet.' She jerks the gun upwards. 'I won't ask twice.'

While Flint weaves between the two of them, he uses the tyre to push himself up off the ground. Once upright, he heaves his bag up onto the roof of the car. It's now level with his chest, a little higher on her. 'Be my guest,' he says. Hands half raised, he takes a hop-step backwards.

Grabbing one of the shoulder straps, she slides the pack along the roof towards her.

He waits.

She whistles on discovering the folded stock of his rifle. 'Nice weapon,' she says. 'Impressively compact. Perfect for the assassin-about-town.' She lays it down. 'What else have you got in here?' Confronted by the buckle securing the main compartment, she's forced to unhitch it with her left hand. She opens the flap and peers inside. 'Wow – is this the AIDP10?' She pulls out the device, sits it on the roof and then turns it over. 'And not just the usual mesh and sat combo, but with AES encryption, integrated ATAK and Smart Grid capability – the whole darn shebang.' She frowns at him. 'In spite of appearances to the contrary, it seems you're a genuine hard guy. Or you used to be.'

She delves further pulling out his clothes along with a few empty wrappers and his water bottle. 'It must come with a nano unit, which I'm guessing is in here somewhere. Unless–'

He lunges, knocks the gun from her grip, drops his wrist so the knife falls down into his hand then puts the blade to her throat. She pulls at his arm with both hands trying to work her way free, but he presses the knife in just enough for her to feel it against her skin.

He kicks the gun further away from them both. He wasn't

raised to be the kind of man who would hold a knife to an unarmed woman's throat. Against his better nature, he says, 'In case you're in any doubt, if you leave me no choice, I will draw this blade across your neck, severing your windpipe.'

His gran will be spinning in her grave. Acting like her representative on earth, Flint begins to snarl and leap at him. 'Call your dog off now before I hurt him,' he demands.

To allow her to speak, he eases the pressure just enough. 'Down Flint,' she croaks. Ears back, the dog drops to his haunches, but keeps those soulful, betrayed eyes glued to him.

Meanwhile Cinders is leaning into his chest, probably calculating that the additional backward force will be enough to overbalance him. He pushes her forward. 'We're both old hands at this game,' he says. 'Right now you must be picturing how this is going to play out. I think we can agree there are several possible outcomes. The first – my personal preference – involves you and me making our way calmly back to the house where, to save me the trouble of hotwiring it, you hand me the keys to this car, and I drive away leaving you and your dog to live happily ever after.'

Though her breathing's a little steadier, her pulse is still racing. 'Or,' he says, 'there's version two – the one where you try to take advantage of my sub-optimum physical condition, but, in our ensuing struggle, I'm forced to slit your throat before I drive away leaving you to bleed out right here on this gravel.'

Though she's got to be as mad as a snake, the blade's too close for her to risk commenting. Meanwhile the damned dog is getting under their feet, growling low like he's trying to intimidate a couple of stray sheep.

He says, 'I'm guessing right now you're conjuring up a different end to that scenario – one where you manage to get hold of this knife and, in the resulting tussle, you stab me and leave me lying in a pool of blood at your feet.'

Ignoring the dog's attempts to intervene, he shoves his knee into the back of Cinders' leg propelling her towards the house. As they stumble forward, he can feel her heart pounding, her muscles tensing like she's ready to make her move.

They come to a halt. He tightens his grip on her arm while holding the knife steady. 'Before you decide to try something rash,' he says, 'in fairness I should warn you of the fatal flaw in that last scenario. Truth is, I was faking weakness earlier on. At the risk of sounding sexist, even on a bad day I'm physically a lot stronger than you and likely to come off best in any fight between us.'

He lets that sink in before adding, 'This is make-your-mind-up time, Cinderella. *You* need to decide which way this will go down.'

Chapter Forty-One

Ash

They're at anchor off Papar Beag island. Tired of carrying it, earlier he'd stashed the Glock in a hidden cubby just under the dash panel. He feels lighter without it.

The cliffs encircling most of its main bay are sheltering them from the worst of the storm. The bilge pumps have helped to dry out the deck and he's unrolled the flapping tarp, securing it like a sail between the aft lockers so the three of them can huddle underneath it while they wait out the weather.

Rocked less violently now, Isla is snuggled up between them with her head against Catriona's chest. He moves a little closer, awkwardly curling his body so that some of his heat might transfer to the child. Isla's exhausted. Her latest intervention must have drained her of energy. Above them seabirds are squawking as they ride the rollercoaster of the squall.

After Isla shuts her eyes, it's not long before quiet regular breathing confirms she's asleep. Catriona's absentmindedly stroking the girl's fair hair, like you might a cat.

Ash clears his throat. Now seems as good a time as any to

broach the subject. Better to begin with the truth. 'I'm worried about her future,' he says, keeping his voice low. 'Honestly, it's not like I can offer her any kind of life. The plain truth is, she'd be a lot better off without me.'

'You're not serious?' Reid adjusts her position, sitting up straighter while trying not to disturb the girl. 'How can you think, never mind say, such a thing? You're her dad – her only surviving parent.'

He gazes at a guano covered sea stack. 'I haven't been entirely truthful about that,' he admits. 'Biologically speaking, I'm not Isla's father.' Saying the words out loud, no matter how quietly, feels like a betrayal. 'There's no genetic link between the two of us,' he adds to clarify the matter beyond any doubt. 'And believe me we're different in just about every way you can think of.'

Reid's sigh is heavy with disappointment. 'Okay, so she's your stepdaughter – so what? When it comes down to it, those distinctions don't really matter. The traditional nuclear family is almost a thing of the past.' While making her point she waves her free hand like she's conducting the gale whistling around them. 'These days, everywhere you look countless displaced kids are being raised by people not biologically related to them. In the end, all children need is someone who's doing their best to take care of them.'

'That's precisely the point I'm trying to make.' He takes a breath before admitting, 'Let's be honest – does she look to you like a kid who's been well cared for?' Surely that bony frame speaks for itself. 'You must have noticed how skinny she is. Not to mention the rag bag of inadequate clothes she's wearing. That jacket of yours is the only thing keeping her warm right now.'

Tinged green by the tarp, Reid's face is a study in disapproval. 'Then do a better job in future,' she tells him. 'For better or worse, you're her primary carer and that little girl loves and depends on you.'

For a trained police officer she's more impressionable than he would have expected. Then again, people see what they want to see. 'Our situation only came about by default.' It's hard to keep his voice down. 'Neither of us got to choose.'

Leaning closer, she says, 'This poor child doesn't speak because her mother abandoned her...' She shelters Isla's exposed ear with her palm before she adds, 'I'm sure she must have had her reasons, but from Isla's point of view her mum chose to desert her when she committed suicide.'

Reid shakes her head as if she'd been the one up to her chest in freezing water pleading with that damned woman not to surrender to the sea. Trembling more from righteous indignation than the cold, Reid says, 'This child desperately needs some continuity in her life and, like it or not, she deserves and expects that from *you.*'

He sets his jaw. 'Your argument would hold sway if I was any kind of... of dependable individual but, as you must have realised by now, I'm not. Look at the dangerous situation I'd dragged the girl into when we met.' He flings up his hands. 'Face it, I'm a self-centred, immoral fuck-up and always have been. She deserves better.'

Reid pops her head out of the side of the tarp and then back again. 'As far as I can tell there are no other applicants on this boat right now. You're the one that's going to have to step up and become the kind of father she deserves.'

He looks her directly in the eye. 'I'm not the person who shielded her when we were under fire. Or during that storm. You're the one cradling her head right now.'

'Are you…?' He waits while the frown lines between Reid's eyes deepen. Then, spitting the words out not exactly sotto voce, she says, 'Let me get this straight – are you asking *me*, someone Isla has only just met, to take over the responsibility for raising *your* daughter so you can cut and run like a fucking coward? Please tell me that's not what you have in mind.'

Holding a hand up in defence, he says, 'It's obvious to me you'd do a much better job of it than I ever could. Plus, like I explained, Isla's not really my daughter–'

'You know, I didn't have a very high opinion of you before, but this… This…' She pounds his arm with her balled fist, does it several more times to make sure it really hurts. 'You utter, utter bastard!'

Isla's eyes spring open and she stares up at them both. Trying not to flinch, he looks away from the indictment he sees in them. He doesn't expect her to yawn, stretch her arms and then wiggle around until she's resting her head against his chest.

Catriona's long look suggests this is all the proof required of their inseparable bond. He waits for Isla to fall back to sleep before he puts her right on that point. 'Like you just said, I'm a complete and utter shit and, as such, the last person suitable to care for any child, never mind this mind-blowingly amazing little girl.'

'You're putting words in my mouth.' With the hint of a smile, she says. 'You do have *some* redeeming features.'

He shakes his head. 'Nice of you to pretend but believe me I don't.' Then, before she can interrupt, 'The best thing I can do for Isla is to leave her in the care of someone who's a far better role model.'

'Why can't you try to be that role model?'

'Too late. Can't change my spots now. Besides, they reckon it takes a village to raise a child and from what you've told me, Pailteas is a peaceful, self-sufficient community where there'll probably be other kids running around. If it's everything you say it is, Isla will have a much better shot at growing up normal there.'

'Define normal,' Reid says. 'Tagging along with you, hopping from island to island in this boat, is normal for Isla.'

'There are better options.' He brushes a strand of hair from the child's cheek. That innocent, sleeping face might be a near perfect disguise, but to keep her safe it's better if she's someplace well off the radar. 'She needs a lot more backup than I can provide,' he says. 'Trust me, the best way to keep her out of harm's way is to put as much distance between the two of us as possible.'

Before Reid can reply, he lays a finger next to her lips. 'You need to understand this kid here is a very, very special child.' How's he supposed to explain the things he's witnessed without sounding deranged? 'She's unique. You won't believe what she...'

Better to leave that revelation for another time.

'Listen to yourself.' Reid lays a kinder hand on his arm. 'You sound just like any proud father talking about his daughter.'

Chapter Forty-Two

Guy

She's determined. Strong too. It's taking all the strength he can muster to keep the knife against her throat. Into her ear, he mutters, 'Hold still damn it! I thought we reached an understanding last night. Like you said, we could be batting for the same team.' Then, breathing through the pain while she's kicking at his injured leg, 'Stop struggling for fuck's sake and I'll make you an offer.'

He waits for her to calm down before easing off the pressure a tad. Pity he can't see her face, can't gauge her response. 'Here's what's going to happen,' he says, taking charge of the situation. 'You're going to hand over the key and I'm going to drive your car away.'

'No fucking way.' She starts clawing at his arm again. While her fingers are trying to prise the blade away, her dog's circling at a safe distance, trying to decide if he's brave enough to intervene.

'Hear me out, damn you!' If she moves a millimetre the blade will pierce her skin. 'Like I said, I'm going to take your car and drive it to the nearest town. I'll let you choose some-place within a half day's hike. If you're serious about wanting this rust heap back, I'll leave the key on the front tyre.'

For now at least, some of the fight's gone out of her. 'In your position,' he says, 'I'd opt for a minor inconvenience over getting my throat slit. But it's your choice.'

Her heartrate's slowing. A good sign. He moves the knife away from her neck just enough to let her respond. 'How do I know you'll keep your side of the bargain? The last man I trusted made off with my flight fund.' So that explains why she was ransacking the bedroom earlier.

'If I wanted to kill you, you'd already be dead.' He can smell her sweat – sweeter than his own feral stench. 'Listen, I'm grateful for the medical kit and your hospitality, such as it was, but that's as far as my goodwill goes. As for your car – no offence but why wouldn't I dump it first chance I get to swap it for an upgrade?'

Taking a risk, he lowers the blade slowly and then lets her go. She stumbles away but not very far, one hand pressed against the other to stem the blood dripping from her cut fingers. She says, 'Yeah, well, hotwiring only works on old cars that don't have immobilisers or transponder keys. Why else would I be driving around in that thing?' She stares at his knife before dropping her gaze to his injured leg. It's not difficult to guess the sequence of events she's imagining.

'Uh-uh.' He shakes his head. 'Don't even think about it.' Her attention flicks to his gun lying in the dirt a pace or two behind him. She'll have to go through him to grab it. Her quivering dog has been creeping closer and has now taken up position in front of her – an impediment she needs to factor in. Meanwhile he spins the knife in the air, catching the handle, weighing it like he's about to aim at a target. 'Face it,' he says, firming his grip, 'I've got all the angles covered.' Eyes darting back to the Glock, she's making the same calculation, reaching the same conclusions – if she's smart.

To de-escalate the situation, he says, 'By the way, you should demand a tech upgrade. With the right scanning capability, all you need to do to steal any vehicle is to pop the door lock, plug into the OBD port, clone the fob code and you're good to go.'

'That easy, huh?' Licking her fingers, she flashes that tiger smile, her front teeth stained with her own blood. 'I've got a better idea,' she says. 'I give you a lift to Lewes and we're done. No recriminations. No need for either of us to look back in anger.'

'I see what you did there.' He smirks, far from amused. 'However, that option's not on the table.' Flint is growling deep within his throat trying to give the impression he's a mean dog and not a coward. To make his point, Guy summersaults the knife again and says, 'If you force me to throw this, I won't miss.'

Driving away, his body still sparked by adrenaline, he concentrates on negotiating the many pain-inducing potholes along the track. A warm day for the time of year, he has to hand crank the windows to let some air in. Above there's unbroken blue sky, ahead an empty, open road and the gentle contours of the South Downs ranged along the horizon. There's even birdsong to complete a picture that's in stark contrast to the one he can no longer see in his rearview mirror.

'Quiet!' His reluctant passenger is whimpering, pulling at the rope he'd tied to the anchorage points intended for child seats.

He punches the steering wheel once and then several more times. If he'd snuck away at dawn as planned, the only thing on his mind right now would be how to avoid running into roadblocks. After their initial tussle over the gun and then the knife, she should have capitulated and watched him drive away. But, oh no, Cinders couldn't leave it at that, couldn't swallow her fucking pride and let him get away clean.

His mistake – make that major error – was to assume they were fighting over this wreck of a car. Taking her at her word, he'd let his guard down because he failed to recognise that, beneath her mendacious smile, she was determined to get her hands on the equipment in his rucksack. If he hadn't been distracted by the pain in his leg or underestimated her tenacity, he might have given more weight to the avaricious gleam in her eyes when she first discovered it.

He runs a hand down his face. If she hadn't lunged at him like that when he was picking up the gun. If his trained reflexes hadn't kicked in…

But they did. And it's done, no rewind possible. Perhaps the outcome was inevitable – she was never going to let that device and its capabilities slip through her bloodied fingers without putting up more of a fight.

Flint begins to bark – feebly at first but growing ever more insistent. In the confined space, all that yelping and yapping sets his ears ringing. 'Okay, I get it, buddy.' Not that he blames the poor animal. This loud protesting is easier to tolerate than his previous cowardly submission.

What was he supposed to do with the dog afterwards? His immortal soul might already be on the fast track to Hell, but he wasn't going to leave her dog there until it got so overcome by hunger it might have…

She deserved more respect than that.

Chapter Forty-Three

Ash

When he glances sideways, Catriona is staring back at him. 'You know you could both stick around here for a while,' she says. 'Who knows, you might find you like having other people about.'

He shakes his head, is about to mention the other women who believed they could reform him, but lets it slide. When he looks up there are larger patches of blue amongst the layers of stratocumulus cloud.

'At least think about it.' She glances at Isla, then back, right into his eyes. If he didn't know better, he might imagine she was flirting.

After clearing his throat, he says, 'We've made good time,' nodding towards their destination which is now visible on the horizon. They watch it grow steadily larger. Viewed from a calm, turquoise sea, with its white beach and verdant shoreline, Pailteas could be an island paradise.

Jury's still out on the reality.

Shading his eyes with his hand, he can pick out the three

distinct landmasses shown on the schematic in front of him. The outer cliffs are mottled cream from so many generations of shitting birds. He can almost smell that guano from here. The sky is full of calling guillemots, fulmars, black-headed gulls and more.

A high ridge runs like a humped backbone along the central and largest of the conjoined islands. Scanning the headland, he can see a sprinkling of hardy Hebridean sheep. As yet no buildings – not even the skeletal remains of an abandoned croft.

A flashing red light on the dash panel prompts him to make a course correction. Squinting, he spies the landmark he's been searching for – the old radio mast protruding from the highest point on the ridge.

Still no signs of current occupation. 'Are you sure this is where your mates have settled?'

'They're not exactly my mates.' She grins. 'But yes – one hundred percent.'

'Is it possible they've moved on to another island?'

'No, this is it.' She chooses not to elaborate on the reason for her certainty. Either way, they'll soon find out.

Keeping the coastline on their port side, they sail on towards the only landing spot indicated on the monitor. It's obvious that even in flat-bottomed boats, the presence of so many rocky outcrops would rule out a beach landing – or invasion.

Closer in, he's able to distinguish between several rock formations jutting out into the sea like the spread fingers of a giant hand. The depth sounder tells him they've entered shallower water while the main display confirms the appropriate speed and heading.

He throttles back ready for the final approach. Nearer to shore the air is crowded with more fulmars and gulls of many varieties – some of them the browner juveniles. Their cries reverberate as they leave their craggy perches to mill around or dive for fish. It's too early for puffins, but they'll soon be swelling the numbers here – man's loss being nature's gain.

High above all the racket and activity, a honking skein of white-fronted geese sails by. He checks on Isla. Approaching what could be her future home, she doesn't seem impressed as she scowls and then shields her ears with her hands to block out the cacophony of bird cries.

Rounding the penultimate promontory, they reach the inlet. A couple of moored boats are hitched to metal rings driven into the granite side of a natural jetty. The 16-footer appears to be a Corsair, the smaller one could be anything. Both boats have been sprayed the same pewter grey – perfect camouflage against the rocks. They're tied up alongside a narrow walkway with a sheer cliff looming over it. A few old tyres provide the only protection against smashing into the side.

Though the noise of their approach is masked by squawking gulls, he was expecting to spot a lookout or two. To slow the boat down, he throws the engine into reverse, churning up the water in the process. With rocks on both sides, it's a tricky approach. They'd never have been able to land here in that gale.

Nodding towards the cliff face, he says, 'Climbing up there every time they arrive home must keep them fit.' Reid gives him a look that could mean anything. He cuts the engine and then, using the paddle, manoeuvres them into a space immediately in front of the other two boats.

Once they're bumping up against the tyres, Reid leaps ashore to secure the mid-line to a cleat he hopes is up to the job.

Before he can retrieve his gun, she faces him from the shore. 'Leave it where it is. We can't arrive here armed.' She's serious – deadly so. 'They're really strict about that.'

'What – with everything that's going on?' Rendered speechless, he can only guffaw, then shake his head. 'Your mates… they must be fucking idiots.'

'Guess you're entitled to your opinion.' She's standing her ground. 'We leave both guns on the boat.' Looking smug, she says, 'I saw you stash yours in that cubby under the instrument panel. Mine's in one of the aft lockers.'

'Yeah, I noticed you doing that.' Sobering his face, he says, 'They'll be no use to us if we leave them here.'

'That's the general idea.' She touches his arm. 'Weapons don't solve conflicts, Ash, they only lead to them.'

'Listen to you with your bumper sticker philosophy. You didn't mind flashing that Glock around before.' He throws up his hands. 'Now all of a sudden you're a convert.'

'I'm starting as I mean to go on. New leaf and all that.' She squares her shoulders at him. 'If you're stepping ashore here, you have to play by their rules. Your choice, Ash.'

Isla is looking up at him, those aquamarine eyes of hers weighing him up, waiting to discover what sort of man he is. 'Okay, sod it. Have it your way,' he says. 'Let's hope neither of us lives to regret it.'

Reid gives him an unfathomable look. 'By the way,' she says, 'I noticed you have a stack of novels back there. Hadn't pictured you as the literary type.'

'Maybe I have hidden depths.' Before she can take the piss, he jumps ashore to fix the bow and stern lines to a couple more rings. Once they're tied fast, he steps back on board before lifting Isla up onto the slippery jetty where Catriona can grab her.

As he steps onto the jetty, Reid says, 'Hold on to your daddy's hand now sweetheart,' transferring the responsibility to him.

At the end of the jetty he's able to pick out a series of steep, uneven steps hewn into the rockface probably by the island's original inhabitants. Isla hangs onto him. She ducks down as a couple of squawking gulls skim their heads in defence of their nest sites.

They begin the climb – an awkward business with him holding Isla's waist from behind. With lots of guano streaking the steps and no sea-edge barrier, one slip would land them on the tooth-sharp rocks below. Halfway up, he stops to survey his boat from this new perspective – it would make a worryingly desirable new addition to the fleet.

Unencumbered, Catriona's made faster progress and, having reached the top, she's studying the lie of the land he can't yet see. For her sake, he hopes she approves of what the place has to offer.

When it comes to defence, Pailteas has some natural advantages, but the fact that they've got this far without being challenged suggests the community's lax about security. With the NSL spreading like a virus across the archipelago, Reid should get them to take better precautions.

Not waiting for them to catch up, she's now disappeared – apparently eager to explore her new home.

Reaching the top he's afforded a panoramic view of the island. He spots Reid striding out along a well-worn pathway leading to what must once have been a sizable settlement. It's laid out in a crescent shape to echo the curve of the beach directly below.

Looming above the village, the dilapidated mast is flanked by a couple of rusting radar dishes – relics from the days when the military peppered these islands with intelligence gathering equipment. The phallic arrangement of this particular array seems deliberate.

From his vantage point he studies the terrain, which is noticeably stony, the total acreage capable of cultivation smaller than he'd imagined. It's difficult to see how they can achieve self-sufficiency here. If they supplement their diet by fishing or eating gulls and their eggs, those activities would be hazardous for even the most agile and experienced members of the community. As he's discovered, trying to barter any surplus wider afield will increase their exposure and potentially attract unwanted attention.

Around half of the standing cottages are still open to the elements – some look beyond repair. Those cramped, single-storey dwellings must once have been thatched. Further along the crescent some of the crofts have been re-roofed with new slates or shiny, industrial cladding.

Dozens of ancient cleits are dotted about the village and

its hillsides like sheep. Constructed a long time before refrigeration, he's noticed these same stone-built storage domes on other nearby islands. He can see lots of tumbledown stone walls, some delineating each cottage's allotted garden. In one of these a couple of figures are at work hoeing or raking.

A more substantial building dominates the main "street" roughly midway along the curve of the crescent. This has to be the old kirk. People are emerging from it in twos and threes – adults and, by the look of it, several children. Mid-afternoon seems an odd time to be holding a service, so maybe they use it for other activities.

Having reached the outskirts of the village, Reid now seems to be heading for the kirk. There's no hostile reception committee advancing to cut her off.

He turns around to check he's not about to be ambushed from behind. There's no one there. He puts Isla down – after being stuck in the boat for so long, she ought to be pleased with a chance to run around. Instead, she keeps hold of his hand.

The figures gathered outside the church don't appear to have noticed Reid yet. How can they not have clocked the arrival of three strangers in their midst? Just how fucking laid back are they?

Reid didn't mention anything about the colony's leadership arrangements. Being a bunch of idealists, they might have decided to reject all forms of hegemony in favour of a more egalitarian model. If so, they'll need to be persuaded that, when push comes to skirmish, one person should call the shots. Assuming that individual knows what they're doing.

Reid passes a square house with an adjacent barn – probably built for the island's former head honcho. More alert than the humans, the horses grazing the paddock next to the barn lumber over to suss her out. Looks like the military unit posted here back in the day had continued to maintain the larger buildings after the original civilian population were evacuated to the mainland.

Bored with standing around, Isla lets go of his hand. She takes off Reid's jacket and hands it to him before she runs on unencumbered. A soft breeze is lifting her hair as she skips along the path in those little black boots. She stoops to pick dandelions and primroses then runs back to hold her tiny bouquet up for his inspection. 'Very pretty,' he tells her with a smile.

When it's sunny – especially in late spring – these tiny, isolated islands are undeniably picturesque. The reality for most of the year is one of scratching a living under dark, brooding skies; weathering ice storms and sometimes hurricane force winds, or enduring days on end when everything is shrouded by a thick blanket of fog or a sea mist that refuses to clear.

It's possible to survive such conditions, but it's gruelling and unrelenting graft; the sort that ages any woman well before her time. For him there was no other choice, but for Catriona it's different. She has other options. Mere survival isn't good enough for her. Or for Isla.

As a trained observer, Reid can't have failed to notice the evidence everywhere here that even those born and bred to this harsh way of life were ultimately forced to capitulate.

Chapter Forty-Four

Guy

As he'd expected, the Fiesta is an absolute pig to drive, and having to constantly change gear isn't helping him to forget the pain in his thigh. At the first opportunity he'll ditch this damned car for a more reliable ride – preferably an automatic with a full tank to get him to the Scottish border.

He pulls over in a deserted spot to consult the AIDP unit. It comes up with a complex route on minor roads that will nonetheless take him almost due north. He also gets an update on the target's current location. Though it's unsaid, they'll be disappointed by his lack of progress since he landed in England.

His first stop is a sprawling, dormitory village a few miles outside Lewes. According to intel, a large proportion of the population are permitted vehicle owners.

So far there's been no sign of the military but they're never going to be far away. Given the heightened unrest, they should be focusing their resources on the major roads to and from Lewes – the main admin and intelligence hub of the region.

Approaching from the south, he reaches the outskirts of the village without noticing any surveillance cameras, though the car's loud rattling draws plenty of attention from early-rising dog walkers. Not the most discrete arrival.

Trees are shedding their spring blossoms like confetti across the roads. The gardens of the more upmarket houses are protected by high evergreen hedges and hefty security gates. He passes one or two vehicles parked road-side, their dash panel alarms flashing like lighthouses warding off potential adventurers.

His first priority is to find an unobtrusive place to abandon the pile of crap he's driving. As he reaches a dense warren of Noughties identikit houses, in a final act of defiance the Fiesta backfires twice, the noise ricochetting like shots fired around the sleepy estate roads. In spite of this provocation, no one comes rushing out to investigate.

The houses become more tightly packed towards the estate's epicentre. Budget cars sit on short, open driveways. Though they've learnt to keep their heads down, he doubts the breakfasting occupants will ignore someone they spot in the act of stealing their precious car.

He turns into a cul-de-sac of cookie-cutter houses, pulls over to one side and kills the engine. His uncouth arrival amongst the locals can't have gone unnoticed. The lack of twitching curtains suggests they practice the usual see-no-evil strategy.

Over on the back seat, Flint is shivering, his head averted in submission. What's he going to do about this wretched animal?

While he's selecting the right car to steal, he'll draw less attention accompanied by a dog. That is providing Flint decides to play ball instead of growing a pair. Once it's done, he'll cut the animal loose to take his chances. Maybe some good Samaritan will take pity on the mutt, though pity, like compassion, is in short supply these days.

Hissing through the pain spike it sets off, he climbs out of the car. If he pulls up the hood of his sweatshirt on such a fine morning it will mark him out as suspicious. Deciding against it, he shoulders his backpack, takes a moment to adjust to the additional weight then opens the rear, kerb side door.

When he reaches inside, Flint shrinks back, his molten eyes full of distrust and accusations. Instead of attacking him like he should, the animal starts to whimper. 'Not going to hurt you,' he mutters grasping the first knot. 'I'm just going to untie these ropes, okay?'

Flint lets him do it. Leaving only the regular leash on him, he says, 'Right then buddy, out you come,' and tugs on it. In an unexpected show of defiance, or possibly abject fear, Flint refuses to budge.

Not wanting to be seen dragging the dog out of the car, he opens his hands and tells him, 'You and me are just going to go for a bit of a walk, buddy. Believe me, it will hurt me more than it hurts you.' Attempting to sound upbeat, he tries, 'Walkies!' with an upward inflexion, though it's not a word Cinders is ever likely to have uttered.

She spoke a number of languages – notably Korean when seriously pissed off. From his scant knowledge of the language, he recalls a phrase. 'Ga-ja!' He repeats it.

Nothing doing.

Aping his neighbour in France, he taps his uninjured thigh and calls, 'Ici Flint! Viens!'

Besides trembling, the dog doesn't move.

Like Charles the fifth, that one-time Holy Roman Emperor, Cinders might have reserved the German language for talking to animals. 'Komm!' he commands. 'Los!'

Still no action.

Meaning business now, he snaps his fingers. 'Out!'

The dog leaps out of the car almost knocking him over. No point locking the Fiesta. In fact, he leaves the key in the ignition hoping someone will drive it away to confuse anyone who might try to track his movements.

Flint sets off at a pace, pulling him along. The dog certainly seems eager to get somewhere. He hauls the animal back to heel then regrets it when, delighted by his relative freedom, his tail wags so hard it keeps whacking his injured leg. He swaps the dog over to his other side.

Nose down, the mutt is straining to follow a scent. Hard to know whether he's on the trail of another dog, or some other creature. What if he's leading him towards someplace Cinders used to frequent? However unlikely, there's no point in risking an encounter with some of the woman's previous associates.

Flint is pulling again. Reasserting his mastery, he clicks his fingers then slaps his side. 'Heel!' It works. With the dog held in check, he tries not to hobble as he crosses the road and heads off in the opposite direction.

After a couple of turns he finds himself in an avenue of ancient trees leading to a church. As a target for thieves and vandals, in all likelihood the building will be bristling with cameras. On the plus side, where there's a place of worship there's usually a car park and the possibility of a few unattended cars. Before reaching the church, he takes the risk of pulling up his hood.

A number of cars are parked near the lychgate. Two have more than a smattering of bird shit on their roofs suggesting they've been parked up for a while.

He leads Flint into the adjacent graveyard where he can keep watch and where the dog promptly cocks a leg and lets loose a stream of piss against the headstone of *Major William (Bill) Leeson 1885 -1917* – a provocative act no doubt caught on camera. 'Sorry about that, Bill,' he mutters. He expects someone to rush out protesting about this blatant disrespect, but no one does.

After keeping watch for a further five minutes, he unclips the dog's lead. 'Off you trot, mate.' Flinging his arms wide, he tries to shoo him away. 'Go on – bugger off.' Flint retreats a few metres then turns around as if curious to find out what he's up to.

Ignoring the daft animal, he makes his move. In less than a minute he's popped the lock on a Ford Puma and plugged the nano into its OBD port. When the instrument panel lights up, the fuel gauge indicates it's almost empty. Bollocks!

Keeping his head well down, he abandons the Puma and hurries over to a Mark 8 Golf. Flint is following some distance behind. Once he's sprung the lock on the driver's door, he goes through the same procedure. This time the tank's almost full. With around 45 litres, and driving on slow country roads, the range will be around 450 miles.

He takes off his backpack and stows it on the back seat glad to be free of all that weight. As soon as the engine starts, the dog jumps up at the passenger side door, paws resting on the window ledge. He scratches at the paintwork, begins to bark and then howl. To shut him up, he leans over and opens the door.

The mutt jumps inside. 'Talk about fucking Stockholm syndrome.' He pulls away, spitting gravel.

Now he's riding shotgun, Flint seems to have a smile on his face. 'Don't get too comfortable, buddy,' he tells him. 'I'm ditching you as soon as I'm well clear of this place.'

He heads back through the maze of estate roads. After checking in the rearview mirror for any repercussions, he lets his window down and leans an elbow out to suggest he's got every right to be driving this car. Before their priorities underwent a seismic shift, the police used to track stolen vehicles and intercept them. Luckily for him, no one bothers to report car theft these days.

To the dog, he mutters, 'Bad mistake back there, buddy. You stood a much better chance amongst those God-botherers.' The animal keeps on staring straight ahead. 'Serves you right if you end up on your lonesome,' he tells him.

Once he's left the village behind, he pumps a fist in the rushing air. 'We're back in business,' he shouts at passing hedgerows. Though the GTI's eager to perform, he'll stick to speed limits on the off chance the civilian police have developed a sudden interest in enforcing traffic violations. No point in drawing unnecessary attention.

Allowing a margin for error, he should aim to swap rides

in about 400 miles. On small roads, and at current speeds, it's likely to take around ten hours to reach a suitable location north of Carlisle. He'll dump the Golf and then, assuming he has no trouble picking up another car with a full tank, he should get to Skye by tomorrow night. They've assured him a boat will be moored up in a small inlet on the island's north-west coast.

He grins. The rest should be plain sailing.

Chapter Forty-Five

Ash

A tall figure peels off from the group of people outside the church and strides towards Reid with arms outstretched. She waves at them – a big overhead gesture. Like a scene from a movie, the two of them rush to meet halfway. Their embrace goes on for a while, suggesting a far closer relationship than Reid had previously let on.

When they break apart, her "friend" finally removes his baseball cap. Black hair, deeply tanned face, dark beard – even from a distance he's an impressive looking individual. The nearer Ash gets, the more good looking the bloke becomes. Why had she downplayed this relationship? He's suspicious and, damn it, more than a little jealous.

With one arm proprietorially encircling Reid's waist, Handsome-bastard leads her towards the rest of his group. Gesticulating with his free hand, he introduces her to the group of islanders standing there. Hands are offered and shaken. One person steps forward to embrace her. He guesses it's a woman since she's wearing a long skirt and tightly wrapped shawl as if cosplaying one of the island's former inhabitants.

He picks out a towering, grey-haired guy with a straggly, pioneer-style beard. This man greets Reid with a curt nod. He could be auditioning for the role of the serpent in this would-be Eden.

Next the whole group turn around to stare at Isla and then, raising their collective gaze, give him the onceover. He's too far away to hear the ensuing conversation. The fact that it's animated suggests they might resent Reid bringing two strangers into their midst.

Holding out her flowers, Isla runs towards Reid who snatches her up, swings her around and then balances her on a hip as any mother might.

Reid's jacket still carries the smell of her. He stuffs it under his arm, takes his time getting down there, his hands hanging loose to suggest he's no threat. He's reached the path running between neat rows of vegetables. It's easy to recognise leeks and various sorts of cabbages. Close enough now, he hears Reid announce, 'This wee one is Isla. My niece. She's had a really tough time of it recently so, for now, she's chosen not to speak.'

Head on one side, one of the women – a petite redhead wearing a navy fleece and jeans, says, 'Och, the poor wee thing.' Isla shrinks back from the woman's outstretched hand. Three serious-faced kids are giving Isla the onceover.

'Best not to crowd the lassie,' Handsome-bastard tells the group.

As Ash gets nearer they all turn to openly stare at him like he's some alien arrived from outer space. Reid makes the introductions. 'Everybody this is Ash. He's a relation of mine – well, sort of. Not sure the brother of my brother-in-law counts as kin.' She follows this nonsense with a giggle. 'It's a wee bit complicated… a long story.' Several members of the group are nodding like they're buying this confection. Reid touches his arm. 'Thanks to Ash we all made it over here safely.'

Handsome-bastard claps him on the back. 'And for that we're really grateful.' He offers his hand – firm grip, soon dropped. 'Welcome to Pailteas. I'm Gilchrist. I suppose you'd describe me as the Jack-of-all-trades around here.' His accent suggests that, like Reid, he grew up in the Edinburgh region. 'I expect Cat's told you all about me.'

'Countless times,' he tells him, shooting her a faux smile. Close up, Gilchrist is even better looking. Late thirties, possibly early forties; when he smiles – which he has the bad habit of doing – his perfect teeth glint in the sun.

'You can't have had an easy journey to get here,' Gilchrist says. 'I look forward to hearing all about it, in due course.'

The grey-haired guy has wormed his way to the front of the group. Older than the rest, standing with his legs splayed, arms crossed, his rolled-up sleeves showcasing his muscular forearms, he awaits his intro.

Gilchrist turns to Reid and says, 'Cat, I don't believe you've met my friend Magnus here.' They could be at some crowded social event back in the day.

Magnus doesn't even crack a grin. 'I've heard a lot about you, Catriona.'

She turns to smile at Gilchrist. 'Nothing bad, I hope.'

Keen to establish his mate's credentials, Gilchrist pats him on the back. 'Magnus and I go way back. He served in the

Medical Corp as a doctor, so as you can imagine, he's a real asset to our community here.'

After modestly rubbing at some stain on his palm, Magnus looks up, 'Which makes me the island's quack, amongst other things.' His accent has a Nordic inflexion. Could be a Scandi blown off course or maybe a Shetlander.

Holding out his hand, Ash says, 'Good to meet you, Doctor.' He gets a nod instead of a shake like this medic's worried they might have brought contagion with them.

Gilchrist covers for him. 'No one stands on ceremony around here. Formality is one of the many things we've left behind with our old lives.' He winks at Isla, then goes back to ogling Catriona. 'Now you're here at last, I hope you're planning to stick around.'

'I'm considering it,' she tells him.

His beaming smile fades a little. 'You'll find us a friendly, helpful bunch. Everyone mucks in with the tasks in hand, but we still find time for things like music and storytelling.'

'Some folk have welcomed the opportunity to reinvent themselves,' Magnus says, somewhat pointedly.

Cosplay-woman butts in with, 'Though most of us still call him Doc.'

Magnus shrugs. 'I also get addressed as Cracker or Saw-bones or sometimes just Bones. I'm happy to answer to all the above.'

'I dinnae know how we'd have managed here wi'out you, Doc,' Cosplay-woman feels the need to say.

'Anyway…' Gilchrist claps his hands. 'I expect you're all thirsty.' He gestures to the kirk's porch with its built-in stone benches. 'Take a seat while I fetch you some water.'

Mentioning various pressing chores, the rest of the group disperse with cheery calls of, 'See ye later.'

Magnus decides to stick around. Instead of sitting down, he leans against the porch wall.

Ash sits out of politeness though the chill from the cold slabs soon seeps into his arse cheeks. He lays out Reid's jacket for Isla to sit on, but she scrambles up onto his lap instead. The flowers she's gripping are already beginning to wilt. Magnus continues to peer at him from beneath impressively hairy eyebrows. 'I didnae catch your last name.'

He shrugs. 'Unlike you, I'm a little short on aliases. Everyone just calls me Ash.'

He turns away from the doctor's unblinking scrutiny to peer through the open door at the kirk's interior. It seems to be empty. No chinks of telltale sunlight coming through the roof, though he can smell the damp even from outside. Patches of green mould decorate much of the walls. It's been a while since he stepped inside a church, but naïvely he'd expected the odd flower arrangement, maybe a few embroidered kneelers. Instead, one half of the building is laid out as a workshop while the other half seems to be a schoolroom. Or a sparse library.

Sensing Magnus's eyes are still on him, he turns to meet the man's gaze. Their eye contact is broken when Gilchrist returns with a jug and some chipped enamel cups. 'From our spring,' he says, pouring the water. 'Is there anything more refreshing?'

The water passes Isla's sniff test. Ash downs his then holds out his cup for a refill. 'Almost as good as a cold beer,' he says.

Gilchrist grins. 'What wouldn't I give...' The handsome bastard sits down next to Catriona. Looking into her eyes, he says, 'I'm guessing you must be hungry, Cat.'

'I'm ravenous.' Reid follows this with a coquettish smile. Hungry for what, exactly? Her sudden decision to leave Ben Faoghla makes a lot more sense now.

Grinning like the cat that just got the mouse, Gilchrist glances at his vintage wristwatch. 'We should be eating in around forty-five minutes,' he tells her.

'We all share the same evening meal,' Magnus chips in.

'Usually it's some sort of stew,' Gilchrist says. 'Or some other concoction today's cooks have dreamt up from whatever fresh meat or fish they have, plus some of the veg we've grown. Occasionally they throw in a few wild plants or fungi if they've managed to forage some.'

'Sounds delicious,' Reid says, between gulps of water. She wipes her wet mouth with the back of her hand. 'I'm looking forward to meeting the others.'

Gilchrist takes and squeezes her hand. 'I'm so thrilled you've finally made it over here, Cat.' He gazes up at the kirk's vaulted ceiling and, by some acoustic trick his words seem to gain gravitas, 'Here we've shown that the sum of the whole really is greater than the parts.' Then, 'But of course this way of life doesn't suit everyone.'

Was that aimed at him? He waves his baseball cap in the direction of the nearby cottages. 'We've got a lot to discuss. Important decisions to contemplate. Your arrival will have created quite a stir – set the proverbial cat amongst the pigeons.'

Stroking his beard, Magnus leans forward to speak. 'Forgive my curiosity Catriona, but since your friend's accent suggests he hails from a lot further afield, I can't help wondering how the three of you happened to wash up here together.'

Before Ash can conjure up a credible lie, Reid says, 'As I tried to explain earlier, Ash is the brother of my late brother-in-law, Sam. Which means, technically, he's not a relative of mine, as such. After poor Sam died, Ash decided to bring Isla to visit me on Ben Faoghla. I should explain that the girl's mother – my older sister Sarah – passed away some time ago.' Her dramatic pause is followed by a masterful little sniff. 'Since Isla's now an orphan, Ash has been acting in loco parentis.'

Are they buying this garbage? 'I admit to being more loco than parentis,' Ash quips.

Reid's the only one who smiles at his joke. Tough crowd.

'I didn't know you had a sister. Sorry to hear she passed.' Gilchrist slaps his thigh. 'Anyway, I'm sure you're all weary after your long journey. We'll need to sort out tonight's sleeping arrangements. Meanwhile the three of you are welcome to wander around, get the lie of the land, so to speak.'

'Or maybe go back to the boat you came here on,' Magnus says, before adding, 'To fetch whatever belongings and supplies you've brought wi' you.'

Reid shakes her head. 'We were forced to leave in a hurry – which is another long story. I managed to pack a wee case, but these two left with nothing but the clothes on their backs.'

Eyebrows furled, Magnus is about to speak but Gilchrist gets in first. 'With a bit of juggling, I'm sure we'll be able to provide you all with a roof over your heads and some blankets.' He jumps up, his hand lingering on Reid's shoulder for a moment. 'See you all later.' With that he walks away.

Before joining him, Magnus wants the last word. 'On these milder evenings, we always eat together around the fire while we amuse each other wi' tall stories. I've a feeling yours will be most entertaining.'

Chapter Forty-Six

Opening his eyes, the first thing Ash is conscious of is his stiff neck. The rough blanket against his cheek still carries a slight whiff of sheep. He sits up, mouth dry, head foggy from the homebrew they'd passed around at the evening meal. Apparently made from fermented dandelions, it tasted bitter with unfortunate undernotes of urine.

Naturally, he'd drunk it all the same. Sitting around a fire, looking up at that old Milky Way had rekindled memories from when he was a young squaddie. Unlike back then, he'd struggled to absorb so many names – Logan, Esme, Malc, Fi, not to be confused with Fiona, Evander, Andy and so on. Too many to reliably pin identities to every individual. Aside from Jaden and his little daughter, Ayani, most of the others had the fair skin and red or sandy hair typical of northern Scots.

With the firelight glowing on faces young and old, and spurred on by drink, Andy – a lanky red-headed lad in his early twenties – staggered to his feet to deliver a eulogy on the joys of living close to nature. A fair number of people nodded along to these sentiments while a few remained stony-faced. Could trouble be brewing in Shangri-La?

The high point of the evening was the lamb stew. Ladled out generously, it smelt great and tasted better than anything he'd eaten in a long while. After wolfing hers down, Isla fell asleep with her head resting against his thigh. Noticing this, Fi-possibly-Fiona, had sighed and called her "your angel-child".

If that wasn't off-putting enough, his appreciation of the food was dampened by Magnus's attempt to pick holes in Reid's cover story. Addressing the wider circle, the doc wondered out loud why, with a small child in tow, anyone would be foolhardy enough to embark on the perilous journey from the mainland all the way to Ben Faoghla.

A good question.

Everyone stopped chewing to listen to his answer. 'Should have thought it through more before I set off,' he told them. Then, raising his mug of bitter wine, 'I'm the first to admit that grief must have clouded my judgement. I guess the sea gods were on our side because, against the odds, we made it there safely.' Prompted by their applause, he'd played to the crowd declaring, 'When Cat persuaded me to head over here, we took a chance our luck would hold and, halleluiah, here we are, folks!' Magnus's response was drowned out by the rest of them stomping and drinking to their continued good fortune.

For once Reid had the sense to keep schtum. Reaching a wall of exhaustion, he remembered to thank them for their hospitality before leading Isla away to their makeshift beds. While he stumbled over unfamiliar ground, with renewed energy the kid skipped rings around him.

He suspects it was Gilchrist who arranged for Reid to bed

down in another house. Chances are she didn't object. Today he'll need to pull her aside and make damn sure that, from now on, they're singing from the same hymn sheet. At some point, Magnus, if not others, will demand a full debriefing.

Stretching his arms, he looks around expecting to see some of those who woke him when they came in singing. He's alone. Isla had been lying beside him, now there's only her airbed and discarded blankets. Funny how he's grown used to her being there at his side.

A sense of unease creeps over him. Who's she gone off with?

Last night they made it clear that there's no such thing as a free meal here. They're expecting him to help with this morning's chore which is – drumroll – planting seed potatoes. That must be why the others have buggered off. Odd that they didn't wake him.

He'd slept fully clothed – jacket and all. Standing up, he rakes back his hair before pulling on his boots and lacing them up tight. Now it's daylight, he takes a closer look around. Aside from rows of neatly-rolled bedding, the cottage is a shell – four bare stone walls and a roof open to the rafters though he can see the underside of the zinc sheeting covering it. Waterproof, but with no insulation. It's chilly. The stone hearth is swept bare. Maybe, at this time of the year, they rely on their combined body heat to warm the place up. It must be a hell of a lot colder in winter.

Outside the air's noticeably warmer, the clear sky promising another fine day. He rubs at his sore neck while he walks some distance away to take a piss. Is there a washhouse somewhere?

A shower would be amazing, but maybe they swim themselves clean.

The settlement looks quaint bathed in sunshine – archive film transposed into colour. He turns towards distant voices and the activity going on further up the hill.

Heading there, he could be approaching some Old Master painting. Spread out on a quarter acre of bare soil, heads covered by hats or colourful scarves, a dozen or more bent figures are either hoeing or carrying buckets of potatoes to drop into furrows. A few half-grown kids are half-heartedly lending a hand while the rest chase each other around. Within this group of noisy youngsters he spots a child who might be Isla.

Nearer, he can see it really is her running about with the other kids. She looks different because she's clean and wearing a new blue top instead of Reid's jacket. Someone's combed her hair and worked it into two long plaits. At first he fears the other kids are trying to chase her away, then, before he intervenes, he realises they're playing tag and Isla's laughing and enjoying the game. 'Well I'll be damned,' he mutters, overcome by something close to parental pride.

'You still have a chance at redemption.'

How had Reid managed to sneak up behind him? While he's annoyed at being caught off guard, she's noticeably pleased with herself. There's a light in her eyes that's probably down to fucking Gilchrist – literally. She's tied her hair back in a blue and orange scarf secured by a bow at the front. Quite the transformation. 'Looks like you've already drunk the Kool-Aid,' he says, with an undisguised edge.

Nodding towards the workers, she rubs soil away from her

hands. 'Just doing my bit. You know, you could try taking off your jacket and rolling up your sleeves the same as the others.'

'Maybe I will.' He takes her by the arm. 'But first, me and you need to talk.'

'No need.' Rotating her arm, she frees herself. 'Everything's been sorted and settled.'

'Just like that? What sort of nonsense did you spin them this time?'

'Listen, I've had a long chat with Magnus and Gilchrist, and they're satisfied and more than happy to have us here. Oh and, by the way, being neither stupid nor naïve, they can tell you have reservations about this setup and they will totally understand if living here doesn't appeal to you.' She shrugs. 'Feel free to leave anytime you want.'

'Should I be relieved they're not preparing to stone me to death for heresy?'

Reid gives a cheery wave to Cosplay-woman. Davina – he seems to recall. Their nothing-to-see-here smiles convince the woman to carry on dropping spuds into a shallow trench.

Reid says, 'I've been considering your earlier suggestion – what you proposed to me on the boat.'

'Did I propose?' He plays at frowning. 'Seems a bit premature since we've only just–'

'Ash, I'm being serious.' Her expression confirms it. 'Like I said, I've been thinking it all over and, well, from now on, I'm prepared to take responsibility for Isla.'

Something's off here, a piece of this puzzle he's missing. 'So, just like that, you go from being outraged by the idea to yeah, okay, I'll be her new mummy?'

This time Reid is the one leading them away from eaves-droppers. At a safe distance, she turns him around to face the potato field again. Then she points to the hill beyond where Isla and a couple of other kids are leaning against one of the cleits to get their breath back. 'Look at those wee ones having fun together. This is the first time I've seen Isla behave like a normal kid.'

Choosing his words with care, he says, 'You know next to nothing about Isla. She's different. And I do mean *really* bloody different…' No, he shouldn't say more out in the open like this. 'Who's to say what's right for her future?'

'Every kid is different,' she parrots. 'Like you said before, it takes a village not just one individual to raise a child. Staying here with me in *this* village is her best option.'

He looks around at the settlement's hard-won crops, the sheep grazing the green hills above; then, past the curved row of cottages, the white sandy beach and shining water below. Sod it – there's barely a cloud in that perfect sky. He says, 'The problem with pretty pictures is they invariably turn out to be illusions. Reality is almost guaranteed to be grimmer than anything you've imagined.'

Reid's frustration is starting to show. Red in the face, she says, 'Talk in metaphors all you want, Ash, it doesn't change the fact that Isla is better off here with me than sailing away to who-the-hell-knows-bloody-where with a man who doesn't give a shit about her.'

'Sounds to me like you've managed to convince yourself with that story about being her aunty. In your *fictional* version of events, I'm merely the unrelated conduit responsible for bringing the two of you here to this – this fucking outdoor museum.'

Up close he can see tiny gold specks in her grey eyes. She says, 'You know Ash, it crosses my mind that your cynicism about this place is due to something else entirely.'

'Oh yeah, and what might that be?'

'Jealousy – plain and simple.'

He comes back with, 'Of what, exactly?', turning away before she can answer.

'Of other people's happiness.' Being Reid, she can't leave it there. 'You must hate seeing Isla so happy.'

'That's bollocks.'

'Then why won't you accept that she's much better off here with or…?' She waits a beat. 'Without you.' Reid takes a step back, obviously hoping her words will finish the job for her.

A suspicion creeps up the back of his neck that he's been blindsided. 'I see,' he says, studying his feet. 'Guess you've opened my eyes.'

He peels off his jacket and lays it down on the grass. 'Let me give you a hand,' he calls out to no one in particular.

Hoeing stony soil is harder than it looks. Finishing the final row, he hears screams, looks up to watch the kids all rolling sideways down the hill and landing in a confused heap of arms and legs at the bottom.

Seeing him, Isla waves. She stops playing to run over, Ayani and her other playmates following like ducklings in a row. He sees flashes of yellow about her ankles – a new pair of socks showing above her boots. Where the other kids hold back, she rushes up to grab his legs. Scrubbed clean, she holds up the plaits someone – most likely Reid – has teased her flaxen hair into. 'Very cute,' he tells her.

She spins around to show him the parting at the back. There's a tiny, star-shaped scar at the base of her skull – a mark he's never noticed before.

Chapter Forty-Seven

North western peninsula, Isle of Skye.

Guy

Due to the mountains and narrow, twisting roads, it's taken Guy a frustrating amount of time to reach the southern end of the peninsular. A fine day – perfect for a sea crossing if he ever manages to get to the bloody boat.

The sickly smell of yellow gorse steals in through the open windows. If this was later in the year, he'd have everything shut to stop the midges eating him alive. In a few weeks those little bastards will begin to emerge looking for blood.

Alongside him in the passenger seat, Flint is upright and alert, his shaggy fur ruffled by the wind. His ears always seem to be pricked in anticipation of danger. He pats the dog's head. 'Chillax mate, we're not at Defcon One. At least, not yet.'

He should have ditched the damned mutt back in England. Or, failing that, as soon as he reached the Scottish border and switched rides to this Nissan pickup. Except, he'd convinced himself that he'd blend better with the locals accompanied by an animal that might be mistaken for a sheepdog. Truth is, having a four-legged companion reminds him of simpler times. Must be getting sentimental or something, to be looking back on his childhood at a time like this. He shakes his head. 'Get a grip.'

Though he's left the formidable obstacle of the Cuillin range behind, there's still a long drive ahead across seemingly endless stretches of moorland bordered by steep, craggy slopes. Houses here are few and very far between. From a distance, it's hard to tell which ones might be occupied since they're likely to park any vehicles well out of sight. Someone must be responsible for all the grazing sheep and roving herds of big-horned Highland cattle, but he hasn't passed another vehicle since a long way back.

He drums his fingers on the wheel. This is the arse end of nowhere; if it wasn't for the prospect of 500k in crypto, he'd turn around right now. On both sides there's nothing but the kind of soaring scenery that ought to be confined to paintings. Here and there he spots the derelict walls of former crofts – relics from another troubled time now returning from whence they came.

A fingerpost points him towards an actual village. With no alternative route, it's unavoidable. The reality turns out to be a collection of whitewashed cottages, each protected by high fences and barking dogs. Chances are the inhabitants are watching him right now through their rifle sights. With a coward's instinct, Flint has dropped low onto his front paws.

He keeps a steady pressure on the accelerator – pulling up in an unfamiliar vehicle in a remote place like this would be tantamount to suicide. He passes the former village shop now boarded up, its blank windows showcasing multicoloured messages all urging him to FUCK OFF. Opposite the shop, a larger, derelict building sports the faded signage of "The Crofting Museum". He picks up speed.

A few miles down the road his device pings. Guy checks through 360 degrees before pulling over. To help him locate the tiny inlet, they've sent supplementary directions mentioning a derelict lighthouse on an adjacent headland and a valley containing the remains of an ancient village. Overkill – they must be getting anxious about his odds of success. He likes to think he's their go-to for a mission like this, but it's possible they'd activated other operatives for the job and he's now the last man standing. If communications weren't strictly one-way, he might try to renegotiate his fee.

An hour or so away from his destination, he decides it's safe to stop for a piss and some hydration. No new patches of blood on his jeans. Putting weight on his injured leg hurts a lot less than it did. Both are encouraging signs that the wound isn't infected. Another bullet dodged.

Flint bounds out of the truck; he throws him leftovers from last night's rabbit. The mutt hoovers this up. Satisfied he's searched out every last scrap, the dog wanders off to cock his leg against a fence post.

Before they set off again, he checks the AIDP unit with its pulsating marker. Some analyst with too much time on their hands has included a historical footnote. He shakes his head in disbelief. Those dudes should leave their bunkers more often. How does it help his mission to know that the ruined village he'll pass through was "cleared" in the 1830s? Seems that, once they'd torched all the cottages, the families were forcibly transported to Nova Scotia. New Scotland – my arse. The landowner thoughtfully exempted those over 70, sending them off to the workhouse instead. He mutters one of Arnaud's favourite sayings, 'Plus ça change, plus c'est la même chose.'

The more things change, the more they stay the same.

The old man wasn't wrong about that.

Flint has found himself a puddle to lap from. Guy walks some distance away, shuts his eyes and listens for micro-drones, helicopters, any nearby flying objects. Not a thing. He can't hear or see any vehicles approaching, not even a tractor. The countryside is still and soporific, silent except for some far-off bleating and bees bumbling about their business. Hearing a mournful call, he looks up to where a couple of white-tailed eagles are circling high on thermals.

Back at the pickup, he gulps down some water, then whistles to Flint. 'Time to go, buddy.' The dog doesn't need telling twice.

Soon the road surface deteriorates to the point where calling it a road is a joke. He turns off onto the track he's been looking out for. Much of its surface tarmac has been washed away by floodwater leaving deep channels and craters to negotiate The pickup grounds and graunches its way along. He tries not to flinch at the damage being done to its suspension. Just as well he's not planning to keep it.

Cresting the brow of the next hill, the tip of the lighthouse comes into view. The track down to the abandoned village is precipitous, eroded here and there but just wide enough to traverse.

By taking it easy and slow, the truck makes it down to the valley floor. They've entered the narrow cleft between the valley's steep sides – the butthole. Once he's through this, he gets his first glimpse of the beach and beyond that breaking waves and the sea. Above him the grimy lighthouse sits on a rocky promontory. He hopes it's only the angle that's hiding the promised boat from view.

Before the pickup gives up the struggle, he runs out of road – the end coming sooner than expected. He pulls on the handbrake. Unable to abandon the vehicle by the side of the track, he's forced to leave it where it's come to rest – a full stop at the end of the line.

Overhead, dozens of seagulls are screaming and wheeling. Grabbing his rucksack from the back seat, he jumps down before a stab of pain reminds him about his wound. He walks around to open the passenger door like some dogsbody chauffeur.

Flint leaps down wagging his tail in anticipation. The dog runs ahead, stopping periodically to sniff the ground. Even the most hard-hearted bastard wouldn't leave the mutt to fend for himself this far off the beaten track. Catching up, he ruffles the fur on the dog's head. 'Believe me, you wouldn't last five minutes, buddy.'

The onshore breeze is tousling his own hair as they follow a narrow sheep track that winds down towards the shoreline. On the way they pass through what's left of a dozen or so stone cottages. He can't help but imagine those long ago crofters being driven out of the only homes they'd known and eventually herded aboard a stinking, overcrowded ship heading for a strange place on the other side of the world. An information board still stands. It's now illegible – history erased by the elements.

He's startled when a sheep wanders out from behind a stone wall followed by a couple of lambs. Confronting Flint, she thumps the ground ready to defend her offspring from the big bad wolf.

The dog comes to cower behind him. 'Jeez!' He stops dead. 'It's just a sheep, Flint. How are you such a bloody wimp?' The daft mutt looks at the ground, tail wedged between his back legs like he's fully aware of his character flaw.

This is ideal ambush territory, and he's let his guard down. If anyone was going to, they would have shot him by now.

He pulls the AIDP from his rucksack. On the screen a pulsating marker confirms he's closing in on the boat's location. Some way off the coast, opposing forces are shown as steadily moving clusters of red or blue dots, depending on their allegiances. A broken orange line indicates the course he'll need to follow to avoid running into trouble. This line continues on through the rest of the archipelago, giving the larger islands a wide berth. His journey's end is not much more than a speck in the ocean near the edge of the map – there-be-dragons territory. It's an island that was designated as uninhabited after the military listening post there was abandoned. The latest sat. images confirm it now has a population of approximately twenty to twenty-five individuals. No intel about who the fuck these people are. And, as yet, no info on the identity of his target.

He scratches his beard. His immediate course of action couldn't be clearer. With intel assistance, and assuming the element of surprise, the task he's facing doesn't appear to be overly challenging. Which begs the question – if this op is as straightforward as it seems, why are they paying him the big bucks?

Chapter Forty-Eight

He'd hoped for something sleeker and faster than the vessel awaiting him. They haven't exactly pushed the boat out with this one. From the outside it looks like a regular, rather elderly fishing boat. Maybe looks deceive.

The short jetty she's floating alongside is made up of large boulders those long-ago crofters must have had to manhandle into position. The boat's tied up to an iron bar which, Excalibur like, is embedded in a massive stone.

Abandoning his customary caution, Flint runs ahead and leaps onto the deck.

Before stepping on board, Guy runs his eye around the exterior of the boat. Approximately six and a half metres long, her fiberglass hull has picked up a few minor scuffs here and there. She seems solid enough to undertake what's likely to be a long journey in notoriously fickle seas.

Forgetting about his injury, he jumps down onto the deck. The resulting pain is minor, tolerable in fact. While the boat sways and creaks under his weight, he begins by checking the navigational equipment inside the open wheelhouse. The basic instruments are there, but there's no autopilot and no

ARPA. On the plus side the auto I.D. system has already been disabled. If he's boarded by hostile forces, he'll need to concoct a story to explain that. Under those circumstances, the absence of advanced tech would make them less suspicious, provided he's had time to dump his portable devices overboard.

The fuel gauge indicates the tank is full. To be certain, he removes the cap and rocks her from side to side until he hears and has visual confirmation. After he's screwed the cap back on, the stench of diesel lingers. When he checks the oil with the dipstick, it's at the right level. Somebody's been thorough.

Opening the first of the aft lockers, he finds a wet suit and flippers. Below these there's a heavy coil of rope, a retractable grappling hook, a bunch of pitons and a compact hammer. Guess who's going rock climbing again?

In the next, he finds they've supplied him with two, twenty-five litre cans of diesel as insurance.

He springs the catch on last locker. It contains a small buoyancy raft and a waterproof sack big enough to carry a few essential items. Tucked in alongside are cans of drink and a bumper pack of energy bars.

Meanwhile the dog's been enthusiastically sniffing around the deck most likely smelling traces of fish. Once he's completed his next round, the mutt curls up beside one of the lockers – naturally, it's the one with the food in it. Satisfied with his new position, Flint gives an exhausted sigh and shuts his eyes.

'Don't go making yourself at home,' Guy tells him. A serious point. What kind of sniper brings a tag-along dog to work? The mutt's a liability – one he needs to rid himself of, and pronto. If he puts Flint ashore here, most likely he'll be shot on sight by whoever tends the flock of sheep they just walked through. Even if those sheep are running feral, the daft mutt's likely to starve to death. Better to wait until they're out at sea, shoot the dog in the head while he's sleeping and dump his body overboard.

As he's picturing this scenario, Flint opens one eye and gives him a look that runs straight through him. 'Cruel to be kind,' he mutters to himself while unhitching the boat.

When he turns the ignition key everything lights up. A good start. He flicks the glow plug switch down, waits twenty seconds, then holding his breath, pushes the starter. The engine comes spluttering to life. Once he's flicked off the glow plug, he puts her in gear and opens the throttle. The exhaust fumes are beginning to run clear as he steers her away from the jetty.

They head out into deeper water. A gentle swell begins to rock the boat like it's a cradle. He keeps a close eye on the shore in case the engine's noise has flushed out potential opposition.

Once they're well away from the shore, he relaxes a little. Behind him the coastline of the peninsula is beginning to recede. Buoyed by this easy getaway, he reminds himself about the dangers of complacency, the need to stay alert. It may be as well there's no autopilot.

An hour in, he checks the AIDP for the latest intel update. This leg of his journey ought to be plain sailing.

Meanwhile, Flint has grumbled himself awake. Slipping and sliding, he comes into the wheelhouse, sidles up and settles down against his leg. Fortunately, it's the dog's warmth and not fresh blood seeping through his torn jeans. That dinosaur bandage could probably go now. He tries not to picture Cinders, how he'd left her lying lifeless in the dirt.

'Sod it!'

He consults the AIDP, zooms in on that "recommended" broken orange line. It's not the fastest sea route to his destination. Though he's supposed to keep well away, he studies the coastline of the nearest of the larger islands. Sources confirm that, due to the formidable obstacle of its mountain range, the southern tip is currently "non-militarised". Looks like there's a fishing village. Nearest maritime forces are a long way away and heading in the opposite direction. At most, this will be a minor diversion adding little to his voyage time. If he sails into port, drops the dog off, then hops back on board, he can be away before anyone really notices – in theory at least. As risks go, it's a minor one compared with what this op has thrown up so far.

Flint stares up at him. 'Stay of execution, buddy,' he tells him. 'Keep practicing that doe-eyed look and maybe some other sucker will succumb to your charms.' Guy reaches down to stroke one of the dog's velvet ears. 'I'm giving you a sporting chance, buddy,' he tells him, owing him that much.

Operation Offload Flint had gone without a hitch. Now, much later in the day, his destination is looming less than eighty metres away. He drops anchor then looks up at the rockface he'll need to climb. A formidable sight.

He shoves all the essentials into the waterproof sack and

straps it to the float. While stripping off, he casts aside the dinosaur bandage to check his wound. The stitches are holding well. There's not much swelling or redness around it. With luck, it shouldn't be much of an impediment. He pulls on the wetsuit taking extra care when easing it up his thighs.

The temperature steals his breath as soon as he lowers himself into the water. Though the flippers help a lot, it's a freezing, arduous swim. He comes ashore dripping seawater, takes off his flippers and then, balancing on the slippery rocks, begins to unpack the raft.

The light is already waning. Shivering, he unpeels his wet suit and checks the wound hasn't sprung open again. It's no worse than it was in spite of his exertions. He dries himself as best he can before dressing. Finally, he pulls on his now mismatched socks and laces his boots up tight.

Choosing a rocky shelf that's well above the highwater mark, he stows the raft along with everything he doesn't immediately need, then weighs it all down with some cobbles.

The sheer face of the cliff towers above him. Climbing it carrying an injury as well as a pack with a rifle strapped to it and wearing less than ideal footwear, will be no easy matter. He shuts his eyes to summon up the blood. 'You can do this,' he says.

Scaling the hard, igneous rockface proves as gruelling as he'd anticipated. Once he's finally made it over the top, he throws his pack and rifle down and flops onto the grass. Not the actions of a pro, but he's past caring.

It takes him some time to recover, longer to roll over and reach for his rifle. It's now dark enough to use infrared mode. He hauls himself onto his elbows and checks out his surroundings.

The settlement down below lies mostly in darkness. Light, though not much heat, is spilling out from several of the old houses. Further up the hill towards him, a glowing figure is lying out on what looks to be a bench. Not moving much, so they're almost certainly asleep.

He scans the terrain to his right and then his left but sees no other guards. There are none along the surrounding ridges and all the rooftops down below are clear. 'Big mistake folks,' he mutters. Given the remoteness of their island, they must assume that one useless guard is all that's needed. The only other objects emitting a heat signature on the hillside are the sheep and a couple of scurrying rodents.

He's already wrapped the hammer head in the dinosaur cloth to deaden the sound. Extracting a piton from his pack, he sets about driving it into the rockface, wincing with the noise of each blow. When he checks that so-called guard they haven't moved. All's still quiet down there. Once he's secured the rope to the piton, he leaves it there ready for a quick exit.

Crouching low, he runs along the ridge to the base of the old radar dish – the perfect vantage point. His heart begins to race when a glowing figure emerges from one of the cottages down below. It would be impossible to identify them even if he knew who he was looking for. The newcomer walks up the path and shakes the guard awake. New-guy waves his hands around – rightly giving that useless guard a hard time.

The accurate range of his rifle is around 1500 metres. To be sure of the shot, he'll need to get closer. He grins. Unless the target conveniently decides to head his way.

Having made his point, New-bloke wanders back down the hill and disappears inside. Old-guard trudges back and forth for a bit then gives up and assumes his previous resting position.

Switching from infrared, he can just make out a number of small, stone-built domes scattered around the landscape – squatter versions of the Provencal bories he's so often used as cover when stalking wolves or deer. None of the domes have doors. One of them seems to be the ideal distance above the village, its entrance perfectly angled. Back on infrared he checks it, and then the other domes, to be certain they're all empty.

That guard down there is unlikely to prove a problem. All the same, he plans to wait until it's fully dark before he relocates to his chosen position. After that, it'll be a matter of watching and waiting.

He yawns. It's been quite a day. With nothing much going on, he has time for a nap. Though it's hard to get comfortable on stony ground with an injured leg, exhaustion is likely to do the trick.

Thinking about the mutt, he wonders if Flint's soulful eyes will work their magic on some other sucker. Funny how you can miss a dumb animal's company.

Tomorrow will decide a lot of things. His employers are being ultra cautious with the intelligence they're sending through. He's been promised more on the target's I.D. once the final order to terminate is confirmed. They've issued standing instructions to avoid collateral damage "if possible" – a caveat that allows for some flexibility.

Chapter Forty-Nine

Ash

He wakes early, before the others this time. Serenaded by someone's regular snoring, he rolls over onto his back and stares up at the rafters spot-lit by the sun streaming through the windows set high in both gable ends. This far north, such fair weather never lasts long.

Biding his time, so far he's going with the communal flow and ignoring the negative vibes he's been getting from Magnus and a handful of others.

Turning onto his side, he studies Isla's face as she sleeps – the fresh crop of freckles across her nose, how peaceful she looks when those pale, ever-vigilant eyes are closed. Wrapped in her woolly cocoon, she could be any normal child of her age. He's the only one here with an inkling of what she's capable of.

Yesterday, after the potato planting, it was no rest for the wicked. They roped him in to the task of rebuilding the stonework on one of the roofless cottages. Living alone on his small island, he'd survived well enough without the need for this much hard graft.

Maisie, the middle-aged woman he was working with, told him that, once they've rebuilt more of the old cottages, they will begin allocating them to families or groups of friends. With no decent sized trees on the island, it's difficult to see how they're going to acquire all the timber they'll need for the new roofs.

According to Maisie, the cement in the mortar came all the way from Barra – bartered for, amongst other things, some hand-knitted jumpers. He's noticed these itchy-looking garments on some of the islanders. Maybe those Barraighis felt the need to atone for their sins by wearing the equivalent of hairshirts.

So far he hasn't seen Gilchrist or Magnus labouring alongside the others. For all the rhetoric about this being a community of equals, he has a sneaking suspicion they're beginning to replicate the hierarchy they've supposedly left behind.

All of which is none of his concern. To hell with prevaricating – time he decided on his next move.

He rolls onto his back. Looking up at the beams and their pegged joints, he tries to decide whether to leave, or not to leave. *That* is the burning question du jour. Thinking about his future from here on, it's difficult to put aside his concerns about Isla. Yesterday, in a surprise volte-face, Reid made a solid case for the girl remaining here. Maybe she sees herself and Gilchrist playing mummy and daddy to the kid. That still leaves plenty of what-ifs to fret about.

He's startled when the outside door is flung open. 'Okay lads and lassies, time to shake a leg.' The rouser-in-chief is Evander – never shortened to Evan. Does he insist on that? If yesterday's anything to go by, he's the working-party foreman. Hard to know whether his job is to implement the collective will of the people or pass on instructions from above. He suspects it's the latter.

Resisting the urge to salute, Ash gets to his feet. Every muscle in his body is complaining about the previous day's exertions.

The general commotion wakes Isla. Opening her eyes, she smiles up at him. Her plaits have come adrift in the night hiding that little scar of hers. Instinct tells him that can only be a good thing. He turns away, cursing himself for becoming too involved.

Still blocking the light, Evander hasn't finished with the motivational bollocks. 'Let's make the most of this weather,' he says, rubbing his massive hands together. 'We'll make a start by sorting through that pile of salvaged timber. Bill will have the final say on which beams are okay to re-use. After the breakfast break, some of you will be cutting and jointing roof trusses. The rest will be raising them. Have a productive day everyone.' With that final flourish, he buggers off.

Obediently, the others are rolling up their bedding or pulling on extra layers. 'Go!' he tells Isla. 'Have some fun while you can.' She looks blank. 'Off you go.' He shoos her away. Giggling, she runs out of the door leaving her bedding in a tangled mess. 'Good for you,' he says, under his breath.

The cottage getting a new roof is at the other end of the crescent from the one they were working on yesterday. Which seems a bit random. Though it's also single storey, it's wider than the others. Timber strips have already been fixed along the top of its stone walls ready to carry the roof.

Whether they're drawn to activity or simply curious, a gaggle of children is never far away from where they're working. From time to time he catches a glimpse of Isla playing hide and seek around the tumbledown garden walls.

Much of the piled up wood that's been collected is good only for fires. They'll be lucky if they can salvage enough for this one cottage.

He's assigned to the truss-raising team. This is led by Logan – a man built like the offspring of an ox and a military tank. Their group's first task is to carry the timbers that have passed muster over to where the woodworkers are measuring, sawing and jointing. The trusses are being put together in a shape that looks a bit like a capital A that's been sat on.

After breakfast break, Gilchrist and Magnus put in an appearance. Arms folded, they study the carpentry team's work as if they're paying for it. The doc then saunters over to say something in Logan's ear. His reply is animated, but at a distance and against all the background noise of chopping and sawing, Ash can't hear what they're saying. Both men's overgrown moustaches make it impossible to read their lips.

Around midday several women turn up carrying baskets. Everyone stops work while water and buns are passed out. The buns prove to be dense and slightly sweet. While chewing on his, he spots Reid amongst the crowd. Instead of acknowledging his raised hand, she turns and walks away.

Once the break is over, Evander announces that the first truss is ready. Sensing that a spectacle is about to occur, the kids run over to join the onlookers gathered at a safe distance.

Carrying the weighty truss between the five of them is difficult; manhandling it above their heads until its two ends sit on opposite walls even harder. Faced with this massive, inverted triangle, Logan and Evander step forward wielding lengths of wood with V-shaped ends attached. Using these, they push, prod and manoeuvre the truss until they've rotated the whole thing on its axis and the apex is sitting upright against the sky.

General applause breaks out along with whooping and whistling as this first truss is fixed into place. Backs are slapped, including his, hands are grasped and shaken. It's hard to remain unmoved by their camaraderie.

As soon as the next truss is ready, his team hauls it up. With it hanging upside-down, they step back. Beckoning him forward, Logan says, 'Give me a hand wi' this one.' He thrusts one of the push sticks at him.

'You want me to help you get that thing upright?' Ash pulls a face. 'Not sure that's a good idea.'

'Let's get on wi' it.' Everyone's watching and waiting.

'Okay then.' He shrugs. 'On your head be it.'

They've managed to get the damned thing semi-upright, when his end begins to slip and then slide along the wall beam. Struggling under the sudden increase in weight, he stumbles. His legs buckle.

He hears gasps. Someone cries out.

And then he's face-down on the stone floor and badly winded. When he dares turn his head, the truss is hanging only millimetres above his skull. From the corner of his eye, he sees Isla with her eyes closed in concentration, one hand outstretched.

During the stunned silence, the truss begins to move. Before Ash can scrabble out of its way, the whole thing floats up above the cottage walls, spins on its axis, then drops into place alongside the first.

While the crowd is erupting, Ash scrambles to his feet. Around him people are screaming, or crossing themselves, or just staring open-mouthed. There's pandemonium everywhere he looks. Some are running away, while others stay cowering. Several are calling out to Almighty God proclaiming a miracle.

Standing quite still amongst the mayhem, Magnus is staring directly at Isla.

Chapter Fifty

'We're going,' Ash says, scooping Isla up. He's forced to stop while he transfers her onto his shoulder. Carrying her in a fireman's lift, he dodges through the screaming, scattering crowd.

Leaving the chaos behind, he hurries uphill, heading for his boat. There'll be time enough to figure out the rest once they're well away from the island.

He hears running footsteps. When he snatches a glance behind, Reid is almost upon them. 'Wait! Ash stop!'

Still recovering from that winding, with Isla's weight, plus the steepness of the slope, he's struggling to keep up the pace, but can't risk slowing down. Reid must have put on a spurt because she's drawn level. Out of breath, she says, 'Stop a minute. Why run away?'

With no spare energy to argue, he says, 'We're getting out of here.'

'You're tired.' Reid tries to grab his arm. 'Hand her to me.'

No way is he falling for that. He digs deep, keeps on up the path. Once they've reached the ridge, it'll be downhill all the way.

'What happened back there?' she asks.

'Your guess is as good as mine.' He's panting a bit now. 'Some weird physics shit… Archimedes stuff… To do with triangles… Fulcrums… and all that.'

'You could've been crushed to death,' she says.

'But I wasn't.'

Reid's in good shape, he concedes that much. She keeps trying to slow him down. 'But aren't you even curious?'

'Better we leave now.' He can't keep this up for much longer. 'Listen to that… fucking commotion… going on down there.'

Spurred on by the way Magnus was staring at Isla, he keeps going. 'They're already dragging… God into it. Next it'll be the devil… Or some other… mythical entity.'

Reid's managed to get in front. Facing him, she's jogging backwards matching his pace. 'So you're planning… to leave with her.'

'Yep, that's the idea. Come with us… if you want… Either way, we're off right now.' With the gradient getting even steeper, he's grinding to a halt. He pauses to catch his breath. They're all still milling around down there, no one paying them any attention. Getting a second wind, he sets off again.

'You're behaving irrationally,' Reid says. 'Stay. We can talk this through.'

'No thanks.'

'Why not?'

'Because I don't intend to stick around… for the bloody witch-hunt.'

Reid's in his way, in his face. 'What witch-hunt? This isn't the seventeenth century.'

He sets Isla down and straightens his back. 'We've just

been raising a fucking roof *by hand*. Look around, Catriona, these people have already gone back in time. Soon they'll be desperate for an explanation, and that's when all the bad shit will hit the fan.'

Reid crouches down, both arms extended for Isla to run into them. Instead the kid backs away.

'That's my girl,' he says, stroking her hair.

'Can't we sit down for a minute and talk this through?'

Shaking his head, he picks Isla up and slings her over his shoulder again. 'I know all about frightened mobs.' He jerks a thumb towards the village. 'That lot down there will listen to anyone, swallow any garbage, however far-fetched, if it offers an explanation for what they've just seen. Then comes the blame game. We're the new kids on the block, we'll make the perfect scapegoats – no pun intended.'

He pushes on up the hill. 'Isla needs to be gone… before that happens.'

'You make it sound like they're savages,' Reid says, running around to get in front of him again.

'Not saying that… I'm just saying… that like all isolated populations… they're vulnerable to manipulation.'

He's getting closer to the top with every step.

'Stop, damn it.' Hair flying in all directions, Reid blocks his path. 'Think about what's best for her.'

'You need to look out,' he says. 'There's a sheer drop right behind you.'

She turns to face the sea, the breaking waves rolling in. Narrowing her eyes, she goes for the cheap shot, 'I'm guessing running away is your usual response when things get tough.'

He laughs in her face, sets Isla down again then fills his lungs with the sea air. The steps leading down to the jetty should be off to their left.

With the kid safely behind him, he stares over the edge. Down below he can see no sign of his boat or either of the ones that were tied up there before. 'Arghhh!' He clamps both hands to his head. 'My fucking boat's gone. Some bastard's stolen it.'

He looks at Catriona, straight into those grey eyes of hers and sees something he wasn't expecting – guilt. 'You knew they'd taken it, didn't you?' She doesn't bother to deny it. Through clenched teeth he says, 'Better step back from that edge, Cat, because right now I'm so tempted to push you over it.'

She retreats to a safer distance before uttering two words, 'We know.'

He frowns at her. 'What the hell are you talking about?'

'About Isla.' Her face is stony. 'Between us we've figured it out.' She waves an accusing finger at the kid. 'That cute little girl there is a PK. And that scar of hers – the one on the back of her neck – it's from the chip they implant in all of them.'

He catches her glance downhill. Turning, he sees Magnus and a couple of others striding up to join them. 'So you were the advanced party,' he says. 'Sent to soften me up before the big guns move in.' If only he had that Glock.

She says, 'Ash, you need to listen to what they have to say.'

'About what? All that nonsense about implants and PJs? I don't think so.'

'PKs!' She squares her shoulders. 'They're called that

because of their psycho-kinetic abilities. Feign ignorance all you want, Ash, I don't believe you don't know what she is.'

The three reinforcements have come to a halt further down, reluctant to get any closer because Isla's staring right at them. He chuckles. 'Seems those three hairy-arsed blokes are frightened of a little girl.'

Reid's undeterred. She raises her voice, so her words will carry. 'A while ago I received an alert about a breach at a classified facility just outside Ullapool. Seven inmates had been freed during a military-style raid. I was asked to report any suspicious strangers arriving on the island but warned not to approach them. They mentioned a distinctive, star-shaped scar on the back of every inmate's neck. I remember wondering how I was supposed to spot that while keeping my distance.'

Trying not to show it, he's joining more than a few dots. The suicidal woman and Isla must have been amongst those set free. The man he found dead was possibly one of their liberators.

'Later, I got an update saying all escapees along with the raiders had been shot dead. When I asked who shot them, the answer was' – she supplies the air quotes – '"unspecified forces".'

Like a couple of fielders, Logan and Evander are standing off. But Magnus has dared to venture a few steps closer. 'An old army pal of mine was a guard at that Ullapool facility,' he says. 'One night, after we'd had a few bevies, he let it slip that the people being held there could move things using only their minds. It was such a daft notion that, at the time, I laughed out loud. My pal reckoned those boffs were conducting a human selective breeding program to increase their telekinetic abilities.'

Reid butts in. 'Yesterday, when I was doing Isla's hair, I spotted her scar, and it got me wondering about all the unlikely escapes the three of us had before we got here. I thought Magnus and Gilchrist had a right to know.'

Ash scoffs. 'So you've put two and two together and made a hundred.'

'I told them the truth about how we met. Then another question occurred to me. Why would an escaped PK be travelling with you, of all people? Unless you were involved in the raid that freed them.'

'Neat theory,' he says. 'Shame it's utter bollocks. So Isla happens to have a star-shaped birthmark on the back of her neck, so what?'

He needs to stay calm if he's going to flip this around. 'I knew you were keen for her to stay here Catriona, but this…' He shakes his head, genuinely disappointed with her. 'You've concocted this utter nonsense based on her birthmark. What's it meant to prove? That she can move a tumbler around like drunk adolescents with a Ouija board?'

He throws his hands up, turns to appeal to the onlookers' common sense. 'Have you ever heard such a load of crap?'

Magnus drops his gaze like he's diagnosed a terminal illness. 'I grant you it all sounds preposterous.' Then, back on full beam, the doc says, 'I'd be the first to agree with you, Ash, if our experiment back there had failed. Logan here may have gone a bit too far, but I think we can all agree it proved the point rather spectacularly.'

Chapter Fifty-One

Guy

The stone dome he'd chosen had a layer of hay inside. It made such a comfortable mattress he's slept longer than intended. It's well past sunrise when he comes to. Yawning, he stretches himself awake – a hard thing to do in such a confined space. When he rolls onto his belly his wound stings, though there's no fresh blood on his jeans.

The dome's entrance frames an uninterrupted view of the cottages as well as the old kirk in the middle of the village. It's a fine, clear morning with tiny, shoal-like clouds drifting sedately across the sky.

He screws the silencer onto the end of the barrel. No need to factor in the wind. He's close enough to make the shot yet far enough away to beat a hasty retreat while they're still running around like headless chickens wondering what hit them. Well, just one of them, with luck.

His rifle scope roams over each house in turn. Some have been recently re-roofed. Habitable enough, he'd imagine, if your expectations are on the low side. He chuckles. In his current position, who's he to criticise?

The turf roof above his head is intact except for one or two ragged holes. Looking up through the gaps, he sees nothing but sky. He checks the time. Ten minutes to go.

Raised voices float up to him from down below. He zooms in on the commotion going on outside the church. Young and old are milling about. He imagines the usual dress code on this island is on the casual side, yet today they've all made an effort to look smart. A few of the kids are sporting flowers in their hair. Could this be a saint's day he's never heard of? Plenty of those to choose from. Or are they about to celebrate an old Celtic festival? He can't see a maypole. Is he about to witness some hocus pocus ceremony to bestow fertility on their veg or whatever. If they all start prancing about, it'll make his task a whole lot harder.

After checking the time again, he flips up the antenna on his sat. device, aligns it with the largest "ceiling" hole and waits. If this doesn't work, he might need to crawl outside. He's relieved when the green light comes on. This is followed by the standard "confirmation of signal" message.

After another short pause the instruction he's been waiting for appears on the screen. Finally, he's been given the official go-ahead. This is it. Next second the message disappears, presumably leaving no digital trace of its existence.

He continues to stare at the blank screen until it's lit up by a series of photographs taken from a variety of angles. There's no accompanying name or information since there's no need. His target is clear, his orders unequivocal.

He sits up. 'Fucking hell!' If there was a way he could query this order he would do it now. Hand over his mouth, he recalls everything he's been through since leaving his sleepy village in France, all the effort he's put into this mission, the bullet wound he sustained, everything that's led to this moment and the order he's expected to execute today.

Now it makes sense why they chose not to use any "in house" agents. They've hired him because he's way off-book and, as such, can't be traced back to his paymasters and the order they've just issued. A textbook strategy to ensure complete deniability.

He's proved his reliability and accuracy many times over. Aside from that, they must have earmarked him as a man unbothered by conscience or ethics; someone guaranteed to carry out orders for the right price and no questions asked.

Right now, lying flat on his belly with the smell of last year's hay in his nostrils, he needs to decide if he is that man.

Starting as a faint, far-off buzz, the noise begins to grow louder and more intrusive. He scans the sky through his scope until the approaching object comes into view. As it gets closer, the noise grows until the air is vibrating with the heavy thrum of its rotating blades. The downdraft is raising a cloud of dust that begins to creep up the hillside towards him. He watches the helicopter bank around then approach the village green where it gently puts down.

If they've spotted his boat, will they bother to wonder why it's at anchor so far offshore?

The locals all rush towards the copter before its blades have stopped rotating. Four black-suited agents emerge first – the armed security detail. They usher everyone back to a safer distance then form a protective semi-circle between the onlookers and the helicopter. Next, two impeccably-dressed VIPs descend to earth like beings from another world.

He gets his first glimpse of the target, though she's immediately obscured by someone else's head. All parties begin to drift towards the kirk – the largest building in the settlement. Instead of going inside, they gather at the churchyard gate.

He hears a drone approaching. Through the lens he sees he's mistaken – it's not a drone but another, smaller helicopter. It must have just taken off from a ship anchored off-shore. As it circles, it kicks up more dust clouds before coming to land right alongside the other copter.

What the hell is going on here?

More security guys jump out – only two this time. They form a defensive shield around the two men who step out next. No one could fail to recognise the taller of the two.

Holy fuck!

Like the chorus line, the locals surge towards the star arrivals. It doesn't take a genius to figure out this is a leaders' summit. Peace talks, he assumes, taking place away from public gaze in an edge-of-the-map location. His employers, for reasons of their own, are paying him top dollar to sabotage these negotiations. Assassinating the target could be the catalyst for who knows what – another Arch Duke Ferdinand moment.

By chance, a gap opens up and his target is exposed while her hand is stretched out to her political enemy. He moves the crosshairs to bisect the woman's skull. Whichever way this goes from here on he's a marked man. He inhales. Holds his breath.

Chapter Fifty-Two

Ash

Logan looks at Ash, 'I didnae mean for that beam to slip as far as it did. Believe me I wasnae trying to kill ye, pal.'

Ash says, 'I'm sure you're about to use the excuse that you were only following orders.' He wags his finger at Magnus. 'And he was the one who put you up to it after all.'

Reid says, 'Trust me–'

'I don't trust any of you,' he tells them. 'And neither should Isla.'

Gilchrist is trudging up the hill towards them. Meanwhile Magnus feels the need to declare, 'We're not your enemies, Ash.'

'Great, thanks for clearing that up,' he says. 'So, since we're all good pals here, you won't mind returning my boat so my little girl and I can piss off out of here.'

'If only it were that simple.' Shaking his head, Magnus makes a show of regret. 'These may be troubled times, but it doesn't change the fact that I swore an oath to serve my country. That promise, and my commitment to it, still holds.' He looks nobly into the middle distance. 'It's my duty to return that wee girl to the Ullapool facility.'

'Wait – I never agreed to that,' Reid says. 'Those PKs must have been virtual prisoners in that place. That can't be right.'

'What about your other oath, Doc?' asks Ash. 'The Hippocratic one. I seem to remember there's a bit in there about not doing harm to others.'

'One has to bear in mind the common good,' Magnus says.

'Does one?' Ash laughs out loud. 'And there it is folks – the ultimate get-out-of-jail-free card.'

A little late to the party, Gilchrist clears his throat. 'We must prioritise our community's safety.' He jabs a finger towards Isla. 'As a hunted fugitive, that wee girl over there is a threat to us all.'

Ash takes a step closer to that handsome face of his. 'Then tell me where my fucking boat is, and I'll rid you all of that risk right now.'

'Hold on a sec,' Logan says. 'I'm guessing that wee lassie there must be worth some serious cash.'

He can almost see the dollar signs lighting up Gilchrist's eyes when he says, 'Given what she's capable of, I suppose certain parties might be prepared to–'

'Let's get this straight,' Ash says, his voice shaking. 'You're seriously considering selling this child right here off to the highest bidders?'

Isla's aquamarine eyes range from one to the other like she's taking this all in.

Raising his hand classroom style, Gilchrist says, 'I merely meant it's something we might want to consider.'

'I don't believe what I'm hearing.' Reid is close to tears. 'I thought the plan was to keep her here with us where she'll be safe.'

They're so busy deciding on her fate, none of them have noticed how close to the cliff edge Isla is now standing.

'Catriona, I swear to you that wasn't my plan when we spoke about this yesterday.' It looks as if Gilchrist will struggle to get back into her good books. Glancing at Magnus for backup, Gilchrist says, 'We agreed that, for everyone's safety, the girl should leave here as soon as possible.'

'Aye,' Logan says, 'I ken we'll sleep sounder in our beds wi' her gone.'

When Ash checks, Isla is another step closer to that sheer drop. All the pressure she's under might be giving her suicidal thoughts just like the woman who drowned herself.

'The NSL would pay a tidy sum tae get their hands on that wee lass,' Evander says. 'And that's nay something tae sniff at.'

'Aye,' Logan says, 'and just think what we could achieve here wi' the dosh.'

Reid's fists are bunched – always a good sign. 'You'd sell out that wee lass there to a bunch of wicked, murdering bastards?'

Careful not to spook her, Ash is edging ever closer to Isla.

'She cannae stay here, that's for sure,' Logan says. 'And we'd be mad tae send her back tae where she came from wi'out considering the potential benefit for the folks here.'

For all his oath of allegiance bullshit, the doc hasn't dismissed the idea out of hand. 'Just listen to yourselves,' Reid says. 'Have you lost every shred of humanity?'

Ash is about to grab her arm, when Isla's eyes flick from

him towards the sea below and then back again. She does it a second time. Has to be a signal. She's drawing his attention to something down at sea level.

'I thought we might harness her abilities, put them to good use here,' Reid says. 'We all saw what she did with that truss. What else is she capable of?'

'Isn't that child exploitation?' Ash asks. 'I told you this place was fucking backwards, and I was dead right about that.'

When they all start shouting at once, he risks a peek over the edge. The jetty down below is still empty.

'Stop this!' Magnus shouts. 'We need to discuss the matter in a civilised fashion.'

'And then put it to a vote,' Gilchrist adds.

'Who gets to vote?' Reid wants to know. 'By rights, it should be everyone.'

'I agree with that in principle,' the doc says, 'but people will expect and want some guidance in the matter, and they've come to regard Gilchrist and myself as their de facto leaders.'

Ash risks another glance over the edge. Isla must have spotted something down there, but he can't see what it is.

Holding up three of her little fingers she begins a silent countdown.

Three.

Two.

One.

His body thrums and vibrates with energy. Those raised voices begin to fade. He realises that his feet are no longer in touch with the ground.

He's burning, falling down and down, all light extinguished. So this is what death feels like.

He's on the deck of his boat with Isla, his body fizzing with a strange power that's slow to leave him. Gulping air, he registers the solidness of the deck under his feet, the smoothness of the gunwale he's gripping. Now he can move, he lifts his arms to emulate the gulls squawking and wheeling as they ride the wind. Under a near cloudless sky, the surface of the sea is barely being ruffled.

Ash is laughing so hard he bends double, eyes streaming. 'Wow!' he says, straightening up, 'If this is the afterlife then it's not half bad.'

Isla grins, then shakes her head. Shading her eyes, she switches her attention to the island behind them. Above Pailteas's steep cliffs, five figures are peering down at the rocks below.

Whoever moved his boat has clipped a faded red float to her anchor line. He knows he should do something about that but can't think where to start.

The kid goes into the wheelhouse. She struggles to climb up into the captain's chair. Coming out of his trance, he watches her turn on the ignition. When the instrument panel lights up, she claps her hands together with glee before going through the start-up routine exactly as he would have done. Using two hands, she pushes the throttle forward, then straining to turn the wheel, steers them straight out to sea.

He makes it to the wheelhouse without falling. 'Move over,' he says. As she jumps down from the seat, he pulls back on the throttle. 'You've forgotten two things. One – the anchor. Two – this is *my* boat.' Today the water is the exact colour of her eyes. 'Okay, now watch that red floating ball,' he tells her.

Once the anchor float starts to follow them, he turns the boat about. Engine idling, he pulls in the line before heaving the captured anchor up and onto the deck.

'Right then.' He rubs his hands together the same way his granddad used to. Genetics must have something to do with it.

When he thrusts the throttle forward, the water churns beneath them – white circles overlaying turquoise. 'I have no idea where we're heading,' he says. 'I suppose you and me will just have to make it up as we go along.'

She holds up one hand. Her tiny thumb and index finger come together to make the okay sign.

Grinning back, he's about to say something when she opens her mouth. At first, she gulps like a fish, then, rocking forward a little, she utters her first word to him: 'Okay.'

Chapter Fifty-Three

Guy

The target's on the move. They're done with the handshaking bit and now, flanked by their deputies, the two leaders are walking side-by-side towards the church. Hell, he could take both of them out. Two for the price of one – wouldn't that turn the world on its head. Or its political axis.

They've stopped to acknowledge the small crowd of islanders kept at arm's length so far; smiles and waves that could lead to a sea change. He's tracking them, still has the shot though not for much longer. So what's stopping him?

Logic – that's what. This island should have been teeming with security when he arrived. Instead of last night's lone and sleepy guard, there ought to have been at least four professionals spread out around the perimeter including a sniper lying more or less where he is now, with another on the kirk roof providing cover from that angle. So why wasn't it?

That half-mil in crypto was always a fantasy because this was, and is, a suicide mission. Was this op initiated and run by a minority within it, or is he doing the bidding of the whole organisation? Either way, he needed to be expendable. Plausible deniability would be crucial in the aftermath. He's the "lone wolf"– motive unknown. As soon as he squeezes the trigger his finger is resting on, he's as good as dead. And what would his legacy be? Here lies the guy who was stupid enough to royally fuck everything up.

Hmm.

The decision makes itself.

Through the lens he can see the two leaders are deep in conversation as they walk into the kirk and out of sight. Safe, for now at least.

He lays his rifle on the fetid hay then lays his head down beside it. Pinned down by daylight, he has time to rest his leg and figure out what to do next. He's got quite a journey ahead of him – that's if he's lucky enough to make it off this island alive.

It's dusk, many hours since those two copters lifted off, each time disturbing more clouds of sand and soil before leaving a strange silence in their wake. The people living here, whoever they are, have gone back inside their cottages. On a clear night such as this, those lit up windows down there make the old houses look cozy, if you didn't know better. Looks like they're not in the habit of partying into the night.

Will what happened today make a difference? Or what didn't happen? Jury's out on both counts.

Focusing on the smaller picture, he needs to get the hell off the island while he still can.

With all the excitement over, another lone and bored guard

is resting his lazy legs on that bench. In case he wakes himself up with his snoring, he'll need to be quiet.

He stows his water bottle, straightens out his limbs and shoulders his pack. Better make sure he's left nothing behind. Switching to infrared he checks again that no one's heading his way or walking along the ridge behind him.

Time to go. He breaks cover, crouched as he runs towards the radar dish silhouetted against the sky. There's enough ambient light to be sure he doesn't run into any obstacles on the way.

From the base of the dish, he retraces his footsteps along the ridge to the approximate point where, twenty-four hours earlier, he'd flopped down exhausted on his back. The metal end of the piton shines up at him in the moonlight. He checks it's still firmly embedded then pulls on the rope to be sure he can trust his weight to it.

Dropping down the cliff is a lot easier and quicker than climbing it. Reaching the rocks below, he looks out past the breaking waves to where he can just make out the white ball-float he'd tied to the anchor line of his boat. A marker to aim for in the black expanse of the sea.

In the darkness, it takes him a while to locate the raft float he'd stowed on a rock shelf. Pulling on the wet wetsuit is quite a struggle, especially getting it over his injured thigh, but he's soon got it zipped up. He checks the raft, makes sure everything is safely stowed and strapped on before he takes a deep breath and enters the water.

The cold is a shock that doesn't last long. Despite the pain in his thigh, it feels good to be exerting himself, concentrating only on keeping a steady rhythm to his strokes as he heads towards the boat with the float raft bobbing along on the surface beside him.

He's alongside the boat when it occurs to him that his employers might have planted explosives timed to go off once he's completed his mission. A neat way to tie up loose ends – him being the annoying, still-alive end they'll want to tie up.

Guess it's time to find out.

The boat's reached what used to be classed as international waters. It's a calm, star-spangled night – which may or may not work in his favour. Even though he's had hours to think about it, Guy has no idea where he'll head next.

He throws the satellite device as far as he can, grins when he imagines all that clever tech fizzing with seawater. Before he even got in this boat, someone had made sure the auto I.D. system was disabled. They might not have blown him up yet, but they will have placed a tracker onboard. How else will they know where to send the kill team that must already have been despatched?

Being small, a tracker can be hidden behind one of the navigational instruments, or somewhere unobtrusive on deck, or even below the waterline. Hell, he'd probably need to dismantle the whole boat to find it.

He's already switched off the AIDP unit. Locked in its metamaterial container, it should have gone totally dark. There's no way to check that. Cinders died attempting to steal the damned thing. Given its advanced capabilities, it's worth assuming that it will remain untraceable unless, or until, he chooses to remove it from its container. For now, he has to assume the genie is safely contained.

Without it he's running blind. Any moment an NSL patrol could pop up on the horizon. And it's not like there's a shortage of other hostiles. Take your pick – everyone's a potential enemy.

To stand a chance of surviving, he's going to have to do things the old-tech way. He sets a south-easterly course towards one of the larger islands. Once he sees shore lights, he'll look for a harbour where he can steal a boat and leave this one in its place. With luck, its new owner will decide to test this boat's sea legs leading his pursuers on the first of many breadcrumb trails he'll need to scatter on the water.

Assuming he successfully switches boats a couple more times after that, what then? He's used to laying low between assignments. Southern France was a good choice the last time. Before he chose that option, he'd checked out several alternatives. They'll know that he tends to opt for somewhere with a decent climate and off the beaten track but offering at least some of the things that make life more interesting. Putting themselves in his shoes, they'll imagine he'll try to get as far away from here as possible.

This time, he'll need to lie lower than ever before. So low that, if it was a limbo bar, only a snake could sliver underneath it. All of which means he needs to consider the more extreme options he'd previously rejected.

His latest boat is hidden inside a rusting old boathouse surrounded by trees and so far up a tiny creek it can't be seen from the shoreline. At least that's the theory. It's raining hard – the sort of rain that assaults your bare skin like a million tiny daggers. His backpack weighed down with the first lot of his supplies, he begins the soggy trek over to the opposite side of the island.

He follows a sheep track up and along a winding route until he's standing up on the headland with a swirl of alarmed seabirds crowding the skies above him. Time to take in the bleak, 360 degree view out to sea. Apart from a couple of protruding rocks, in all directions there's nothing but water to the horizon. He was aiming for isolated – tick that one off.

Continuing on, he enters an area of woodland – the result of a once-upon-a-time scheme to reintroduce more trees to the archipelago. He disturbs a group of feral sheep sheltering under the trees. Unused to humans, they watch him pass showing curiosity but no fear. 'I'm the top predator around here now,' he tells them.

The old settlement looks exactly as he'd expected in that there's not a lot of it left standing. Struggling to scratch a living, the last of the dwindling population here left for the mainland with all its advantages some 150 years ago.

The substantial walls of an old tythe barn still stand senti-nel above the beach. Harried by wind and rain he heads down towards it. Even though he's aware of its existence, he doesn't see the hut until the last minute. To preserve the authentic appearance of the island, the conservationists who constructed it had deliberately hidden it from view.

The lock on the door has rusted away. He pulls the door open and steps inside a time capsule. Everything is as they must have hurriedly left it once birdwatching in remote places became a dangerous occupation.

They'd built the place to last, making sure it was substantial enough to keep out various four-legged intruders. Over in one corner there's a wooden bunk, its blankets neatly folded at the foot of the mattress. Cooking equipment is arranged on the shelves where they'd left them to gather dust. There's several rows of paperbacks and even some writing materials. Along one wall there's a pinned chart showing a comparative tally of bird's spotted. By far the biggest bonus is the woodstove – which looks to be in working order, a pile of wood and old paper still lying beside it. 'Thank you very much,' he tells the ghosts.

He takes off his backpack. So this is it – home for the foreseeable future. Quite a thought and quite an adjustment to make. It's not like he's a prisoner here in his own little Alcatraz. Or Elba. He has a boat after all – if the isolation gets too much, he has options. In fact, when all the stuff he's brought here runs out, he'll have to leave to get more supplies.

Which means he'll need a new identity. Time to wave goodbye to good old Guy. The trick is to sink into the new persona like a method actor would. Become a new character – though, face it, he's unlikely to be all that different from the old one. Answering to his new name needs to be a knee-jerk response. Choosing something simple tends to work best.

Looking along the spines of the books they left, the name Will leaps out at him. Where there's a Will, there's always a way.

Or Frank for a man hiding nothing.

Looking around the cabin, he wonders if he can pull off Woody. Not really – sounds too American.

In any case, right now he's cold and wet. If he gets that fire going, he might feel more cheerful about his new situation.

When he opens the stove, the remnants of the last fire are still sitting there – archaeological evidence of a previous civilisation. Did the bird watchers know this was going to be their final night here? Or, given how much they left behind, did they imagine they'd be back for the next breeding season? Such an innocent occupation in a world where innocence is growing ever harder to find.

He shakes his head – he's the last person qualified to complain about lack of innocence.

In front of him a half burnt log sits on a little pyramid of ashes. Ash. Hmm… works as a first or a last name. And appropriate in these destructive times. Yeah – Ash does have a certain ring to it.

The End

About the Author

Before becoming a writer, Jan Turk Petrie taught English in inner city London schools. She now lives in the Cotswolds area of southern England. She holds an M.A. in Creative and Critical Writing from the University of Gloucestershire.

As a novelist, Jan likes "to mix things up a bit". Of her twelve published novels, **'Falling Apart'**, the **'The Eldísvík Trilogy'**, and the **'Cotswold Time-slip Quartet'** can all be loosely categorised as works of 'speculative fiction'.

By contrast, **'The Truth in a Lie'** and **'Still Life with a Vengeance'** are contemporary, domestic dramas, while **'Too Many Heroes'** and **'Towards the Vanishing Point'** are thrillers set predominantly in the 1950s.

Jan has also written numerous, prize-winning short stories. She is a big fan of Margaret Atwood, Kate Atkinson, Kurt Vonnegut, and Jennifer Egan – authors who also like to take risks in their writing.

Author's Note

I really hope you've enjoyed reading 'Falling Apart'. Thank you so much for buying or borrowing a copy – this book means a lot to me.

If you would like to help other readers discover it, please consider leaving a review anywhere readers are likely to visit. It doesn't need to be a long review – a sentence or two would be just fine. Many thanks in advance to anyone who takes the time to do so.

To find out more about this book, or any of my other published novels, please visit my website: https://janturkpetrie.com

If you'd like to follow me on X (formerly Twitter) my handle is: @TurkPetrie.

My Facebook author page: https://www.facebook.com/janturkpetrie

Instagram: @jan_turk_petrie

Contact Pintail Press via the website: https://pintailpress.com

Goodreads: If you'd like to ask me a question about this book or have any other queries, please visit to my author page on Goodreads.

Acknowledgements

I can hardly believe this is my twelfth published novel. This one took even longer than usual to write and presented me with many new challenges. Whenever I had moments of doubt, my wonderful husband, John, urged me to keep going. I'm indebted to him more than anyone else for reading and commenting on each hot-off-the-press chapter. His feedback and cups of coffee kept me going during the long and occasionally arduous process of writing and rewriting 'Falling Apart'.

As always, I am grateful for the unfailing love and support of my family – my brilliant daughters Laila and Natalie, lovely sons-in-law Ed and Sam, and my endlessly entertaining little grandsons Leon and Lucas.

Grateful thanks must also go to my wider family especially my sister Jenny, brother-in-law Geoff and my mum, Pearl Elizabeth Turk – renowned for her highly prized "Pearls of Wisdom".

Writing is a solitary occupation and so considered, insightful feedback from other writers is invaluable. I'm enormously appreciative of the comments and suggestions made by the highly talented members of the Catchword writing group based in Cirencester. Your feedback most definitely helped to make this a better book.

I'm indebted to my talented and sympathetic editor and proof-reader Johnny Hudspith for all his comments and corrections.

Final thanks go to Jane Dixon-Smith, my brilliant cover designer, for her outstanding work on yet another arresting cover.

www.ingramcontent.com/pod-product-compliance
Lightning Source LLC
Chambersburg PA
CBHW010020200726
48283CB00015B/3069